"Are you coming on to me?"

Jon's question was soft, intimate.

There was a two-year-old sleeping a couple of feet away. A child Lillie couldn't take any further into her heart.

"No." Was she? "At least, I don't think I am. I'm just... the other night you said...we both acknowledged..." For someone whose entire life was dedicated to finding the right words to help people, to soothe them, Lillie was failing miserably. "But I really don't want anything more than friendship...."

She *couldn't* take on Jon's son. Not as her own. She'd smother him with her love and constant concern. Worry herself sick over every little hiccup.

She honestly did not want to marry again. Ever.

Dear Reader,

We get to spend more time together in Shelter Valley! I love it here and love that so many of you do, too. I hope we'll be able to keep meeting like this!

Jon's new to Shelter Valley this semester. He's a man who was on the periphery of my mind after his appearance in *It's Never Too Late;* the real story in *Second Time's the Charm* was going to be Lillie's.

Lillie first came here to attend college. And then, when tragedy took away everything that was dear to her, she came back to Shelter Valley to live. She's a child life specialist who's had a very successful private practice here for the past five years. She knows what she's doing, what life is about and she believes she has all the answers—or knows how to find them.

Then Jon shows up. He has answers, too. But he raises questions. Jon needs Shelter Valley as much as anyone who's ever been there. He doesn't know that yet, but it's as if Shelter Valley was made for Jon. He has secrets, though. And because of that, our town might not be safe with him in it....

It seemed to me, while I was writing this book, that I was going to have to choose—between a town that's come to mean so much to me and to many of us, and a man who'd sacrifice everything for his two-year-old son. And I learned, right along with Lillie, that I don't have all the answers.

I hope you enjoy this visit! And remember to plan time in your schedule for another Shelter Valley vacation. We'll be here again later this fall in *The Moment of Truth.*

I love to connect with my readers. Please like Tara Taylor Quinn on Facebook, and follow me on Twitter so we can get better acquainted! You can also reach me at tarataylorquinn.com.

Tara Taylor Quinn

Second Time's the Charm

Tara Taylor Quinn

HARLEQUIN® SUPER ROMANCE®

Recycling programs
for this product may
not exist in your area.

ISBN-13: 978-0-373-71871-9

SECOND TIME'S THE CHARM

Printed in U.S.A.

www.Harlequin.com

ABOUT THE AUTHOR

With fifty-nine original novels, published in more than twenty languages, Tara Taylor Quinn is a *USA TODAY* bestselling author. She is the winner of a 2008 National Reader's Choice Award, four-time finalist for an RWA RITA®Award, finalist for a Reviewer's Choice Award, a Bookseller's Best Award and a Holt Medallion, and she appears regularly on Amazon bestseller lists. Tara Taylor Quinn is a past president of the Romance Writers of America and served for eight years on its board of directors. She is in demand as a public speaker and has appeared on television and radio shows across the country, including CBS *Sunday Morning*. Tara is a spokesperson for the National Domestic Violence Hotline, and she and her husband, Tim, sponsor an annual inline skating race in Phoenix to benefit the fight against domestic violence. When she's not at home in Arizona with Tim and their canine owners, Jerry Lee and Taylor Marie, or fulfilling speaking engagements, Tara spends her time traveling and inline skating.

Books by Tara Taylor Quinn

HARLEQUIN SUPERROMANCE

SINGLE TITLE

MIRA BOOKS

*Shelter Valley Stories
**Chapman Files
***It Happened in Comfort Cove

Other titles by this author available in ebook format.

For Mindy

Thank you for all the parts of your life that you share with me. And for having the strength and endurance to do what you do every day for those children. You are not only my inspiration, but my heroine.

CHAPTER ONE

Five years ago

HOT AND HEAVY with baby, Lillie Henderson knew the pains would pass. She wasn't going to deliver for another month, at least. False labor was common. Birthing class said so. The pains weren't acute enough to be labor. They were symptoms of dread. Alone in the elevator, she held the basketball-like protrusion that used to be a flat tummy and pushed the button for the eighteenth floor.

"We have to talk, Lillie," Kirk had said when he'd asked her to meet him at his office—a top-floor suite with a windowed view of Camelback Mountain in his father's Phoenix PR firm.

Jerry Henderson, Kirk's father, and his third wife, Gayle, were out of town for the summer. Which made Henderson Marketing Kirk's sole territory. He'd called a meeting on his ground—not on mutual or neutral ground. Lillie didn't miss the ploy. In the almost three years they'd been married, Lillie had figured out that many of Kirk's actions were strategically devised to get the results he wanted.

The elevator slowed to a smooth stop and the door opened, showing her the plush blue-gray carpet that covered every inch of the Henderson offices except the kitchen and bathrooms. Original Picasso sketches lined the walls in between solid mahogany doors that remained open—unless private business was being discussed—to get the maximum benefit from the walls of windows inside the rooms. The entire floor had been designed to convey a sense of openness that was meant to translate to an atmosphere of trust.

Lillie had been breathlessly nervous the first time she'd visited the offices as Kirk's fiancée. She'd been a college senior then, studying child and family development.

In the three years since, she'd graduated and become employed as a child life specialist, but the nerves were as bad as ever. Some things didn't change.

Her long, chocolate-brown hair curled loosely down her back and she could feel its weight on her shoulders. She'd left it down for the interview, in spite of the triple-digit heat outside. And she'd donned her one pair of expensive maternity dress slacks, purchased before Kirk had learned that the baby she was carrying was going to be born with serious birth defects.

The nice thing to do would have been for Kirk to meet her at the elevator. She'd texted to let him know she'd arrived, just as he'd instructed. He'd texted back, telling her to come on up.

Since the doctor's distressing diagnosis two months ago, Kirk hadn't shown any deference to her pregnant state. He hadn't spent many nights in their mountain-view home, either, leaving her to tend to her grief and worry and growing discomfort alone in their elite gated community.

He'd spent a lot of nights away before the doctor's pronouncement, too. Just not as many.

Kylie, the firm's latest blonde receptionist, smiled from behind the massive, curved desk directly across from the elevator.

"Good morning, Mrs. Henderson," she said in her lilting saccharine voice. "He's expecting you." Kylie's smile didn't quite reach her eyes, but Lillie had never felt any animosity from the receptionist, who was likely a year or two older than Lillie's twenty-three. What she felt coming from the other woman was more like pity.

She was sick of pity.

Kirk's was the third office on the right—directly across from his father's. His door was the only one closed. And, based on the rooms she'd passed on her way in and the morguelike silence of the space, his was the only one occupied, too. Not unusual for July in Phoenix. Half of the population left the scorching desert temperatures in the summer for cooler climates.

Standing in the hall in front of that closed door, her black Coach purse hanging from her shoulder, Lillie contemplated turning around and heading back the way she'd come. She was not a possession, or a pet, who had to perform on command.

It was possible Kirk wasn't alone, but not likely. Kylie didn't usually make mistakes.

That closed door was as deliberate as everything else Kirk did. As orchestrated as his smooth-talking charm had been during their senior year of college when he'd wooed her—an orphan without a home to visit during holidays—into his bed.

He was making her knock on her own husband's door. Making her ask for permission to enter his abode. Treating her as little more than a stranger.

He was going to ask for a divorce.

She'd come because she didn't want the conversation to happen at home, where she'd found a measure of peace.

Knocking, she thought about one of her patients, little Sandra, the six-year-old who'd recently undergone surgery to fix the damage done to her back in a car accident the previous spring. Employed by a local children's hospital, Lillie had supported Sandra through every procedure since the accident, and had learned far more from the spirited redhead than she'd been able to impart as Sandra's child life specialist.

No matter how much pain she was in, Sandra never lost the smile on her face—even when there were tears in her eyes. She never backed down from her willingness to take life head-on.

Kirk kept her waiting a full minute. She heard him clear his throat once as he approached from the inside.

"Lillie, come in," he said, pulling open the door.

Without meeting his gaze, she entered, taking in the spectacular view, the pristine room and the uncluttered desk before settling in an armchair on the other side of the room. She'd be damned if she was going to be dumped sitting like a client in front of his desk.

Couldn't he have waited until after the baby was born?

Her husband, dressed impeccably in the gray suit he'd purchased the summer before and a deep maroon shirt she didn't recognize, stood, hands in his pockets, just to her right. He walked to the window and over to the bar.

"Can I get you something to drink? A glass of wine?"

Glancing at her stomach, at the evidence of the baby Kirk had already written off, she said, "I can't drink. You know that."

He had the grace to look chagrined—and she had a feeling that his remorse, the regret that shadowed his eyes, was sincere. "I just figured…you know…with the way things are, it wouldn't matter…."

Her chin ached with the effort it took to keep her expression placid. "His heart is malformed, Kirk. He isn't dead. Alcohol consumption could cause brain damage."

This time the pity was in his eyes. "The doctor gave him a ten percent chance of living through gestation. And no chance at all of surviving more than a year outside the womb."

"He also said they won't know for sure what we're dealing with until he's born and they can run more thorough tests."

As a child life specialist, a trained and certified child development advocate who helped children and their families through times of crises, she'd witnessed medical miracles. Some things weren't up to professionals.

And he hadn't summoned her to this lunchtime meeting to discuss their son's fate. "I'd like some cranberry juice, if you have it."

Nodding, he filled a glass with ice from the bucket on the bar and, reaching underneath, pulled out an individual-size bottle of juice, opening it to fill the glass.

Pouring himself a shot of Scotch on the rocks, he brought both glasses over to set them on the table next to her and sat in the armchair on the opposite side. Taking a sip of his drink—a stiff one even for him—he leaned forward, his forearms on his knees, hands clasped, and turned toward her.

"You know about Leah."

His mistress. "Yes." She'd suspected, when Kirk had started coming home late, that he had a lover. She'd confronted him about it and he'd told her the truth. He'd also told her that the woman meant nothing to him and that he'd already ended the affair. He'd sworn that he loved Lillie. That she was his life. He'd agreed to go to counseling. He'd had tears in his eyes.

She'd just found out she was pregnant.

And she'd believed him.

"She's pregnant, Lillie."

Pain shot through Lillie's lower stomach. She stared at Kirk, her mind completely blank.

"The baby's mine."

"How far along is she?" She should be feeling something.

"Three months."

He hadn't ended the affair.

"I wanted you to hear it from me."

She nodded. Made sense.

Braydon Thomas—named for Lillie's father, who, along with her mother, had been killed in a car accident when she was nineteen—kicked against her, the feeling faint, almost like air bubbles, in spite of the fact that she was at thirty-two weeks' gestation.

"She asked me to move in with her."

"She knows you're married."

"Yes."

The girl had no scruples. No ethics.

"I told her yes, Lillie."

"You're married," she said again, numb. Fueled by whatever force it was that got her through the hard times, she sat there.

"I know." His brows drew together and his eyes shadowed. "I feel horrible about this but she loves me and I love her."

One usually asked for a divorce before falling in love and starting a family. She'd have liked to point that fact out to him, but didn't see any good that would come out of doing so.

"Is that where you go when you don't come home at night?"

She'd kicked him out of her bed when she'd found out about his affair—until she could welcome him back with an open heart.

"Yes."

What more could she say?

"It's not as if you're head over heels in love with me," he blurted into the silence.

He was right. She'd married him because she cared about him deeply. Because she loved his father and Gayle. The family they all made together. Because they had so much in common, enjoyed being together. Because they'd wanted the same things out of life. Because he'd been her first lover and she'd found him incredibly attractive.

She didn't want her marriage to end. But she couldn't live with infidelity. Couldn't be in a relationship without trust.

She couldn't settle.

"I'm not going to file for divorce," Kirk was saying. "You'll have full insurance coverage throughout the rest of your…term."

He was having another baby. Presumably a healthy one.

"Leah has her own insurance," he said, continuing to fill her silence with information she didn't want.

And had to have.

"I'll still be paying the bills, the house is all yours, the car…"

"I cover my own car payment," she reminded him, just to keep the facts straight. She paid the utilities on the house, too. Kirk might live like a wealthy man, but the money belonged to his father.

The elder Henderson kept his son on a tight budget. For Kirk's own good, Lillie had discovered.

"Braydon's medical bills are going to be exorbitant," she said. "We'll have co-pays."

His upper lip puckered. "Do you really think it's wise to run up bills when the doctor says there's no hope? Why put ourselves in debt, or put him through all kinds of tests, if there's nothing they can do?"

"Until he has the tests, we don't know for sure that there's nothing they can do."

This was her field of expertise now. She spent her days advocating for and providing for the needs of children who were suffering in a long-term care unit at one of Phoenix's largest children's hospitals. She was there during treatments, to see that the patient suffered as little as possible, to make certain that environments were best suited to the comfort of the child. To be soothing when pain was impossible to avoid.

But with her degree, she was qualified to work in schools, in the court system, even at funeral homes to help children cope with the trauma of losing loved ones. She was trained to make sure that everything possible was done for the good of the children. Her own included.

With a heavy sigh, Kirk stood, hands in his pockets again, his mostly untouched drink on the table.

"You haven't said anything about me moving in with Leah."

"I don't want you home with me if you don't want to be there."

"You're okay with it, then?"

"No, Kirk, I'm not okay with my husband moving in with his pregnant lover," she said, her shaky voice evidence that she must be feeling something. She stood, too. "How could I possibly be okay with that?" she asked, tears in her eyes as she finally faced him. Stood up to him.

"I'm also not foolish enough to believe anymore that you want me or our marriage, and I know that you always get what you want."

That didn't come out as she'd meant it to. "I…don't want you in my home wishing you were with someone else. Thinking about someone else."

He nodded. "I'm sorry, Lillie."

She believed him.

And two months later, on the day Braydon breathed his last, she filed for divorce.

CHAPTER TWO

Present day

JON SWARTZ KNEW everyone in the room was looking at him—with horror not admiration. He might have cared. If his heart hadn't been fully engaged with his red-faced little man. Two-year-old Abe was clearly not planning to have a good time at day care that Thursday in October. The boy's screams had reached at least eighty decibel levels—a feat even for him.

"Noooooo!" The shrieks were continuous.

Jon, struggling to pry his son's small but surprisingly strong arms from their locked position around his neck, was speaking continuously, as well. "It's okay, son. It's okay." But he was fairly certain that Abraham Elias Swartz couldn't hear him. He couldn't even hear himself.

Pumpkins bearing smiling faces hung on the walls around them. A larger lit up jack-o'-lantern sat on the counter behind which sat a young woman with a frown on her face. Four women with various-aged children stood in front of him.

"It's okay, son," Jon said again.

He had to be at work in less than an hour and could not afford to be late. Jobs with flexible hours for students who were also single parents in a town as small as Shelter Valley were not easy to come by.

Holding on to Abe's butt and back with one arm, he

reached up to pull his son's hands down from his neck with the other—disengaging the death grip without bruising the toddler's tender skin.

"Abie baby, let go. Daddy wants to talk to you," he said directly into his son's ear.

"Nooooo!"

Tears soaked Jon's neck. He knelt down, putting the boy's feet on the floor.

"Noooo!" Abe picked his feet back up, kicking as Jon tried to take hold of one of the boy's ankles and put his foot back on the floor.

What in the hell was he going to do?

When he'd first brought Abe to Little Spirits Day Care a couple of months before, his little guy had whimpered a bit, but he'd been happily engrossed in playing before Jon had made it to the door.

"Noooo!" A tennis shoe caught him in the groin, taking Jon's breath away. Abe's red short-sleeved shirt had come loose from the beige cargo pants he'd chosen from his drawer that morning and the skin on Jon's arm was sticking to his son's sweat-slicked back.

"Abraham," he spoke again in the boy's ear as soon as the pain in his lower region dissipated enough to allow conversation. He spoke more firmly this time. As firm as Jon got. "Daddy has to go and you have to stay. It's not negotiable."

Abraham kicked. And wailed.

Jon picked him back up, encased once again in a death grip.

"Let's go in here." A female voice sounded from just beside him.

An angel's voice?

With a hand on his elbow, a jeans-clad woman led him

through a door off the day care reception room—a door that had been closed every other time he'd been there.

Abraham quit kicking and screaming long enough to look around.

"Hey, little guy." The woman's smile was warm, her tone nurturing, as she offered a finger toward Abe's hand.

The boy snatched his hand into his chest and whined— a sure sign that more histrionics were on their way.

"My name's Lillie." The beautiful, long-haired brunette who'd rescued them from the day care lineup apparently hadn't received Abe's imminent tantrum memo.

"Noooo!" Abraham said, the word breaking on a wail. Jon would be damned glad when his son's vocabulary progressed beyond the three or four words he'd been using clearly to express himself over the past six months. Even a slight progression, a one-word addition—*yes*—would be nice.

"The itsy bitsy spider climbed up..."

The woman started to sing. Abraham's cries were building back up to full force—and the strange woman was singing.

Standing in the small room with a cluttered desk and a couple of chairs, Jon had no idea what to do. Who the woman was. Or if he should have automatically followed her just because she'd told him to do so. At least in here Abe wasn't upsetting the other kids.

The toddler's fingers were digging into Jon's neck as Abe engaged in full-out wailing.

The woman continued to sing. Her voice was good. He'd give her that. And rising in decibels equal to Abe's. But...

"Down came the rain and..."

Abe stilled long enough to turn around and look at Looney Lillie.

"Out came the sun and..." Her volume lowered but she didn't miss a beat.

The toddler stared at the strange woman. Jon did, too. Who the hell was she?

Jon had never seen her before. But she had the most compelling violet-blue eyes.

"Climbed up the spout again."

Letting go of Jon's neck Abraham pinched his little fingers together on both hands and, holding them out in front of him, twisted them together.

"That's right," Lillie said, matching her thumb and index fingers from opposite hands and switching them back and forth in a crawling motion. She started to sing again.

Abraham watched her, his little fingers moving. By the time the song was done he was sitting calmly on Jon's hip—looking around as though waiting for the adults in the room to figure out what they were doing so he could get on with his day.

"Thank you." Jon didn't know what else to say.

Lillie smiled, rolling up the sleeves of her white oxford. "Abe and I met last week," she said. "Didn't we, buddy?"

Abe stared.

The slender woman, only a few inches shorter than Jon's six-foot height, held out her hand.

"I'm Lillie Henderson."

"Jon Swartz," he said, meeting her gesture with his free hand. And...getting a stab to his gut. It had been too long since he'd touched a woman's skin. In any capacity. "You work here?"

"Yes and no." The woman's smile was unwavering. And all-encompassing. He just didn't have time to fall under her spell as his son had done. He had to get to work.

"I'm a freelance child life specialist," she said, as though he knew what that meant. "I have a small office at the clinic in town, as they pay the largest part of my salary and take up the brunt of my time, but I work out here at the day care and with some other private clients in the field, as well."

"In the field?" He didn't have time to be ignorant, either.

"Doctors' offices outside of the clinic, the funeral home, schools. I go anyplace a child might need support getting through trauma."

He nodded. And noticed that the entire time she'd been talking, she'd been softly rubbing the top of Abe's hand.

"You ready to come with me and play for a while?" she asked the boy, switching her focus from father to son without missing a beat.

Prepared for the next onslaught, Jon tensed. And felt his son lean toward the arms outstretched in front of him. Without so much as a peep, the little boy made the switch from Jon's arms to Lillie's.

Acting as though he and Abraham had intercessions from heaven every day, Jon nodded and slid his free hands into the pockets of his jeans. Did he just leave now?

The woman, Lillie, was running a finger along Abe's lower lip. "Let's see if we can find you some juice, shall we?" she asked, and as the toddler nodded, she turned and headed through a door on the opposite side of the office leading into the day care. Just before the door closed behind her, she glanced over her shoulder at Jon, winked and was gone.

With no time left to spare, Jon hurried out to the front desk, confirmed that Lillie Henderson was permitted to have physical custody of his son and left.

But not before making one very clear determination.

He had to see her again.

LILLIE PULLED INTO the parking lot of the Shelter Valley Clinic a little past three on Thursday afternoon. She was early. Bailey Wright's blood work wasn't scheduled until four, but she wanted to make certain she was there to greet the six-year-old when her mother brought her in.

Bailey's doctor suspected the little girl might be anemic and the six-year-old was deathly afraid of needles. Lillie's job was to explain the blood draw procedure to the little girl in nonthreatening, nonfrightening terms—the pinch and pressure she would feel—and then to support her through the procedure, distracting her from anything and everything that upset her.

If Bailey tensed, the procedure would hurt. Lillie was there to see that the child stayed relaxed.

Her cell phone rang and she answered immediately, as always. "Lillie Henderson, can I help you?"

"Ms. Henderson, Bonnie Nielson gave me your number." Bonnie, the owner of Little Spirits Day Care, had her permission to pass out all of her contact information. "This is Jon Swartz. You helped my son, Abraham, this morning."

The gorgeous guy who'd had his ass whupped by a two-year-old.

"Yes, Mr. Swartz." She and Bonnie had talked about Jon and Abe over lunch. Bonnie thought Lillie could help the single dad. Lillie wanted to try. For Abe's sake. "Thanks for calling."

"I owe you a huge thank-you," the man said. "Abe's going through a rough time with separation anxiety right now, but his pediatrician says it's all part of the terrible twos. He assures me we'll get through it."

"Of course you will." Grabbing her bag, she locked her car and, entrance card in hand and ready to swipe, headed toward the service door at the back of the clinic.

"I just didn't want you to think he's like that all the time."

The man was on the defensive, she ascertained, distracted by the even timbre of his voice when she should have been 100 percent focused on his son's issues.

"I've seen Abraham a couple of times over the past week," she assured the harried father who, in all fairness, sounded completely calm. "He's a very sweet, responsive boy," she added, because it was true. "Except when he's, as you say, exhibiting anxiety."

"Usually he's a prince," Jon Swartz said as though they had all the time in the world, which she didn't. Curiously, she didn't tell him so. "He does whatever I ask of him."

"He's not a discipline problem at the day care, either, if that's what's concerning you. He does what he's told, when he's told. He doesn't have altercations with the other children. But he has been experiencing seemingly inexplicable moments of extreme anxiety."

Tantrums that in no way seemed to be a result of temper upsets. And because, a couple of times, they'd happened in the middle of the day, she wasn't sure they were separation related, either.

"Mrs. Nielson suggested that I call you. She says that, as part of your work for her, she asked you to observe Abraham. She says you're certified at what you do. And I need to know, do you think my son has a problem?"

"I think he's struggling and I'd like to help, Mr. Swartz." Holding her phone with one hand while she swiped her card and quickly pulled open the door with the other, Lillie lowered her voice in deference to the office suites opening up off both sides of the hallway.

From a therapeutic masseuse to an orthopedic surgeon, a dentist, several general practitioners, counseling services and three pediatricians, the Shelter Valley Clinic was home to more than forty health care professionals—including Lillie.

"I'd like a chance to speak with you. Is there a time we could meet?" she asked the father who'd been on her mind for much the day.

"With or without Abraham?"

"Without would be best, but either is fine. I understand that you don't have a lot of free time. I will make myself available to fit your schedule. Early morning, late evening…"

She didn't mind the long hours. She didn't mind time off, either.

"I'm a little in the dark here about what we have to discuss."

She'd reached the small room designated for Bailey's procedure and had to go. Had to get the room ready for Bailey. She didn't have time to explain what she, as a child life specialist, did.

"I'm trained to help little ones deal with anxiety—from trauma, separation or even just the stress inherent in learning to share. I'm at the day care a few hours every week, and Bonnie calls me in more when she thinks I can help. She's noticed Abraham's escalating stress in your absence and asked me to observe him. I have some ideas where he's concerned," she said, still on the phone when she shouldn't be. Pulling stuffed animals out of her bag, she placed them around the room.

"You want to talk professionally?"

"Yes." Her work was her life. Professional was pretty much all she was. The purple bear with the heart on his chest toppled over and she righted him.

"I can't afford another bill right now. If he's sick or exhibiting some symptoms that concern you, I'll get him to his pediatrician immediately."

"I don't think your son is sick." She was fumbling this entire conversation. Which wasn't like her at all. "I'm talking about observations, not symptoms…" Placing the portable music player in a corner of the room, she scrolled through songs until she found the lullaby she wanted— soft, soothing.

"…and Bonnie pays for my services," she added. Occasionally she took on private clients, but she made most of her money from the clinic, which used her services on behalf of its young patients. Shelter Valley schools called her in on occasion. And she got the weekly stipend from Little Spirits, too, but only because Bonnie wouldn't let her work there without pay. Lillie had more than one client that she'd helped on a pro bono basis. And that was nobody's business.

Turned out Jerry Henderson, Kirk's father, had had different ideas than his son regarding Kirk's mistress, Leah. And Lillie, Kirk's wife. Lillie's divorce settlement had been generous.

Which was nobody's business, either.

Lillie could hear voices at the end of the hall. It sounded like Bailey's mother.

"I have to go right now, Mr. Swartz. But I'd love to talk more if you're interested."

"I'll be at the university in the morning," he said. "I have a break between classes from nine until ten. We could meet there if you're free."

She had a procedure at the clinic at eight. And another, a PICC change for a little preemie who'd been released from a hospital in Tucson, at ten-thirty. "I'll do my best," she told him. She could make the date if the procedure at eight happened on time and without problems, and if she left the university by a quarter to ten.

Arranging to meet him outside the student center at

nine, or to call him if she couldn't, Lillie shoved her phone into the pocket of her rainbow-colored scrub top just as an extremely frightened-looking blonde sprite came hesitantly around the corner.

A genuine smile on her face, Lillie moved toward the girl and took Bailey's small hand in hers. She spent the next half hour engrossed in the six-year-old's trauma and doing everything she could to make the experience better for her.

Bailey made it through without shedding a tear.

CHAPTER THREE

"GOGGLES ON," JON said as he stood back from the apparatus he and his lab partner, Mark Heber, had just built inside a safety-glass room at Montford University. If all went well they would soon know how quickly glass would craze when set five feet from a fire started by nail polish remover, and if, in the same amount of time, the same type of standard window glass would craze from a ten-foot distance.

"On," Mark said, grinning as he joined Jon. "Light the fuse."

Shaking his head, Jon motioned toward the long piece of fuse protruding from the puddle of accelerant. "It's your turn," Jon said.

A little more than halfway through the semester, the two "old men," as they'd been dubbed in the freshman chemistry lab, had gained a bit of a reputation for the ingenuity, scale and success of their experiments. Jon's lab partner, Mark, who'd worked as a forensics safety engineer for years without the title, and who was now in school to get the degree that would allow him to officially work in the field, deserved most of the credit.

Mark stepped forward, lit the fuse and ducked as a whorl of flame exploded from the puddle, bursting in front of them.

"Whoops." Mark wasn't smiling.

"Guess our calculations were a little off on this one."

"The velocity of the fire was greater than we'd calculated for the amount of polish remover," Mark said.

Straight-faced, they looked each other over.

"No singeing," Jon declared.

"Make a note that idiots should not be allowed to play with fire," Mark said as they stood, watching their piece of window as the fire burned down.

On the upside, the glass at the five-foot distance crazed—bearing spiderweb-type cracks that would allow arson investigators to determine that the fire had been set by an accelerant and that the glass had been close. The point of their experiment was to help arson investigators determine how long the fire had burned.

The glass at ten feet did not craze.

Another correct prediction.

"Nice experiment, gentlemen." Professor Wood came up behind them. Several students had found their way to the room at the back of the lab to take a peek.

"A little less velocity," Jon said, "and we'd have been perfect."

"At least it didn't burn out of the controlled area, or burn anything other than the intended substance," Mark added.

Professor Wood nodded and, without another word, turned and left. "I'll bet he'll have some choice words for us when he tells his wife about this one," Jon said.

"Is he married?"

"Hell if I know."

Marriage wasn't something he thought a lot about. Didn't spend much time thinking about women at all these days. Or he hadn't until the past twenty-four hours.

"Abe threw another fit yesterday at the day care," he offered casually as he and his lab partner set to work cleaning up the mess they'd just created. He had half an hour before he was supposed to meet up with Lillie Henderson to find out what she had to say about his son.

"Yesterday was Thursday."

"Yeah."

"I thought he only threw fits on Saturdays. When you went to work instead of school."

Jon had told Mark about the first fit. More than a month before. At work at the cactus jelly plant outside town where Mark, a supervisor, had gotten Jon a job as a janitor. They'd been having lunch.

He hadn't seen Mark much at the plant since then. After one of the plant's machines had broken down and Jon had been able to repair it and get it back up in time to make shipment, he'd been promoted to maintenance engineer. A fancy title for a guy who could fix things.

"That theory, that his tantrums were the result of an extra day of day care, proved to be false," Jon admitted.

Frowning, Mark sprayed water on the metal piece that had held the puddle of accelerant. "You didn't mention that you're having more problems with him."

Jon shook his head and, with gloved hands, lifted the crazed glass and put it in the trash receptacle. "I'm not," he said. "Doc says it's just the terrible twos, and from what I've read, we're getting through it a lot easier than some."

The room was half-clean. He had another fifteen minutes before he had to leave.

He'd pulled on his nicer pair of black jeans that morning and had been thinking about looking responsible, respectable, as he'd buttoned up the oxford shirt and rolled the cuffs to just below his elbows.

"He's never had a problem when you leave him with us," Mark pointed out. The thirty-year-old, together with his fiancée and grandmother, watched Abe one evening a week, giving Jon time to do whatever the hell he pleased.

Which usually meant homework but he was good with that.

"Maybe it's the day care," Mark offered. "Must be something there upsetting him."

"Tantrums are normal. All I have to do is stay calm, not give in to him and this phase will pass. He's testing his limits."

Mark glanced his way for a long minute and then shrugged. "If you say so."

His doctor said so. And he trusted his doctor.

JON DIDN'T TRUST Lillie Henderson. He found her attractive. But he didn't trust her. He didn't believe in angels. She'd told him that his son was not a discipline problem—Abe followed instructions and got along well with others.

But she'd said they needed to talk.

Like Abraham's terrible twos were different from everyone else's?

She'd also said that she'd met Abraham the week before, yet he hadn't been told about a child expert being called in.

And that had his mind spinning noises he didn't like.

Was someone making charges behind his back? Questioning whether or not Jon—a single guy in his twenties who worked and went to school full-time—was capable of providing for the needs of a two-year-old child?

Someone outside Shelter Valley?

Had Lillie been hired by someone other than Bonnie Nielson? Hired in secret by an older woman she wouldn't ever mention?

An older woman with enough money to stay at Jon's back until she got what she wanted?

The thought could be considered paranoid. He might even be able to convince himself of that if he hadn't learned the hard way, more than once, about the duplicity of women.

At least, the women in *his* life.

Even then, he wasn't afraid of the power of the opposite sex. What scared the shit out of him was his own culpability.

He'd made mistakes. Big ones. He wasn't kidding himself. His past could be used against him—but only if his present supported the theory that he was still the loser he'd once been.

Had Lillie been hired to watch him? And his handling of his son? Could Abraham's crying bouts—and Jon's ineffectiveness in controlling them—be used against him?

One thing was for sure, university scholarship or not, he'd leave Shelter Valley immediately if anyone thought they were going to take his son away from him. Clara Abrams could follow him forever and he'd just keep moving one step ahead of her. She was not going to get Abraham.

Abraham. Named for the mother who didn't want him, Kate Abrams. Jon's first mistake as a parent.

His second had been in offering to let Abe's maternal grandparents meet their grandson.

Abraham might not have everything life had to offer—he might not have designer clothes, or a mother who wanted him—but he did have a biological parent who would go to the grave for him.

Kids needed that.

And Jon was going to see that Abraham got it.

He'd learned a thing or three during his years of growing up in a system that didn't always listen to the children in its care. He'd learned that the best way to find out what was being planned for you was to pretend to cooperate.

He had to meet Lillie Henderson. He had to appear to

agree with her suggestions, whatever they might be—to accept her at face value. He had to pretend he had no suspicions regarding her sudden advent into his life.

And all the while, he'd be watching his back. His and Abraham's. And be ready to leave at a moment's notice.

He'd pack the bag again. The one Kate had helped him pack when she'd come to him over a year ago to tell him that her parents—mainly her mother—were planning to take Abraham away from him. She'd only found out herself in enough time to give him a few hours to skip town.

He'd played the disappearing act before. He knew the score.

He'd had to leave another town before Kate had managed to blackmail her mother into leaving him alone.

But Clara was crafty—her daughter had come by the talent naturally—he'd give her that. She could be on the warpath again.

After all, as Kate had told him on more than one occasion during the months they'd lived together, Abramses didn't give up.

He'd pack the bag. Keep it ready in the closet. He'd put aside enough money to get them by on cash for a while if necessary. With the toddler, he'd need diapers and non-perishable food, too. And a warm blanket.

His mind spun, plans forming with a familiar clarity.

Running wasn't new to Jon.

He'd just been fool enough to hope it was over.

WITH ONLY A minute to spare to get from the back of the public parking area to the Montford University Student Union, Lillie ran the entire way, thanking her joy of jogging and the serviceable rubber-soled shoes she wore to work for allowing her to sprint half a mile without passing out. She'd texted Jon Swartz, letting him know that she was on her way. She didn't expect him to leave. She just hated to make people wait.

Spotting him leaning against the trunk of a paloverde tree, she slowed to a walk and took a second to smooth the blouse and jeans she'd put on when she'd changed out of her stained scrubs twenty minutes before. Her hair, in a ponytail, thankfully was still presentable.

"Sorry I'm late," she said, her breath even as she approached.

"No problem. I have an hour."

Less than that, actually, if he wanted to get to class before it started. At least according to what he'd told her.

Not that it was her business.

Nor were those big brown eyes or the ease with which he held his body. The man was…all man.

And she wasn't one who generally noticed. Or cared. Except in the most superficial sense.

She would walk away from this meeting and have nothing more to do with him, except as it pertained to his being Abraham's father. The little guy had been on her mind all week. She couldn't shake him. Which meant that she had a job to do.

"We can walk toward your class if you'd like," she said, and without a word, he fell into place beside her. Not too close. But closer than he might have if they hadn't been on a busy campus sidewalk thronging with students heading to and from classes.

"Bonnie tells me this is your first year at Montford," she started. She had to get a feel for him if she was going to help him. Her job extended to family support as well as client support. Children needed healthy families.

"That's right."

He didn't sound defensive so she continued. "What are you studying?"

"Premed. I'd like to be a doctor."

"So you'd transfer after you get your undergraduate degree?"

He shrugged, his satchel riding against his denim-clad hip with ease. "I've looked at University of Arizona's medical school in Tucson, but that's a long way off. My first consideration is Abraham. He'll be almost six by the time I graduate. I'm not going to uproot him if he's settled in. I can always go to medical school when he graduates from high school."

"So why major in premed?"

He turned, and she had no explanation for what his brown-eyed gaze did to her. "How much do you know about my situation?"

"Not much." Lillie almost missed a step. Something else she didn't usually do. "I just know that you're raising Abraham by yourself. And that your son obviously means a lot to you."

Jutting his chin, he nodded, his gaze turned in front of them again. His hands in his pockets, he continued to head across campus with the ease of a man who knew where he was going.

"I know that you work at the cactus jelly plant," she added, wanting to be completely up front with him. The files of the children enrolled at Little Spirits contained the names of their parents' employers. "And I know that you live in an apartment not far from my house," she added. The complex was less than a mile from the home she'd purchased the previous year.

"That's more than I know about you."

"You're right, it is. And that can change," she told him. Her current life was an open book. "I admire what you're trying to do," she told him.

Was that why she couldn't get the two Swartz men off

her mind? Why thoughts of little Abe—and his dad—continued to pop up throughout her day?

She hardly knew them.

And here she was pushing services that he clearly didn't want. Like she needed the work. Which she didn't.

Another direct glance from him, and she reminded herself to put herself in his shoes, to seek to understand, to listen and find out what he needed so she would know if there was anything she could do. She was not only well trained, she was experienced.

And she knew she could help make his job easier. If he'd let her.

"What exactly is it that you think I'm trying to do?" he asked.

Students jostled against them on both sides, snippets of their conversations filling the air around them. The sun was uncharacteristically absent overhead. Lillie was aware of her surroundings—and not really. The man beside her was an enigma.

"Raising your son, getting a degree and working. It's admirable."

"It's life," he said. "I fathered a child. I was offered a scholarship—a chance to better myself—and I have to work to buy diapers."

"Right. You didn't have to accept the scholarship."

Another glance. Were they growing sharper? "You're kidding, right? You'd expect me to turn my back on an opportunity to be able to provide my son with more advantages as he grows up?"

"Of course not! I'm not saying I thought you should have passed it by. I'm saying that many people in your situation wouldn't have dared to accept the opportunity."

"Oh."

"Especially since you have to work, too."

"The scholarship actually provides living expenses, but only for one. And in addition to Abe's living expenses, I have to pay extra for the student health benefits that are provided to me to cover my son."

"Like I said, I think what you're doing is admirable."

"I don't want to be admired."

She was missing the boat on this one. And running out of time.

"I want to help you." Bonnie paid her to help children adapt to day care life. Not to help single fathers raise their children.

But she knew she could make a difference here. Abe was a motherless baby boy who could benefit from her services and she didn't care about being paid.

"I don't need help."

"Hey—" Slowing, she touched his wrist and stepped out of the flow of traffic on the sidewalk. He followed her, standing facing her, both hands in his pockets. "I'm not judging you, Jon." And then quickly added, "May I call you that?"

"Of course."

"Call me Lillie."

"Fine." He glanced over her shoulder. Presumably at the sidewalk they'd left. He seemed eager to be on his way, but still had time before he was due in class.

"Have you ever worked with a child life specialist before?"

"Never heard of one until yesterday."

"Which makes you like a lot of people," she said, offering him the first natural grin she'd felt since their meeting began. "Child life specialists have college degrees, generally in a child development field. After college, they complete a practicum, followed by an internship, usually at a hospital. Finally they take a national, several-part exam and, upon passing, receive certification. Our goal is to reduce the negative impact of stressful situations on children and on their families. Most commonly, we're found in hospitals or in the medical field, supporting kids and their families through procedures or long-term illnesses, but we work in schools, with the courts, and even in funeral homes." She spoke like a parrot in front of a classroom. Not at all like herself.

And wasn't happy about that. She'd like to have walked away, to put this man, and his son, out of her life, but something was compelling her to press forward.

"Abraham's not sick or in court. He doesn't go to school and no one's died that I know of." Jon started to walk again.

"You just moved to a new town, a new apartment. You've started school and working at a new job. Your situation could be having a negative impact on him."

That stopped him.

"What kind of impact? He's throwing tantrums like a normal two-year-old."

She shook her head. "That's just it. He's not. Other than his bouts of panic, Abraham is probably the most well-behaved two-year-old I've ever met. His tantrums don't seem to be a product of testing his boundaries like you'd normally see at his age. They aren't temper related. He doesn't throw tantrums when he doesn't get his way. He doesn't have problems sharing. To the contrary, he lets the other children take things from him. His tantrums appear to be emotionally based. A symptom of stress, as opposed to part of his normal development process."

"Are you suggesting that I quit work? Or school?"

"What I'm trying to suggest, Mr. Swartz—" Jon just didn't do it "—is that you let me help you. Or at least let me try."

She'd never pursued a client before. Why was she doing so now?

Her schedule was kept plenty full with the clinic and Bonnie and the school, and the once-or-twice-a-year call from the local funeral home.

"How can you help?" He didn't slow down. Or look at her. She wasn't sure if he was just humoring her or not.

"I'd like to spend some time with you and Abraham. To observe you together. I've got some things I can show you to help him to calm down, little things. Easy things…"

"Like singing."

"Music therapy is good, yes," she said, relaxing for the first time since she'd seen him standing by the tree. "I'm not sure what's causing Abe's stress, but I think that if you gave me a little time, I might be able to figure it out."

"You're some kind of shrink, then?"

"Psychology classes were part of my degree, but no, I'm nowhere close to being a psychologist."

Veering off the main path, he approached a classroom building, stopping at the foot of a wide staircase up to a row of doors. "Let me get this straight," he said. "You want to hang out with us, give me some ideas, and that's it?"

"That's it." She had no idea if that would be a good thing or bad thing as far as he was concerned.

"And Bonnie's paying you for this?"

"She pays me to help her clients adapt to preschool and Abe's stress is preventing that adaptation," she said carefully. Money didn't matter here. Abe did.

"Fine."

It was Lillie's turn to stare. "Fine?"

"Yes, fine." That was it. Nothing more. Her heart rate sped up, anyway.

"Okay, then, I'll call you tonight and we can discuss schedules. If that's okay with you."

"I can tell you right now. I'm working tomorrow until three and then Abe and I are going to go to the park and out for a hamburger before coming home to have a bath, read books and get ready for bed. And no, I don't feed him fast food every night. Once a week for a special treat is it."

The next day was Saturday. Traditionally a light day for her as only the emergency clinic was open in Shelter Valley after noon. "Unless I'm called in on a medical emergency, I can meet you at the park at four."

"Fine."

Wow. What had appeared to be a mountain she was going to have to scale had turned out to be a curb. "Fine," she repeated, smiling, getting lost in his gaze when she should have just been getting lost. "I'll see you tomorrow, then," she said and, turning, hurried away from the strangest encounter she could ever remember having.

First rule of child life—the specialist did not become personally involved with the patient or the patient's family. She was there to support. Not to experience.

The designation fit her life to a T.

CHAPTER FOUR

JON TOOK THE last half of his peanut butter sandwich in two bites. A machine had gone down that morning and he'd lost half an hour getting it back up again so the plant didn't miss shipment. Every minute a line was down cost the company five hundred dollars in employee salaries that weren't producing product.

The emergency put him behind on his regular Saturday maintenance work—checks and balances that had to be done on schedule to meet regulatory standards—and he couldn't leave until he'd completed every one of them.

He never liked to be late picking up Abe, but today, with Lillie Henderson meeting them in the park only an hour after he clocked out, he couldn't afford to be running behind schedule. How would that look? A dad who couldn't even get to the day care to pick up his kid on time?

So, Jon was outside on the patio at the cactus jelly plant, standing with his foot on a boulder, gulping down a five-minute lunch, with plans to work through the rest of his scheduled break time.

"Hey, man, I heard you saved the day in there. Good work." Jon's lab partner, Mark Heber, leaned against the boulder next to his, facing the miles of desert and mountain behind them, pulling open a brown paper bag.

He shrugged. "It was a tension issue, mostly—stretched belt that caused a kink in the chain." Mark, a shift supervisor, and three years his senior, would already have known that.

"Management's pleased with your work," Mark said. "I thought you should know."

Nodding, Jon opened the cup of fruit he'd brought along, dumping half of it into his opened mouth. There was a spoon in the bag, but he wasn't out to impress anyone at the plant. He was in a hurry.

"Addy and Nonnie are baking cookies today. You and Abe want to stop by later?"

Mark's outspoken, wheelchair-bound grandmother and his hotshot lawyer fiancée were in love with Abe. Jon figured his son could do worse.

"How about I bring Abe by after dinner and the two of us will visit with Nonnie while you and Addy go out on a date?"

Nonnie lived with Mark. At eighty years old and in the late stages of multiple sclerosis, she was sometimes a handful.

"You got a deal." Mark's grin wasn't masked by the bite of sandwich he'd just taken. And then he sobered. "I assume you heard about the break-in?"

"What break-in?" Jon stared, his urgency to get back to work put on hold.

"I just figured you'd heard," Mark said, dropping his sandwich back into the little plastic bag from which he'd removed it. "It was less than a mile from your place. Sometime last night. A guy lifted the sliding glass door out of the track, took a bunch of cash and left the door leaning up against the kitchen wall. The couple were in Phoenix seeing a play and called it in when they got home. Everyone was talking about it this morning in the break room."

Jon didn't shake his head on the outside, but inside his mind was reeling. Would he ever get used to living in a place like Shelter Valley? It was so different from the neighborhoods he'd grown up in, where a dead body under a bench wasn't much in the way of news, that he sometimes felt as if he were living on another planet.

A break-in would be a big deal here. As would the knowledge that a new guy in town had done time for robbery.

"I guess they don't get much crime around here, do they?" he said, reminding himself that this was the life he wanted for Abraham.

Shrugging, Mark dug out his sandwich again. Took a bite. "One thing about this town—people watch out for one another here. And the sheriff, he makes it his business to get to know everyone."

Wishing he hadn't just eaten, Jon kept the expression on his face neutral.

"A real autocrat, huh?" he asked, mentally calculating how much he'd have to pay back in scholarship monies if he packed up and skipped town with Abe. If they came after him for the money.

"Not at all," Mark said, finishing one lunch-meat sandwich and pulling out another. "He's open-minded and fair. But he's also a great cop, ready to help anyone who needs it."

The statement made him curious. "You're as new to this town as I am. How come you know so much about the sheriff?"

In his world, guys kept their distance from cops. Mark finished his sandwich, bunched the bag into a ball shape and tossed it into a can six feet away. "Addy was born here," he said, as though testing the waters. "She knows him."

Walking with his friend back to the shop, Jon forgot about time, about his impending meeting that afternoon, and frowned as Mark mentioned his fiancée, the woman who watched Abe once a week. "I thought she was new to town, too."

"She's only been back for a couple of months. She moved away when she was six."

There was more to the story, Jon could sense as much. But Mark didn't elaborate, and Jon didn't ask.

LILLIE WAS RUNNING late. She'd been called to the clinic to assist with setting the arm of a ten-year-old boy who'd fractured it playing football. It had been almost one o'clock before she'd been free to change into her jeans and tend to the paperwork and reports that had built up during the week, and she hadn't eaten yet that day.

Which was why she was at the Shelter Valley Diner at three, grabbing a bite before walking over to the city park across the street for her four-o'clock appointment with Jon Swartz.

"Hey, woman, how are you?" The familiar voice greeted her as she stood at the counter, trying to decide what she felt like eating. Salad or sandwich? Or maybe just a cup of soup?

"Ellen? I didn't know you were in town!" There was nothing about the pretty blonde that suggested the trauma she'd lived through almost ten years before.

"Jay and I are dropping Josh off at Mom's. We're heading up to Jerome for the night."

Jerome, an authentic old mining town built into the top of a five-thousand-foot mountain, was a couple of hours north of Shelter Valley. These days, the bustling roadside town was an artists' haven and boasted several B and Bs in addition to a well-preserved twenty-five-room hotel that dated back to the 1900s.

"Are you taking the motorcycle?" Lillie asked, noting

the happy glint in Ellen's brown eyes, the shine to her natural blond hair. Marriage to Jay had done wonders for the woman Lillie had first met through Ellen's son, Josh, when Lillie had first come to town. She'd supported Josh through a routine procedure at the clinic. And bonded with his grateful mother in the process.

Ellen, who'd been born and raised in Shelter Valley, had been a regular to the clinic back then—visiting the counselor whose office was just across the hall from Lillie's—as she fought her way back from the hell of having been raped.

Jay, a masseuse at the clinic, had been central to Ellen's recovery. In ways no one could have foreseen.

"Of course we're taking the bike." Ellen's grin stretched across her face. "Jay's been great about taking the car when we have Josh in tow, so I insist on taking the bike anytime it's just the two of us."

"Admit it—" Lillie grinned back "—you just want to spend the entire trip with your arms wrapped around that husband of yours."

"I also happen to love the wind in my hair, the feeling of flying and the rush of speed...."

Ellen looked happier than Lillie had ever seen her. And for a brief second, she was envious.

Nancy, a mother of six who'd been working at the diner since she was in high school, approached them from behind the counter. Ellen ordered a cherry pie to go. "Jay and Josh are in the car," she told Lillie. "Mom's having the ladies over this afternoon and I told her I'd pick up the pie on my way there."

Ellen's mom, Martha—who was married to one of the preachers in town—and her friends, some of them from as far back as high school, got together every week. They were well-known throughout town because anytime anyone needed anything, the ladies inevitably found out about it and went out of their way to help. It didn't hurt that Becca Parsons, mayor of Shelter Valley, was among their ranks.

Nancy turned to Lillie and she ordered a sandwich—easy to eat in the park—and waved as Mrs. Wright and Bailey walked in, hand in hand. Bailey's lab work hadn't come back yet.

"Did you hear about the break-in?" Ellen asked as Nancy went to the back to collect the pie and put in Lillie's order.

"At the Conklins'? Yeah, Dr. Mueller mentioned it this morning. They just took cash, right?"

"Mom said they think it's one guy working alone. Something about a size-ten footprint. They aren't sure if he was only after cash, or if the Conklins got home while he was still there and scared him off. He left the sliding glass door leaning against a wall."

"I was here four years for college and I've been back for five and the only break-ins I ever heard of were on campus."

"I know what you mean. I read the police report in the weekly paper Mom sends to me in Phoenix and there have been a few accounts of people walking out of stores with things," Ellen said. "But mostly the calls are due to domestic violence or traffic accidents or someone having a heart attack."

But they both knew that, even given Shelter Valley's low crime rates, bad things did happen there. Ellen was living proof of that.

"I'm sure Sheriff Richards will catch whoever did it," Lillie told her friend, and hoped she was right. Knowing that there was a thief living among them was creepy. Shelter Valley was a unique little place on earth. It had been founded by a man who'd sought shelter from a world that condemned him for a mixed-race marriage at a time when such things weren't accepted. The town's growth had been guided by the belief that all good people deserved shelter from life's storms.

And everyone who came to town seeking shelter and stayed was ready to offer shelter to others who needed it.

After saying goodbye to her friend, Lillie paid for her sandwich and focused on her upcoming appointment.

The child. Not the father.

She could get through anything life had to hand her by focusing on work.

"THROW THE BALL, son." Kneeling next to Abe, Jon showed the toddler how to give the plastic orb an underhanded toss. And with a sprint, he made it in front of the ball to grab it as it fell and toss it back toward the little boy. Abraham followed the ball and, tripping over Jon's feet, fell against him. Standing immediately, Abe reached for the ball with both hands and placed them just as Jon had demonstrated, tossed the ball and went running after it again.

"Wait, son," Jon said. "Stay right there and Daddy will throw it back to you." For two Saturdays now he'd been trying to teach the boy the concept of playing catch. Trying to get Abe to wait for the ball to come back to him. And just as Jon was determined to teach him, Abe was determined to play the game his own way.

Still, Jon continued to try. He waited while Abe tossed the ball and then went after it, trying to get the ball heading back to the toddler before Abe's small legs got to it.

"Watch," he said. "Daddy will throw the ball and then you catch it," he said. Backing up, he tossed the cheap dollar-store toy gently in Abe's direction. The boy ran toward it, waited while it dropped and then grabbed it with a laugh.

"Now throw it to me," Jon said. Abraham tossed. And ran. Jon reached the ball first and, scooping it up with one hand, tossed the ball back in his son's direction. Again. And again.

"I'm going to back up farther now," he said as Abe once more picked up the ball. Turning, he hurried a few steps away before Abe had time to straighten. "Nooo!" His heart in his throat, Jon swung back around at the sound of his son's terrified scream.

If...

Abraham stood there, right where he'd been, screaming his head off. No one was around. The ball was still in the boy's hands.

"Abe?" He ran forward. Grabbed the boy's hands, letting the ball drop to the ground as he checked for bee stings. Abe's legs were next, and Jon scrutinized them fully while the toddler gained the attention of everyone else in the park with his full-bodied screams.

Jon glanced quickly around, fearing that Lillie Henderson would observe this latest display, but only saw unfamiliar faces staring back at them. Some were tinged with curiosity. An older woman on a bench several yards away was frowning.

But there was no sign of Ms. Henderson.

Jon picked the boy up and Abe quieted almost immediately.

"Put him back down," a soft voice said from directly behind him.

His first instinct—a strong one—was to ignore the child-life-whatever-she-was. He wanted nothing more than to avoid another screaming match in public. He also wasn't completely convinced that Abe was okay. Something had clearly upset him.

And then he thought about losing Abe. Because the

woman who'd just directed him to put his son down might be a spy—someone employed by Abe's maternal grandmother to observe Jon's parenting skills.

And even if Lillie wasn't a spy, she was clearly someone who knew a lot about raising children. He wanted whatever help he could get. He set the boy back on his feet.

Before his feet had even touched the ground, Abe opened his mouth and started to cry again.

And Lillie Henderson was down on her knees in front of him, shaking her head. Abe, apparently startled to see her, quieted enough to hiccup through his sobs. Lillie put a finger on his lips.

"No more screaming, Abe," she said. "Remember what we talked about? Use your words."

Abe only had four words. Jon started to tell her so, but figured he'd let her find that out on her own.

The boy studied Lillie's mouth. His lower lip was still jutting out and quivering, but he wasn't crying.

"Your Daddy and I—" she turned and smiled up at Jon "—can't help you if we don't know what's wrong."

Yes. That was completely true. And as soon as Abe got old enough to comprehend the concept they'd be home free.

"Instead of screaming, use your words to tell us what's upset you," Lillie said. "Okay?"

Abraham nodded. He didn't say anything. Didn't give Jon a clue as to what had caused his distress, but the tantrum had apparently passed.

Jon wasn't as confident that he'd passed the parenting test.

CHAPTER FIVE

THEY SPENT AN hour at the park. Abe tripped over a root and fell and started to cry. Jon picked him up and faced the woman who'd just given up an hour of her day to explain various coping skills to him.

Things he hadn't found in any of the numerous child-rearing books he'd read. Things like encouraging Abe to use his words, even though he didn't verbalize any yet. According to Lillie, the boy had a full understanding of language, and they had to give him a reason to vocalize his thoughts.

"Time to go," he said, looking at Lillie, hoping to hell that she wasn't a spy. He was grateful to her. "That particular whine means he's hungry."

She looked at Abe. "All you had to do was tell Daddy that you want to eat," she said simply. "Eat." She drew the word out. Said it again. Abe watched her mouth.

He grinned.

And shoved his fist in his mouth.

"Would you like to join us for a hamburger?" Jon asked, and was shocked when she nodded.

"I'd like that, thanks."

Twenty minutes later, after a quick diaper change in the front passenger seat of Jon's small, four-door truck, they were seated across from each other in a booth at the fast-food hamburger place just outside of town. Lillie, who'd followed behind them in her car, had insisted on paying for her own grilled chicken sandwich.

Abe, in a booster seat next to him, was happily shoving French fries in his mouth.

Lillie made a face at the boy. He laughed out loud. She chuckled.

And Jon was struck by how much he was enjoying himself.

Which posed a major problem.

"I have a question," he said, leaning forward over his opened container with a quarter-pound burger inside.

"Ask anything. That's what I'm here for."

"You married?" Not the question he'd meant to ask.

She blinked. "No."

"You said, the other day, that your life was an open book. I'm apparently not much of a reader. You know about me. I know virtually nothing about you."

And he wanted to know. Which was why he had to ask her.

"I graduated from Montford eight years ago. I married a business major I met my senior year. I'm divorced. And I've been back in Shelter Valley, practicing child life full-time, for the past five years. I live alone and am on call 24/7. My choice. Because that's the way I like it."

"No children?"

"No." Something moved in and out of her expression so quickly he couldn't make it out. Sadness, maybe.

Had she wanted children?

Or her husband had and she hadn't?

It seemed kind of strange that a woman who knew so much about kids, and who clearly adored them, didn't have any of her own.

"That wasn't my question."

She grinned. "Whose was it?"

Bowing his head, he tried to hold back his own grin, and lost the battle. "Okay, it was mine. But it wasn't the one I'd meant to ask. Before. When I told you I had a question." If he sounded anywhere near as idiotic to her as he sounded to himself, he should just hang his head and go home.

"What's your question?" Grabbing a napkin, she wiped a drop of ketchup from Abraham's mouth.

"Are we working?"

Frowning, she took a bite of her sandwich. Chewed and swallowed. "I'm not sure what you mean."

"Right now. What we're doing here. Is this work?"

"As opposed to what?" She really seemed confused.

Breaking more pieces of bread and hamburger patty, Jon put them on the paper in front of Abraham.

He felt stupid. "I don't know. Two people becoming friends…" It sounded as though he was hitting on her. Which he wasn't. At all. Not that he hadn't noticed how those jeans of hers hugged her long legs and a backside that— No. He was better than that. "Am I a client? I mean, I know you said I don't have to pay you, but—"

"I'm happy to help you with Abe, Jon. Don't worry about it."

He wasn't worried, exactly. Except when paranoia set in and he thought she might be a spy. "I'm not too sure about protocol for child life specialists."

His burger was getting cold. He loved burgers. And since becoming a father he only got one a week.

"Are you allowed to be friends with your clients?"

"Not according to the books," she said, and then shrugged. "And certainly in some situations, life-threatening medical procedures, for instance, I have to keep my professional distance, but in a small town like Shelter Valley it would be impossible not to be friends with my clients. Most of the parents of young children are my age and I wouldn't have any friends if I couldn't be friends with them. Or conversely, I wouldn't have many patients if I couldn't tend to the children of my friends. I've got a skill set, you know, like a plumber or a doctor. If your pipe bursts and your buddy's a plumber, he comes over to help, right?"

"So you and I—" he gestured toward her with his hamburger-holding hand "—we could be friends. If the idea was mutually satisfying, of course."

"If the idea was mutually satisfying, yes…" She'd withdrawn a bit. Wasn't smiling like she had been.

He got nervous again. "Hey, you do understand I'm not hitting on you, right?"

"I wasn't sure."

"But you are now."

"Yes." She nodded once, slowly.

"Good, because I'd like to offer my services. In exchange for what you're doing here for me. And Abe."

"Your services?"

The idea had occurred to him during the hour she'd spent giving him back some semblance of control where his son was concerned. "I've got some skills, too. I'd like to offer them to you." Especially now that he knew she lived alone. "For instance, do you have a sliding glass door?"

"Yes, why?"

"Does it have a security lock on it?"

"It's got the lock on the door handle. I'm sure it's secure."

He shook his head. "There was a theft in town last night."

"I heard. And I'm sure the thief, if he's still around, will be caught."

What was it about the people in this town? Did they have no street smarts at all? They didn't live behind a locked gate. Shelter Valley was accessible from the highway. All kinds of people took the highway.

"I'd like to install a secure lock on your sliding glass door. If you're okay with that."

"Sure. It never hurts to be safe. I'll pay you for it, of course."

"You're missing the point," Jon said. "This is a trade-off. You help me with Abe and I'll help you."

Being in debt gave people control over you.

She eyed the uneaten food in his container. "But…"

Abraham held up a French fry, looked from Jon to Lillie, grinned and nodded.

"It's good, isn't it?" Lillie grinned at the toddler.

Abe's nod encompassed the entire top half of his body. And then, still grinning, he chewed, French fry showing between his teeth. He picked up another and handed it to Lillie.

"You want me to have it?" she asked, when Jon would have just taken the fry.

Abraham, studying her with seriousness now as he held out his gift, nodded again.

She took the potato from his sticky fingers, said, "Thank you," and popped it into her mouth.

Abe went back to the sections of burger Jon had cut for his son, picking one up and taking a huge bite out of it. He chewed, swallowed and kicked his feet. It occurred to Jon that he looked like a healthy, happy, well-adjusted kid.

One who was communicating.

"Do you want a pickle?" Lillie asked the boy, picking up the discarded vegetable from her take-out container.

"No!" Abraham said emphatically.

Smiling, Jon looked across the booth at their gorgeous companion. "I don't buy that Bonnie Nielson pays you to spend hours on Saturday with the parents of her clients," he said. "Being at the day care, to help them adjust, makes sense, but this?" Sitting back against the booth, he motioned at himself and Abe and the food in front of them.

Lillie's gaze dropped before she once again looked him in the eye. "You're right. I'm on my own time."

"I don't accept charity."

"I understand." She gathered her trash together and Jon thought she might be about to walk out on them.

"But if you'd allow me to return the favor—professional skills in exchange for professional skills…"

Her hands stilling, Lillie studied him and his son. "I have to be honest with you, Jon. I'm not sure why I've been so persistent where the two of you are concerned. It's not my usual way."

So he hadn't been completely paranoid in thinking she'd singled him out. Just erroneous—okay, paranoid, maybe— in his conclusions that she was out to get him.

Maybe. Clara Abrams could afford to hire people who were highly skilled at acting.

"Tell me this," he said, "are you here because you're genuinely interested in helping me help my son?"

"Absolutely."

She hadn't blinked. Hadn't looked away. "Then that's enough for me," he said. "Assuming you'll allow me to reciprocate in kind. Service for—"

"I know, professional service for professional service," she finished, a small smile on her beautiful face. "I agree to your terms."

"Good." He smiled. Her grin grew wider.

Something was going on here. He wasn't sure what. And he was fairly certain he didn't want to know.

"Good," she said.

"Dada?" Abe's voice sounded between them.

He'd forgotten that his son was still eating. He couldn't believe he'd forgotten to watch Abe right next to him.

"Yes, son?" he said, wrapping an arm around Abe's tiny, fragile shoulders as he surveyed the ketchup-smeared table. Abe had pushed what was left of his food-filled paper across to the other side of the table.

"Uh," the boy grunted, bobbing up and down in his chair and pointing toward the door.

"He's ready to go." Jon gathered up the debris from their meal and retrieved a couple of packets from the back pocket of his jeans. The individually sealed antibacterial wipes he'd learned never to leave home without.

"Use your words, Abraham," Lillie said softly from across the table as Jon tended to his son's chubby little fingers and face first before starting on the table.

"Tell us what you want." Lillie's attention was intent on the boy. "Tell us you want to go," she said.

With a small frown marring his brow, Abe's big brown eyes studied the woman.

Jon wiped the table. He knew what Abraham wanted without needing to be told.

"Tell us you want to go," she said again. "Go."

"Gah," Abe responded, bobbing up and down some more. "Gah."

Jon grinned. A new word. *Gah.* It meant *go.*

"Gooo," Lillie said, drawing out the long *O* sound. "Gooo."

"Gah," Abe repeated, grinning. "Gah." The boy stood up on the bench and almost fell backward as his booster seat got in the way.

Jon reached out and steadied his son, feeling as though he'd just been given a new lease on life. He picked Abe up and set him on the ground.

"I was making it easy for him not to learn to talk," Jon

said to Lillie as they made their way through the restaurant. "He didn't have to speak to get what he wanted."

"That's probably part of it. And he's just turned two."

"I do try to teach him words." With Abe holding on to one hand, he held the door open for her.

"I don't doubt that, Jon." Lillie's voice was soft. Tender. And, inside, he softened toward her.

"We're working on potty training, too," he added, still proving himself, just in case.

"Not too vigorously, I hope," she said. "Boys generally train later than girls, closer to three than two. It takes that long for them to feel the sensation that they have to go. And trying to get him to understand what you want when he can't recognize the feeling inside his body yet will only lead to frustration. For both of you."

He'd read all of that.

"But sometimes they're ready early," he said. "I just wanted to give him the chance to move forward if he was ready. It's not an everyday thing. Just an occasional invitation."

He was talking about peeing with a woman he was attracted to.

"So—" Jon cleared his throat "—make a list of things you'd like done around your house," he said, getting back on track. "Tomorrow is Sunday. I have the day off." Except for cleaning the bathroom, washing the sheets, picking up groceries and studying. "I could come over and fix that door for you."

They'd reached their vehicles, sitting side by side in the parking lot. Her newish dark blue Malibu next to his quite a bit older, four-door Ranger.

He wasn't ready to leave her.

And he'd promised Mark that he and Abe would sit with Nonnie so Mark and Addy could have a night out.

"Tomorrow would be great." Lillie leaned into him and, for a second, Jon thought she was going to kiss him.

And knew he'd kiss her back.

She kissed Abe on the cheek. "Anytime after noon would be fine," she said.

What was she doing before noon?

He told himself it was none of his business as he watched her drive off.

Alone with Abe once more, Jon opened the back door of his truck, fastened the toddler securely in his car seat and settled himself in for the drive to Mark's.

All in all they'd had a good day. Fun in the park. Good food.

And Abe had five words now instead of four.

Jon turned the truck toward Mark's house, looking forward to a couple of hours of sparring with Mark Heber's recalcitrant grandmother.

Hopefully Abe would fall asleep soon and Jon and Nonnie could get in a game of penny poker. The old bat had five dollars of his money.

CHAPTER SIX

JON HAD ASKED her to make a list of things she'd like done around her house. She did so, mentally, as she drove to Phoenix on Sunday morning. Overall, she loved the little house she'd bought close to the center of town, but a few of the rooms needed ceiling fans.

He'd have to bring Abe along when he installed them. It wasn't like he could leave the toddler home alone.

She really wanted to have new faucets in the master bathroom. And one in the kitchen, too, with a pull out sprayer....

She'd need to baby-proof her home. She still had the cupboard safety catches she'd purchased when...

Maybe Jon could undermount her kitchen sink—a style of mounting that put the counter on top of the edge of the sink. She had granite countertops, which she'd had in her home in Phoenix and loved, but the sink was traditionally mounted. She'd grown used to undermounting. Preferred not to have to worry about water and other debris spilling over, wetting her outfit as she leaned against the edge of the counter as she worked.

A little boy in her home. Wandering from room to room...

The electrical outlet in her living room, the one behind the couch, didn't work. Could Jon do electric?

She had brand-new sippy cups, still in their plastic. Was Abe too old for those?

There was the sticky latch on the window in the office. And she'd been meaning to get quotes on having a front porch put on....

Wait.

Taking the 202 to the 101, Lillie headed north toward Scottsdale and the little café that made breakfasts good enough to compel rich and famous people to wait for a table.

This thing with Jon. And Abraham. She wanted to help them because she knew she could. Because something about Abraham, the serious way he looked at her, as though he was trying to tell her something, haunted her.

But the time she was spending with them was nowhere near equal to the time that would be required to complete the list of jobs she was compiling.

She had to scale herself back. Way back.

Maybe just the ceiling fans. And the faucets.

Or just the ceiling fans.

And they could see about the faucets....

ABE WOKE JON up at six. Laundry was done by seven. Two loads was all it took. One with jeans and pants, the other with the rest of their clothes.

Sitting down with his son for a bowl of nonsugared cereal with fresh bananas and a piece of toast at the little four-seater, faux butcher-block table that had come with the furnished, two-bedroom apartment he'd found for them, Jon checked the strap on Abe's booster seat one more time and, reaching under the table, pulled it more firmly up to the table before placing Abe's plastic bowl within sight, but not reach.

"Eat," he said clearly, holding the big handled little spoon. "You're hungry," he said, leaning down just a bit so that his lips were right in Abe's line of vision. "You want to eat," he said, keeping his voice steady, kind. But firm, too. "Tell Daddy you want to *eat*."

Abe grunted, looking at the bowl of cereal, and kicked Jon's knee under the table. Repositioning himself so that his legs were together and angled away from the little boy, he leaned forward a little more. "You're hungry," he said again. "Tell Daddy you want *eat*." And when Abe grunted again, he repeated the process a third time, putting more emphasis on the word *eat* each time.

Abe's face puckered and Jon could see a bout of tears on the horizon. "I'm not giving in, Abraham." He almost smiled. But this wasn't a game. "It's just you and me, buddy, and if you want to scream to he—Hades and back, you go ahead." In his former life he'd used more colorful vocabulary. It came naturally to him. But he was working on not slipping up. "You want to eat. I understand that. I just need you to tell me."

Slamming his hands on the table, Abraham started to cry. Jon moved the boy's cereal bowl a little farther out of reach. He'd cleaned up enough spilled milk.

And he took hold of his son's little hand, rubbing it lightly.

Abe stared at him.

"Your breakfast is here, son," he explained slowly. "So is mine. And I'm hungry, too. I just need you to use your words. Tell Daddy you want to eat."

With drops of tears wetting his lashes, Abe stared.

"Eeeeaaat," Jon said again. Slowly.

"Eeeeeuh!" The word wasn't offered gently at all.

Jon didn't give a damn about that. He almost spilled the cereal himself in his haste to reward Abe's milestone.

The boy was not stupid. He'd just had a father who'd been too good at reading his mind and not good enough at forcing him to do for himself.

"So…WHAT DO you think?" Lillie stared back and forth between the two people she loved more than anything in the world—her stand-in parents, Jerry and Gayle Henderson, who'd taken her into their hearts long before they'd become her in-laws, and kept her there in spite of the divorce.

"I think you look happier than you have in a long time." Gayle's soft-spoken words settled a bit of the unease deep inside of Lillie.

She turned to Jerry. "What about you, Papa?" Not Dad. Or Daddy. Lillie couldn't give another man that name. But neither could she call Jerry anything but a variation of it.

"I trust you, Lil. You'll do the right thing."

She'd told them about Jon and Abraham. Every Sunday morning over breakfast, she gave them a rundown of her week and they did the same. They were her family.

The only close family she had.

"What does that mean?" she asked, shaking her head. "I'm asking for your opinion, Papa. That's when you tell me what you think even if I'm not going to like it." They'd been over this point before. She needed Jerry's honesty. She wasn't going anywhere, no matter what he said to her.

"I think that you obviously feel something for this little boy. And it could be a bit personal. Frankly, I can't imagine that your personal experience doesn't play some part in the work you do. How could it not? What happens to you becomes a part of you. You can't just leave it behind. No matter how badly you want to."

There was a message in there for her. Unrelated to Jon and Abraham Swartz.

"You think I'm trying to leave my past behind? I thought you approved of my move to Shelter Valley. You encouraged me to branch out on my own."

Gayle's blue eyes were filled with concern. "We did," she said. "We do."

"Papa?"

"Gayle and I fully support your move—and your career choice," he said, his words coming slowly, as if he was choosing them carefully.

Gayle. It was what Kirk had called his father's third wife. So that was what Lillie called her, too, although she'd always been closer to Gayle than to Kirk's biological mother—Jerry's first wife, who'd left him for a man richer than he was back when Jerry had been fresh out of college and starting his own PR firm.

"We thought you'd have found…someone…by now," Gayle's gaze was direct. And filled with love.

Shaking her head, Lillie looked between the two of them, her broccoli quiche and fruit untouched on her plate. "I don't understand." Either they thought the move to Shelter Valley had been a good decision, or they thought she was running away. It couldn't be both.

Taking a deep breath, she reminded herself that she'd asked for this conversation. That she wanted—no, needed—their insight and perspective.

Everyone needed a sounding board.

"Your career choice, your location, isn't the problem, Lil," Jerry said. "It's your lack of close relationships that concerns us."

"You want me to take a lover?"

What did this have to do with Jon and Abraham? She'd asked them if they thought she was crossing a line getting involved with the Swartzes.

During the final months of her pregnancy, Lillie and the Hendersons had had many frank conversations. Gayle had been present during the birth.

Gayle's smile was too knowing, but Lillie wasn't sure what the older woman thought she knew.

"No, Lil, we don't mean you should take a lover," she

said. "Unless you meet a man you're in love with and want to sleep with, of course," she added.

"We just want you to open your heart and let people in again," Jerry said.

Oh.

As far as she was concerned, the conversation was over. "Hearts break."

"When you first came to us, your parents had only been gone for a year," Jerry said. "You had a broken heart then."

She remembered spending nights alone in her dorm room when she'd been so filled with pain that she'd been afraid she wouldn't be able to pull enough air into her lungs to sustain her until morning.

"But you were still you, Lil. A woman with a generous heart who has a special awareness of people and their needs. You're very perceptive to other people's feelings," he added.

"Are you saying I'm no longer generous?"

Reaching across the table, Gayle covered Lillie's hand. "We're saying that while you're busy giving every hour of your life to other people, you aren't allowing yourself to get close to anyone," she said.

"We were talking about Jon and Abraham Swartz. About whether or not I'd overstepped a professional boundary by making that absurd agreement with him—trading skill set for skill set. Letting him in my home..."

"And we're telling you that isn't even an issue, Lil," Jerry said, more serious than she'd heard him in a long time. "What you're doing for that man and his little boy is marvelous. Generous. It's classic you, understanding that in order for him to accept your help he had to be able to give in kind. My worry is that you had to ask if you were overstepping. Are you really that afraid of letting anyone into your heart?"

"Jerry and I have been worried about you for a while," Gayle said. "You've got a town full of friends, but you don't let any of them into your heart. At least, not that you tell us about."

"You two are in there."

Jerry's gaze softened, moistened, as he added his hand atop Gayle's and hers on the table. "And you are first in ours, Lil. Don't ever doubt that. But you need more than two old folks in your life. You need a partner who is worthy of you. Who will look out for you as much as you look out for him. I'm just worried that if he comes along, you won't be able or ready to open your heart and let him in."

Kirk had bolted her heart shut and thrown away the key.

But Papa and Gayle knew that. Lillie was at a loss for words. She'd accepted her lot in life. Had found a way to be happy.

And she didn't want to screw it up by making a professional mistake from which it would be impossible to recover in a town as small and close-knit as Shelter Valley.

"Have you heard from that damned son of mine?" Jerry asked.

Kirk still worked for his father. But they didn't socialize.

Or even chat much beyond clients and accounts. And Kirk dropping his son off to spend an occasional day with them.

"No," Lillie assured him. She didn't need Papa thinking he had to rake Kirk across the coals another time. It hurt Papa and served no purpose. "Of course not."

A couple of years before, when Kirk had come to Lillie pressuring her for a change to their divorce decree that would give him more money, Jerry had given his son an ultimatum. If Kirk bothered Lillie again he would be cut off. Period. From the firm and from his inheritance.

"He left Leah," Gayle said softly.

"I thought they were getting married." Their son was five now—not that Kirk spent much quality time with the boy, according to Papa and Gayle.

Papa and Gayle did more with him the couple of times a month they saw him then Kirk appeared to.

"He said he didn't love her enough to marry her."

Kind of late to be figuring that out. Lillie counted her lucky stars that she'd gotten out before wasting all of the best years of her life with him.

She had to admit, she felt a small thrill of satisfaction, too. Did that mean Kirk really had loved her as much as he'd said he did? He had, after all, married *her*.

"Maybe if Leah hadn't let him move in with her, if she hadn't had his child without expecting anything in return, he would have married her," she said, just to show Jerry and Gayle that she could speak rationally, unemotionally, about the man who'd ripped her apart at the seams during the darkest hours of her life. To show them that it didn't matter to her a whit whether Kirk was with Leah, or Kayla or Marcie or anyone.

Jerry and Gayle were like parents to her.

Their son meant nothing.

Period.

CHAPTER SEVEN

BREAKFAST DISHES WERE done, bathroom cleaned—and Jon hadn't cracked a book open because Abe hadn't gone down for his nap.

And they had an appointment at Lillie's that afternoon.

So Jon improvised. The doctor said that Abe's nap times would change over the next year. If the toddler didn't want to sleep and wasn't exhibiting signs of crankiness due to fatigue, then he should give him a chance at staying up.

But Abe still took two naps at the day care—morning and afternoon. Jon should do what he could to stick to the routine.

He compromised. With Abe in his crib, he hauled out the navy duffel that had seen him through many phases of his life. He could afford to replace it but he didn't care to.

Barbara Bent had given it to him the day she'd told him that she was getting married, planning to have a child of her own and giving up foster care.

He'd been twelve at the time. And had spent the majority of his life in her home.

He'd packed that duffel twice since Abraham was born. He had a system. Knew the ropes. Diapers filled both side pockets—enough to get him through twenty-four hours. They were bigger now, but they still fit. And regardless of whether or not he liked Lillie Henderson, there was a very real possibility that she'd been hired by Clara Abrams to collect enough evidence of his poor fathering skills to persuade the courts that the toddler was better off with his wealthy and well-situated grandparents than he was with a single male with a criminal record.

Jon had learned his lessons the hard way. He wasn't going to forget them. Or get lazy. He wasn't going to sit around and let the courts decide his future. Or the future of his son.

If Clara came after them, he'd grab Abe, the bag, and run.

"Uh!"

Abe stood up in his crib, pointing to Jon, asking what he was doing.

Jon's mouth was forming a reply, something about always being prepared, when he stopped himself. "You want to know what I'm doing?" he asked.

"Uh!" Abe said, reaching toward his father.

"Ask me what I'm *dooiinng* and I'll tell you." Jon enunciated the key word carefully, just as Lillie had done the evening before.

A resealable bag of toiletries—tear-proof shampoo, lotion, body wash, cleaning wipes, thermometer, acetaminophen drops and syrup of ipecac—went in the front pocket.

"Uhhh!" Abe's voice rose in conjunction with the whiny tone that had entered his voice.

"Dooiinng." Jon faced his son. Abe was getting tired. He could tell by his tone. But he wasn't going to give in. He wasn't going to reward bad behavior.

"Uh. Uh. *Uhhh.*" Abe stood his ground.

Jon strode over, gently picked his son up off his feet, laid him down in his crib, told him to sleep well, grabbed the duffel and left the room, checking to ensure that the working light on the baby monitor was engaged on his way out. He could finish packing for the two of them outside the toddler's room.

Half an hour later, most of which was spent enduring demanding—and then just exhausted—screams, he very quietly, so as not to disturb his sleeping son, hid the fully packed duffel in the back of his bedroom closet.

A safeguard.

Just in case life came crashing down on him again.

LILLIE PLAYED OUTSIDE with Abraham on Sunday for the twenty minutes it took Jon to install the security lock on her sliding glass door. Her house wasn't exactly child friendly.

She came home one night later that week to new ceiling fans whirring softly in her living room and kitchen— Jon had finished his lab early and had had an extra hour and a half of free time before he had to go to work. He'd stopped by the clinic for her key.

She'd refused to picture him in her home, among her things, free to explore at his will. Why would he bother snooping? He was there in a professional capacity, that was all.

There'd been another break-in that week. A home on the outskirts of town. The thief had taken everything of value—guns, electronics, jewelry—but he hadn't damaged anything except the standard lock on the sliding glass door as he'd lifted it off the track. It was this detail that had people convinced the two crimes were related. Word was that the guy had special suction cups used by glass installers to remove the doors.

On Friday, after observing Abraham playing happily by himself at Little Spirits Day Care, Lillie phoned Jon and got his voice mail.

Sitting in her car in the day care parking lot, she tried to pretend that she hadn't chosen that particular time to call because she'd known that her chances of reaching him were slim.

"This is Jon. Leave a message."

"Hi, Jon, it's Lillie. Lillie Henderson. I just wanted to call and thank you for your thoughtfulness in installing the safety catch on my sliding door. There was another break-in and I feel a lot better knowing that I'm protected. So…thank you."

She could have said more. Should have said more. This was, after all, an exchange of services and she had some thoughts about his son. But they could talk about Abraham when he called her back.

With her hand on the keys, ready to turn the car on, Lillie froze. She'd left the message unfinished so that he'd call her back.

As though she was playing some kind of cat-and-mouse game.

It was completely and totally not her style.

JON HEARD HIS phone ring. Saw Lillie's number pop up. He was elbow-deep in the belly of a five-foot-tall steel grinder, removing a twelve-inch-by-five-inch steel blade. The third of eight. He was working on his own, and he could have stopped to take the call.

He waited to see if she left a message instead. There was an outside chance that she was calling because of some emergency with Abraham, but it wasn't likely. Bonnie Nielson or one of her full-time employees would be calling if that were the case.

Still, vice grips and pliers in hand, he watched his phone, hit voice mail as soon as it popped up and—after listening to a voice that reminded him of flowers in a garden—pressed nine to save the message.

CAROLINE STRICKLAND, THE mother of a twenty-four-year-old Harvard graduate, a second-grader and a kindergartner, stopped by Lillie's office at just past four on Friday afternoon. "Oh, you're on the phone," she said, backing out the door.

"No! Come on in." Lillie smiled at the woman who'd been one of her first clients when she'd come to town. Caroline's middle child had been two at the time and in for stitches.

Putting her cell phone back in her purse, Lillie swore to herself that she'd leave it there unless it actually rang. If Jon Swartz called, she'd know it. If he texted, she'd know it. She could hear. She didn't have to keep looking at the damned thing.

"What's up?" she asked as Caroline, slim and comfortable looking in her jeans and T-shirt, settled into the rocker in the corner of the room.

"John wants to take me to Italy for our anniversary." Caroline was not smiling.

"You love Italian food," Lillie reminded her. "And you've always wanted to see the Mediterranean."

Caroline and Lillie met early in the morning three times a week to ride bikes on the quiet streets of Shelter Valley.

To exercise when no one was watching.

"I know." Caroline's usually cheerful voice fell on the last word.

"So what's the problem?" There was one; that much was evident. Lillie hated to see her friend so obviously bothered. It wasn't like Caroline, who'd taken her first husband's unexpected death, an unplanned pregnancy and a move across the country in stride.

"I don't know." Caroline looked at the paperwork on Lillie's desk.

"Weren't you just saying last week that you wanted to spend more time alone with him?"

"Yeah."

"So?" She frowned. Caroline wasn't afraid of flying. She and John and the kids spent a lot of time on Caroline's family farm in Kentucky and flew back and forth several times throughout the year as the kids' schooling allowed.

"When he told me…" She grinned, but there were tears in her eyes as she paused. "He'd told me he had a business thing in Phoenix." As an architect of some renown, John Strickland did a lot of business in the city, and often took Caroline to dinner meetings with clients. "But instead, he took me to this fancy restaurant and ordered wine, and when they brought the bottle they also delivered the travel documents…."

"Romantic!" Lillie liked John and found him to be genuine. Still, she'd found Kirk to be genuine, too, back before she'd realized that a man could look her straight in the eye and lie and she couldn't tell the difference.

Kirk had plied her with romance throughout their courtship and after they were married, too. Even when he'd also been plying Leah.

If Caroline was here to tell her something bad about John, to tell her she'd found out that he'd had an affair, Lillie would be surprised. But she'd also believe her.

"It was romantic," Caroline said, still smiling. Still avoiding Lillie's gaze with eyes that were glistening. "He's the best, Lillie. And I love him so much."

Here it comes. Lillie braced herself. Still hoping that Caroline merely had a schedule conflict with John's probably prepaid travel arrangements. And that she didn't want to hurt her husband's feelings and…

"I don't want to leave the children." Caroline looked up, her brow creased. "I don't know what's come over me, but the second I saw the reminder to bring current passports, I thought of the kids and got scared to death. What if something happens to them while we're gone? I'd be too far away to get to them. It's over an eight-hour flight, Lil."

Her friend's gaze begged for understanding.

"Did you tell John how you felt?"

"No! How could I? What he did was so sweet and he was so happy knowing he was giving me what I really wanted."

Had Kirk ever done anything like that for her? Lillie couldn't remember.

"I just…" Caroline's hands twisted in her lap as she started rocking back and forth. And then she glanced up. "What if something happened to John and me? Who'd care for our kids?"

Lillie knew then why Caroline was in her office. Lillie had been a junior in college when her own parents had been killed in a car accident while on a business trip in Chicago.

"I was devastated when I lost Mom and Dad," Lillie said. "Honestly, I didn't think I was going to make it. A year later, I was still having panic attacks. But then I was also getting ready to graduate from an elite university with a near-perfect grade point average. And eight years later, while I still miss them terribly, I get up every morning with joy in my heart. I'm living a life I love, working in a career I love, surrounded by friends I love."

Caroline didn't know about baby Braydon. She didn't need to know. No one in Shelter Valley did.

Straightening her light pink scrub top, Lillie turned her chair until it was completely facing Caroline, rested her elbows on the arms and gripped the chair with both hands.

"So you think I'm not a bad mother if I take this trip with John?"

"Of course you're not!" She put every ounce of passion she had in that answer. "Quite the opposite. You're doing your children a huge disservice if you let fear of what might happen keep you from living. Because they'll learn by your example…."

Her words faded off.

Had her phone just rung? She'd turned the volume up, but in her purse the sound would have been muffled.

Which mattered not at all. If Jon Swartz called, he'd leave a message. Or call back.

Or not, if he'd decided that she'd helped Abraham enough.

She hadn't.

She thought of the boy's solitary play, of the tantrum he'd thrown at the day care the day before when the teacher announced that it was snack time and all of the other kids hurried to their places on their washable mats. Abe had already been sitting in his spot but had burst into a screaming fit.

And now was not the time…. She purposely pushed all thoughts of Jon and Abraham Swartz away.

Caroline's face was lined and Lillie hated to see her so stressed. Caro was the one who always found the positive in any moment. She was the embodiment of the person that Lillie Henderson strove to be.

"You know that there's as much possibility of something bad happening to you here as there is in Italy."

"Yeah." She shrugged. "But it's so far away."

"It's natural to experience separation anxiety. The kids are going to face it, too, when you go to Italy and when it's time for them to go away to summer camp and, later, college. Or when they get a job offer that's too good to pass up. You want them to give in to that fear and stay home with you and John forever?"

Her friend stuck out her tongue.

"You're five hours away from Jesse. And you don't love or care for him any less than you do the babies."

"I know." Caroline shook her head, her expression unreadable.

"What?" Lillie asked, growing more concerned. "What aren't you telling me?"

Her cell phone rang. She heard it loud and clear, blurting from inside her purse. She looked at the leather satchel under her desk. Caroline stared at it, too.

"Do you need to get that?"

"No. The doctors know I'm here. If there was a medical emergency they'd try my office phone first."

It could be Jon. A client. Requiring privacy.

"This isn't just about a trip to Italy, is it?"

Caroline planted her feet on the floor and leaned forward until the rocker almost tipped her out of her seat. Then she looked up. "Probably not."

"What is it, then?"

"It's just... I've never... My whole life... It hasn't been easy, you know? We never had any money. I had to quit school. There was Daddy's drinking...."

And his rage. Lillie filled in the blanks. Caroline had loved her adoptive father, in spite of his alcoholism.

"Then Jesse's father...he was the jealous type and didn't have any money, either. There was debt when he died. And then I end up pregnant by some guy I don't even know and have to face raising a baby alone, with no money and no education and..."

Lillie knew all of this. Caroline knew she knew.

"Don't get me wrong...I'm not complaining. Or looking for sympathy." Caroline's gaze was direct now as she started to rock again. "Quite the opposite. My past has made me stronger."

"So what's the problem?"

Tell me, Caro. You have an entire town of people here who love you. Who will wrap their arms around you and see you and your family through whatever lies ahead. Good or bad.

"I don't know how to live with so much happiness." The words came out in a rush. "When things were bad, I got up every morning looking forward to whatever possibility the day might bring—whatever possibility I could create to counteract the challenges. Now I get up every morning to John's kiss and that look in his eyes. The kids greet me with squeals and smiles. My biological twin sister is attached to my hip. I feel all the love around me and I'm scared to death."

"Of what?"

"Of losing any of it. I'm afraid to go to Italy. Afraid to take a trip up the mountain or to go to the doctor. I'm afraid that I'm going to wake up and it'll all be gone."

The older woman burst into sobs.

Lillie dropped to the floor at her friend's feet, and took both of Caro's hands.

She could feel her friend's pain as though it were her own. Could remember waking up with that same fear shortly after she'd found out she was pregnant with Braydon.

And look what had happened.

"You're a strong woman," Lillie said, no longer in counselor mode, just being her. She needed Caro to succeed where she'd failed. "You need to use that strength, that courage, and enjoy all of life's blessings without looking back." Someone had to.

Lillie didn't realize she had tears streaming down her own face until Caroline reached out and gently wiped them away.

"Thank you," Caro said. "I knew I just had to talk to you."

She hadn't said anything. She'd blubbered.

"If it would help, I'd be happy to stay with your little ones when you go to Italy," she said.

"I have always wanted to go to Italy."

"I know."

"Life is good."

"Yep."

But it wasn't easy.

Papa and Gayle had been wrong when they'd said that she was too closed off—that she didn't allow her friends into her inner sanctum.

It didn't get much more personal than this.

CHAPTER EIGHT

JON WAS ON campus, heading toward the library after class on Friday night when Lillie called him back.

He answered immediately. Asked her how she was and told her, when she asked, that he was fine.

He'd keep things proper and businesslike, but damn, it was good to hear her voice.

Veering off the main path, he found a bench beneath a tree and sat as he took the call, watching the other students make their way to their evening activities. Even in the dark, he could see clearly due to all the streetlamps. Montford spared no expense when it came to safety.

"You said in your message that you were free tonight," Lillie was saying.

He'd offered to hit another item on her list, but he really wanted to talk about Abe.

"That's right. My friends, Mark and Addy, have Abe. They usually take him one night a week."

"All night?"

They'd offered. More than once. "No. I usually pick him up around ten."

"Does he normally stay up that late?"

Was she checking up on him?

Paranoia, familiar and debilitating, knocked. Briefly.

Lillie had given him a key to her home. She trusted him.

And he'd confirmed that her interest in Abe was just as she'd said, through Bonnie Nielson.

"Jon?"

"Yeah, sorry. Abe goes to bed at eight every night. He goes down at Mark's," Jon said as his fear slid to the back of his psyche once more. "He does much better when I keep him on schedule," he added, just in case.

"Is he cranky when you pick him up?"

"Nope. He doesn't usually even wake up." Campus was well populated, but what Jon saw was mostly couples. Men and women forging bonds. "Mark and Addy bathe him and put him in his pajamas," he continued, and wasn't sure why. Because he liked talking about his son to someone who seemed to be genuinely interested in the day-to-day business of his life? Or because he was still watching his back and wanted to make sure she knew that Abraham was well cared for.

"I secretly think they're using my son as practice for having a child of their own." He sat back on the bench, his ankle crossed at his knee. "Mark and Addy are engaged and in the process of finding a house."

"When's the wedding?"

"I'm not sure. Soon. Probably over Christmas break."

She sighed. Smacking him in the gut. He sat up. "Is it too late to start on the faucets?" he asked, switching mental gears.

She'd emailed her choices and he'd picked them up at the newly opened home improvement store out by the highway on the way to work that afternoon.

Her pause made him uneasy. Standing, Jon hitched his backpack up onto his shoulder and headed to the sidewalk. He was an idiot. A woman as beautiful as Lillie, as sweet as Lillie, wouldn't be spending Friday night alone.

"Or I can just go ahead on to the library like I'd planned and catch you later this weekend."

"I was actually going to ask if you'd like to go get something to eat. You said in your message that you wanted to talk about Abraham and I haven't eaten since eleven o'clock this morning."

She doesn't have a date should not have been the first thought that crossed his mind.

"Sure," he replied. "Do you want to meet someplace?"

The Shelter Valley Diner and campus eateries were the only non-fast-food places he knew of in town.

He suggested the small on-campus pub that served food until midnight. "I discovered early in the semester that the place is virtually dead this time of night. Apparently kids don't start partying until after ten."

"I was one of those kids not so long ago," she said with a chuckle, telling him that she'd meet him at the pub in fifteen minutes.

There was a new bounce to Jon's step as he made his way across campus.

SHE ORDERED A salad. Jon went for the barbecue chicken burger. He longed for a beer. Longed to be just a guy out on a Friday night. But only for a second. Until he pictured the young man playing happily—he hoped—just a few blocks away who'd be a passenger in his truck in a couple of hours. Iced tea was just fine.

And he was not on a date.

"Abe had another tantrum today," he started right in. "A bad one."

"I know. Bonnie called. He had one yesterday, too."

He nodded. Played with his straw wrapper. "Bonnie said you nipped that one in the bud almost as soon as it started."

Sitting directly across from him in the booth, Lillie looked over at him with those compelling blue eyes, and Jon had to take a deep breath and remind himself that they were working.

Only working.

What was it with him? Would he be forever looking for that special woman who'd magically sashay into his life and make it all better?

He'd given up the dream of having a woman in his life before he'd started kindergarten. And he gave it up again at twelve when Barbara gave him the boot. Then a third time when he found out that Abraham's mother had only been using her relationship with him, an ex-con, to get her parents to agree to let her move to New York.

"I'm fairly certain that at least a part of his problem is his lack of language skills," Lillie was saying. "Like most two-year-olds, Abraham understands most of what's said to him. But while it's developmentally normal for him to be much less skilled at verbalizing his own thoughts, he's still behind his age when it comes to speech."

Jon stiffened. Abraham was fine. He was not suffering because Jon was his father. And if he was, Jon would try harder.

That was why he was meeting with Lillie.

It wasn't the only reason he was with her, a voice inside of him said. But it was the only reason that mattered.

"...verbalize needs."

He had no idea what she'd just said, but Jon nodded, anyway.

"At two, he should have a minimum of fifty words, though you should expect only sixty-five percent or so of those to be intelligible."

Abe had fifty different sounds. Jon knew what they all meant.

"Do you read to him?"

"Of course." He had to relax. Lillie wasn't out to get him. This wasn't even about him. Jon leaned back as the waitress set his plate of food in front of him.

"Does he participate?"

A picture sprang immediately to mind. Abe in bed with him, sitting on the pillow, his little diaper-padded butt up against his ear, banging a book on Jon's forehead trying to get his father to read to him.

From now on, Abe would get a story every single night before bed. He just didn't think they could fit one in in the morning. But he'd try.

"I ask him questions. He points," he said. If he was getting it wrong, he'd get it right.

"He does with me, too," Lillie said. "It's clear that he's aware of what's going on in the stories, and that he's interested—at more than a two-year-old level, in my opinion."

He sat back. There you go, then. Jon took a bite of his burger.

They had the place virtually to themselves.

"I wonder if his problem is that he can't make himself understood, except when he's with you." She stabbed at the lettuce lined with chicken strips and Asian noodles, her fingers slender and feminine around the fork.

He and Abe didn't get much of that at their table. The salad or the femininity.

"You said he doesn't have problems when he's at your friends' house."

"That's right." He popped a French fry into his mouth. She was going to think that was all he ever ate.

"And not at home, either."

"Not much. Nothing like the books say he should be having at this age."

Frowning, she ate silently for a couple of minutes. Jon was enjoying sitting there with her.

"In all other respects, developmentally, Abe's either right on track or ahead of his age group." Lillie's words, when she spoke again, eased him even more. "He squats for long periods when he plays, walks up steps unassisted, but still one foot at a time. He grasps crayons with his fist, but draws legible lines more than he scribbles. Scribbling is more likely what you'd see in someone his age. He can balance on one foot. He opens doors by turning the door-knob...."

She didn't need to tell Jon about that. He'd almost died when he'd seen his son heading out to the front yard the week before. He'd since installed a dead bolt on their door, with permission from their very supportive landlord, Caroline Strickland.

Nodding, he took another bite of his sandwich. The thing was almost gone already.

"A lot of what I do involves play, even with my patients at the clinic," Lillie said, still making progress on her salad. "Yesterday, Abe played with this pillow toy Bonnie has for the two-year-olds. It has big zippers and buttons on it and is fun for the kids, but it also helps me assess if a child is developmentally on track. And it begins to teach children how to dress themselves."

"How do I get one of those?"

Holding her fork midair, she blinked as though changing her train of thought, and he realized he'd interrupted her.

"I'm not sure," she said. "But I'll ask Bonnie where she gets them."

Nodding, he motioned for her to continue.

"Abraham was able to button and undo all of the buttons, and to master the zippers, too," she said, "which is in keeping with his age group. He seemed to be really enjoying himself."

He'd see that Abe had one at home, then. Right away.

"What I'm noticing is that Abraham struggles when there are a lot of people around him. It's the only thing that comes together for me." Jon dropped his hands to the table and focused fully on the gorgeous woman sitting across from him.

She was his ticket to Abe's success.

He trusted her to know what was best for his son—at least where this tantrum thing was concerned.

"The lobby in the day care that first time I met you was so chaotic, everyone hurrying to get on with their day. When we were in the park, that big group was passing by. Yesterday he'd been sitting alone on his mat when all of the other kids came rushing over to join him for snack time. Today, Bonnie said that they were going into another room to watch a cartoon movie and Abe's tantrum started as the kids all ran to the door."

"He loves cartoons." Not that Jon let the boy spend too much time in front of the television set.

"It wasn't about the movie," Lillie said. "Or, I'm beginning to suspect, about being left at day care, either. Abraham struggles with coping with large groups of people. Have you had him out in public much?"

He had to think about that. "I don't know. It hasn't been something I've given conscious thought to. But I don't avoid taking him out in public, either." At least not until recently, when he started worrying about these sudden and unexpected tantrums.

"It's okay, Jon." Lillie's touch against the back of his hand was fleeting. Gone in an instant. And it affected him more than it should have.

He wanted her to do that again. To touch him.

"It's not uncommon for a single father to avoid taking his child out in public. Men are more anal than women about needing to maintain control, about fixing every little problem the second it happens, and it's easier to do that when you can control the environment. Which you can do at home."

There was some truth to what she said.

The waitress was back, asking if they wanted anything else. She left the bill at Jon's elbow. Lillie reached for it, but he grabbed it before she could get her hands on it. "I'll get this."

"I asked you to dinner."

"To talk about my son."

She reached for her purse. "Then at least let me pay my half."

"Let me get this, Lillie, please." He looked her straight in the eye. He didn't understand why it was suddenly so important to him to pay her way, but he knew that it was.

"Okay, but only if you'll let me make dinner for you one night this week—even if I have to drop it off at your house." Her expression was dead serious.

And lovely enough to catch his breath.

"Okay."

She stood, waited for him while he laid a tip on the table and again at the register while he settled their tab.

Jon liked knowing she was there. Waiting.

"You want to walk a bit?" he asked as they left the pub. There had been some couples out before. Now the campus seemed to be swarming with them.

It was probably just his imagination.

"Sure, I guess," she said, a note of tension entering her voice again as she looked around.

And he remembered that she'd met her husband on Montford's campus. Remembered that she was divorced.

"Or I can walk you to your car," he offered.

"Would you mind?"

"Not at all," he said, falling into step beside her.

But he did.

"I HAVE A suggestion," Lillie said, keeping her gaze on the sidewalk and her mind on Abraham Swartz as she walked beside Jon across campus.

Friday night had been date night when she'd been in school.

And somehow, anytime she was on campus, she felt like that college kid again.

"I'm listening."

"What would you think about the two of us taking Abraham on some outings in Phoenix? We could go to the zoo. To the mall. To a children's museum that I know about. They have hands-on exhibits for toddlers. If I'm right, and all he needs are some skills to help him cope in large groups of people, a few outings should take care of it."

"I'm good with that," Jon's answer came just before they reached her car. "I'll give anything a try if it'll help Abe."

Lillie relaxed again, smiling up at Jon as she opened her car door. "How about Sunday afternoon? Are you off again this week?"

"Yeah. I don't work Sundays. No day care. Sunday afternoon would be fine."

She would be in the city, anyway—except that her relationship with Papa and Gayle was her business.

"How about if I pick you up?" Jon asked. "I've got the car seat and all the paraphernalia in the truck. If he throws up, it's on my seat." He was grinning, but Lillie sensed that he was also completely serious. Jon Swartz was nothing if not prepared.

Overprepared, in her opinion.

Which endeared him to her.

So she'd make two trips to and from the city. It wasn't that far. Agreeing to be ready at one, Lillie stood for a second too long, waiting for Jon to say something.

She didn't know what.
He didn't say it.
She got in her car and drove away without looking back.

CHAPTER NINE

JON DROPPED ABE off at day care as soon as they opened at six on Saturday morning. That early on a weekend morning, he and the Saturday teacher, Laura James, were the only ones there. There were only a handful of little ones who even came to day care on Saturday, but Bonnie kept the place open for them.

This morning, with the reception room to themselves, Abe took Laura's hand and walked off to the playroom without so much as a backward glance at Jon.

Maybe Lillie was right. His son had a problem with crowds. They could fix that.

Easily.

Jon arrived at work only to find out that there was no electricity and everyone was being sent home. So, just before nine-thirty, he walked out to his truck and dialed Lillie's cell. Exchanged pleasantries with her because he was in a good mood.

Because he wanted her to like him.

To think he was a good dad.

Even if she *was* working for Clara Abrams on the side, her loyalty could be changed. If Jon did his job well enough. He was the one spending time with Lillie, not Clara. And he'd seen enough to know that Lillie had a good heart. She'd want what was best for Abe. Money clearly didn't matter to her. It wasn't like she lived big or associated with the kinds of people Kate came from.

She was like him, down-to-earth, working for a living, wearing regular clothes, cleaning her own house.

Jon just had to prove to her that he was what was best for Abe—not Abe's rich and influential maternal grand-parents.

Except that Clara knew about Jon's past. Which meant that Lillie might know, too.

"You're at home?" he asked, stopping in the parking lot with his hand on the door handle of the truck.

Why hadn't he thought of it before? What if Lillie knew about the years he'd spent in juvenile detention?

And then he started breathing again. She'd given him a key to her home. There was no way she'd have done so if she'd known he was a convicted burglar.

"A rare Saturday morning off." She answered his question with a chuckle. "Unless someone breaks something or needs stitches or falls unexpectedly ill," she added. "As long as the clinic is open, I could get called."

He realized she didn't get much more sleep than he did.

"So what's up?"

"A semi lost control on the highway and ran into the transformer that supplies our electricity at the plant. Management wants to preserve the backup generator for perish-able food and have shut down the production lines for the rest of the weekend." *TMI, man,* he reprimanded silently as he climbed behind the wheel of his truck.

"I thought maybe I could get those faucets changed for you," he said. "But if you're home, I can always do them another time."

"Now's fine," she said easily. And Jon refused to think that her ready acceptance of his offer meant she was in-terested in him.

He refused to consider the idea.

She hadn't been alone with a man in her home since her divorce. She dated. She'd just never brought her dates home.

She'd left her door unlocked for the cable guy. Had Caro meet the carpet people for her when she'd had her bedrooms redone. They hadn't been conscious choices, just the way things had worked out.

And now here she was, with a six-foot-tall, dark-haired specimen of male perfection and her palms were a little sweaty.

She washed them. And the bathroom sinks, too, while he worked in the kitchen. Wouldn't be proper to expect him to deal with traces of toothpaste spit when he installed her new faucet.

He'd asked, the previous week, if they could be friends.

She didn't know what that meant.

Her curiosity bothered her.

"All done." The subject of her thoughts stood, tools in hand, at the door to her bathroom. His jeans and T-shirt hugged his body and the way they fit turned her on.

Uh-uh. Not happening.

Except it was.

Which pissed her off. Or something.

God, what was the matter with her?

"I can come back and do these later if you're busy in here," he said, his big brown eyes seeming to see her, the sink and tub, and probably any hair she'd lost while she'd hurriedly showered during the time it had taken him to drive from the cactus jelly plant to her place.

"No!" Giving the counter one last swipe with the paper towel in her hand, she took a deep breath. "Really, it's fine. I'll just go."

She retreated to her office to look at the pile of bills she put off paying until they were absolutely due because she hated the paperwork involved.

Kirk hadn't minded household bookkeeping. He'd been good at it. And good at spending whatever was left over each month, too.

With her computer screen open to her online bill payment screen, Lillie was typing in the last amount when Jon's voice sounded behind her.

"I'm really sorry to bother you," he said. "But I could use your help if you've got a second."

Lillie jumped. Bought herself a breath of time to calm down as she minimized her screen. And followed him out the door.

"There's hard-water corrosion on your shutoff valve." He chatted as he led her through her living room and down the hall toward the bathroom. His ass was rock solid, sitting above thighs that were clearly muscled. And perfectly proportioned. Probably had a lot of hair on them. She'd seen the dark chest hair curling at the opening of his shirt the other day.

She was a hair girl—liked it gone on her but all over her man. Her preference was natural, instinctive—necessary for the procreation of the human species.

It had nothing to do with Jon Swartz.

"I'm going to have to replace the valve," he was saying. "I had one in the truck, just in case."

His tight ass preceded her down the hall. And turned into her bathroom.

"If you could just turn on the shower while I hold this bucket under here…" Now he was lying flat on his back on her floor, scooting himself beneath the sink. "I'd have done it myself, but the bucket I have won't fit under the lines. I have to hold it at an angle."

As he shifted his body, her gaze collided with his zipper. And it stuck there. She couldn't help herself. She looked.

Her body reacted.

And on the floor not too far away, in a very neat pile, was her bin of nail polish, her hair spray, a container filled to the brim with hair ties. And a brand-new box of tampons.

"Why do you need the shower on?" Her words came out more sharply than she'd intended, so she added, as she stepped over the tools and opened her shower curtain, "I thought you shut off the water to the house."

"I did, but there's always water left in the lines, and if you open the shower faucet, the pressure will release the water that's resting in these pipes. I catch it now, or catch it in the face later when I change the shutoff valve. If everything was working properly, I'd just shut off the valve and that would take care of any excess water in the lines. Since it isn't, it's less messy this way."

Without another word, Lillie turned on the shower. Water gushed. And then, almost immediately, slowed to a mere trickle.

Jon emerged from under the sink with a bucket sloshing a couple of inches of water.

"Thanks," he said, reaching for a heavy-duty-looking wrench from the big toolbox he'd carried in.

Those same hands had moved her personal items.

"If you don't mind hanging around, I could use your help again in a minute," Jon said from beneath the sink. Steel clanged against steel—tool against pipe. "It'll be a lot easier to fasten the new faucets if you could hold them straight for me while I'm under here tightening them."

He knew what brands of products she used.

"Sure. No problem." She'd just stand there. Waiting.

There was that zipper again. Lillie tried to swallow, but there was nothing there. Her throat was uncomfortably dry. Other parts of her were uncomfortably wet.

Because a good-looking man was in her bathroom? Changing a faucet?

Lillie definitely had to get out more.

CRAZY AS IT seemed, Jon had never been to a zoo. His foster mother until he was twelve had not been one for extracurriculars with the kids she took in. The money she made from the state was for their health, their well-being and for her pocket. Not for fun.

After that, he'd never spent enough time in one home—or one school—to be present for a zoo trip.

"Look, Abie baby!" Kneeling beside his son, he pointed to the monkey hanging from a branch in a landscaped enclosure. "See the monkey?"

Abe's gaze followed Jon's finger and the toddler nodded. Turning, the boy looked for Lillie, who was standing right beside them. He pointed.

"See?" she said. "You want me to see?"

Abe nodded. Lillie focused on the boy. "Say, 'look.' Lllooook. You say 'look' and then I will see. Use your words, Abraham."

The monkey had switched trees and was no longer hanging. But, God love her, Lillie had a job to do and she was doing it.

"Lllooook," she said again. Jon was looking. At her.

In a pink sweater that hugged her full breasts, jeans that encased long, perfectly shaped legs, pink patent leather tennis shoes and her long luscious hair held back with a clip, the woman exemplified femininity. His body responded. Her open-eyed gaze and hint of a smile while she talked to his son hit him someplace else. Someplace much deeper.

"Lllooook," she was saying.

"Ooook." Abe's voice was loud, excited, as he finally gave her what she wanted.

"Good, son!" If his tone mimicked his son's overstimulated emotions, he hoped their companion put the response down to fatherly encouragement.

That was all it really was.

That and the fact that everyone was looking at them as though they were a family. And more than just about anything else at that moment, Jon wished it was true.

CHAPTER TEN

THE ZOO WASN'T all that crowded that late on a Sunday afternoon, but still, there were enough people around that Jon was conscious of hanging on to his son every second they were there.

And as much as he liked the place and wished he could explore every exhibit, every cavelike structure, he was glad when it was time to head for the gate.

His tummy full with hot dog and ice cream, a clean-faced and freshly diapered Abraham promptly fell asleep in the car seat as Jon entered the on-ramp to the highway that would take them home.

"We made it through without a single tantrum." Might as well put it right out there. His son was fine. Lillie's presence that afternoon, while nice, had not been professionally necessary.

He was a good dad.

"You never put him down unless you were kneeling down with him."

"He's two years old. He'd have been trampled."

"That's what strollers are for."

"He doesn't like strollers."

"You were afraid he'd throw a tantrum if you put him in one."

More like, Jon knew he would have.

"I wanted him to have fun." He'd been having fun.

But Lillie had been there to work.

A mile went by. "You could have said something," he told her. "You could have suggested we get a stroller."

"I wanted to observe the two of you together, doing things your way, as you normally would without my interference."

Had he been stupid to believe that she was there to help him and Abe? Not to separate them?

"And I'm not saying you should have rented a stroller," Lillie said slowly, as though she was thinking hard about something.

"What are you saying?"

"I'm not forming opinions yet. I'm just watching. Assessing. I'd like to be out with you a couple more times to see how things go before I give suggestions. If that's okay with you."

Jon's heart leaped. Not a comfortable feeling. "That's fine," he said, putting a wrap on the part of himself that still stupidly longed for baby and dad and mom makes three. Longed for a woman who'd give her time to them just because she cared and wanted to help them be better together.

"If you'd rather not have me tagging along, we can work out something else...."

Taking his eyes from the road for only the briefest second, Jon glanced at his companion. Her eyebrows were drawn, her mouth a straight line.

And he felt like a fool—painting his happy-family pictures oblivious to what others wanted.

He'd been enjoying a Sunday outing while Lillie had been busy working and probably thinking of all the other things she could—and should—be doing.

Just like Kate had done.

Worse, she might have been spying.

"I'm sure you have better things to do than hang out

with us," he said, letting her off whatever hook she was on. One thing Jon Swartz knew was to let go of women who were finished spending time with him.

She moved and he could feel her looking at him. A mile marker flew by. And then another.

"There's nothing more fulfilling than helping a child."

He shot her another glance. She was staring straight at him and he had no idea what to say. "I'm more concerned that I'm pushing myself on you and your son because I believe I can help, than because it's the appropriate thing to do."

He didn't know what to make of that, either.

"You aren't pushing yourself on us. We've agreed upon a fair trade."

"It's just that…you have the right to raise your son as you see fit, Jon. I feel like I'm overstepping my professional boundaries here."

She wasn't spying. She was just who she said she was. For that moment, his gut knew the truth. Knew, too, that for Abraham's sake, he had to trust her.

He had to trust someone.

"I need the help." The admission was tough. Because she was right—they'd made it through the day without a tantrum because sometimes Jon knew how to avoid them. Not because Abraham knew how to cope with life.

"You're a good father."

"I'm a single guy learning as I go. It was nice today, having a woman around. Abraham turned to you several times. He was glad to have you there. And it's occurred to me that maybe that's part of his problem. He's a boy, but he's also a baby. He needs a woman's influence. Her nurturing…"

More mile markers whizzed past. He'd scared her. He'd

done that before, too. Luckily for him, unlike his son, he had the coping skills to deal with it.

"Is his mother in the picture at all?"

Kate Abrams? He'd named their son after her, hoping against hope that some kind of maternal instinct would kick in.

He thought of Clara again. If the worst happened, if Lillie *was* on Clara's payroll, he had to trust that she'd realize Abraham was better off with his father than with family money.

"No, Kate's not in the picture."

"She's alive, though?"

"Yep. Lives in New York City. She's in advertising." At least, the last he heard that was where she was, what she was doing. It wasn't as if he kept track. Once she'd been satisfied that her parents were off his back, she'd disappeared just like she'd said she was going to do.

And if he wanted Lillie's help, she probably should understand a few things.

"I was working for a construction framing company when I met Kate."

He didn't like to think about those days. They served no purpose. The first few months he'd thought he'd died and gone to heaven.

The bump back to earth had been more painful than any that he'd experienced before. But he learned something, too. He wasn't going to go through that again.

"Framing companies are hired by construction bosses—contractors who get the jobs and then hire smaller, more specialized companies who specialize in the various skills needed to put up buildings."

"So your specialty is framing?"

He shrugged. Started to say, "When I got out," and caught himself. "I worked two and three jobs back then," he said. "I'm trained in framing, plumbing and electrical work, though I don't have the certification to run big jobs. I was the guy who laid the pipes and put the wires in place, and the boss would check my work before turning on the juice."

"What does it take to get certification?"

"Classes. A test." He'd have gotten there one day—though more slowly once Abraham came along—if the Montford scholarship hadn't changed his course.

She'd asked about Kate. They were trying to solidify Lillie's role in Abe's life.

For his son's sake he said, "The contractor, a man with more money than I'd know what to do with, was a decent man. I rented a little two-bedroom house from his property management company, which is how I got the job to begin with."

His parole officer had referred him to the contractor when he'd been set free. A young kid with a sealed record, a GED earned while serving time for armed robbery and no references didn't just walk out into the world and get received with open arms. The contractor had a history of hiring newly released juvenile offenders, his civic duty, he'd said, to give them a trade and a chance to be a contributing member of society.

"Kate was the guy's niece," he said out loud. "She showed up on the construction site to see her uncle and asked me out." She'd just graduated with a degree in marketing and had been bored, he'd later found out, waiting to land her dream job and leave Atlanta for even more populated pastures. The only problem was, her parents wouldn't let her go. Kate had been determined, though. She'd been looking for trouble so that her father would agree that it would be a good idea for her to get out of town.

Jon withheld that part of the story. Either Lillie already

had the information, or she didn't need to know about it to help Abraham.

"Six months later she told me she was pregnant."

He'd never forget the day. The...

"I'm assuming that was unexpected."

With a quick glance in the rearview mirror, an instinctive reflex assuring himself that his son was right there with him—not a heavenly dream—Jon said, "In more ways than one."

She was looking at him again. His peripheral vision told him her face was turned toward him.

"The morning Kate found me on break to tell me that we were going to have a child, I jumped off a four-foot-high block wall and hugged everyone in sight. Understand this, professionally and every other way, I wanted my son. I was ready to shout the news to the world. I imagined we'd get married. She'd move in with me and we'd buy a house...."

He'd been a fool. There was no point in hiding the fact.

Lillie gazed out the front window. He wondered if she thought he was lying to her.

And thought again about her childless state. About a husband who maybe hadn't wanted children.

"Kate had come to tell me the news with one goal in mind—asking me to put up the money for the abortion so her family wouldn't know she'd had it."

They were supposed to know that she'd hooked up with an ex-con, not that she'd produced an heir to the Abrams throne.

"Wow."

He'd been poleaxed himself. "She wasn't a bad person," he said. Because Kate was Abraham's mother—and because the words were true. When Kate had caught wind that her mother was petitioning to take Abe away from him, she'd moved hell and high water to make certain that didn't happen. Of course, she'd done so partially because if Clara had Abraham, Kate would be forced to see her son, to be at least a part-time mother. But Jon also knew that Kate wanted Abraham with him. She'd had tears in her eyes when she'd told him how lucky Abraham was to have a father who cared as much as Jon did.

"Kate just had different goals. She was going to New York, to make it big in advertising. She wanted to travel. She'd grown up under the strict thumb of an overprotective father and yearned for freedom more than anything else."

Logically, he understood it all.

"Her worst nightmare, as she'd put it, was to live in the town where she'd grown up, changing diapers and wiping noses."

Lillie still wasn't saying anything. Just staring out the windshield. Jon tried not to care about what she might be thinking.

He checked again on Abe instead, satisfied to see that his son was still sleeping soundly, his head propped against the travel pillow Jon kept in the truck for such occasions, his little mouth open and wet with drool. God, he loved that kid.

"I know it might sound like Kate's heartless," he told Lillie, what he'd told himself over and over during those early days. "But she's not. As soon as she saw how much our unborn child meant to me, she agreed to have it. As long as I'd take full custody and release her from any obligations or responsibilities, legally as well as any other way."

"A surrogate mother." Lillie's voice sounded far away.

"Right. She moved in with me while she was pregnant—" although they'd slept in separate bedrooms "—and followed through with excellent prenatal care. I was present for every doctor appointment and was there when Abe was born."

A small cough sounded from Lillie's side of the car. When Jon glanced over, he saw a tear slide down her face.

He focused on the road in front of him. "A couple of hours later, she signed the baby over to me, checked herself out of the hospital against doctor's orders and moved on with her life. I stayed at the hospital with Abe that night, and when I brought him home the next day, all of her stuff was gone."

Lillie didn't say anything for so long, Jon wasn't sure they were going to speak again for the rest of the trip. He wasn't sure he wanted to.

Pulling a tissue out of the pack on his visor, he handed it to her. She took it without saying a word.

The woman cared enough for his son to cry for them. If he wasn't careful he was going to fall right back into his own trap and make too much of that.

They'd been driving without conversation for more than twenty minutes when Lillie's words, "She was a fool," fell softly into the silence.

Shrugging, Jon said, "Or she was smart, and decent for being honest with me, rather than pretending that Abe and I were what she wanted and then being unhappy and eventually divorcing us. She did right by us. She had him."

Her gaze was on him again. "Do you ever hear from her?"

"No. At her request, we went through the court and had her name removed from his birth certificate."

She'd also done it to make her mother's quest to get custody of Abe a bit harder. But not impossible. Kate couldn't do anything about the Abrams DNA running through Abe's veins.

"She could change her mind."

She wouldn't. Because, in the end, Jon was an ex-con. And Kate Abrams was still an Abrams. She wanted a blue-blooded father for her children.

"You never know. You might hear from her someday."

Was Lillie telling him something? Or just being her usual compassionate self?

Either way, he hoped she was wrong. Because if he heard from Kate it could only mean that her mother had decided that Kate's threat to keep her away from her future grandchildren was not enough reason for Clara to leave Jon and Abe alone.

CHAPTER ELEVEN

"L<small>IL</small>?"

Hearing her name on her way to her car in the mostly deserted clinic parking lot Thursday night, Lillie paused and continued to walk. She was exhausted. Hadn't sat down since her bike ride with Caro just before dawn.

"Lil!" The voice came again. Kirk's voice. Louder this time. She hadn't imagined that unmistakable tone of voice. She just hadn't heard it in years.

Turning, she saw her ex-husband, looking as perfect as always.

"Kirk? What are you doing here?" Besides walking toward her from the other side of a brick wall where he'd evidently parked his car. In jeans and a blue-and-white long-sleeved shirt, he appeared younger than she remembered. More like the Kirk she'd known in college—back when she'd thought she wanted nothing more than to spend the rest of her life with him.

"I didn't think you'd take my call." He reached her, standing a bit too close for her comfort.

He'd been right. If he'd called, she wouldn't have answered. The late-October evening breeze wafted from him to her, carrying the slightly musky scent that used to fill her nostrils every night and greet her at the breakfast table every morning.

She'd liked it.

"Why are you here?" she asked again, irritated that she

was rumpled, still wearing her scrubs. After a ten-hour day between the day care and the clinic, her makeup would be worn away. And her hair was falling out of its ponytail.

Kirk liked it loose and curling down her back.

"I wanted to see you, to make certain you were okay."

She wanted him to look at her and eat his heart out.

"I've been here five years," she said. She was too tired to deal with him, to listen between the lines for the truth he didn't speak. One thing she knew, Kirk took care of Kirk. If he was in Shelter Valley, it was because he needed something from her.

"I just heard about the break-ins you've been having here," he said. "The one last night made the news in Phoenix."

Truth be known, she was a tad unnerved by the latest break-in herself. Everyone in town was. An older woman who lived alone had been in bed asleep and never heard the intruder who'd removed her sliding glass door, helped himself to the money and credit cards in her purse and left. She'd woken early that morning to a chilled house and gone out to her kitchen to find the sliding glass door off the track and her purse contents dumped on her kitchen table.

Nothing else had been disturbed.

"According to the news, the thief's getting more daring," Kirk told her. "Until now the thefts have taken place when people weren't home."

He was right, which still didn't explain his presence there.

"I'm not giving you any money, Kirk." It was the only reason she could think of for him to have made the almost-hour-long drive from his home in Scottsdale, the high-end suburb north of Phoenix where she'd last heard he was living.

"I broke up with Leah."

She knew. But didn't want to feed his ego and let him know that she and Papa and Gayle ever mentioned him. "I'm sorry to hear that," she said, proud of her even voice, her expressionless face.

Because inside, she was seething. How dare he show up in her new hometown? So what if he'd attended college there. They'd met and fallen in love in Shelter Valley. He shouldn't have the balls to show his face there. Not anymore.

"I couldn't marry her."

"Oh? Why not?" The question slipped out because she was too tired to stop it. But she wished she had. She didn't give a rat's ass about Kirk Henderson. Didn't want to know anything about him. And didn't want him to think she did. "Is she already married?"

The dig was beneath her. But the small part of her that lived in a lower place liked the justice that would have been served if that were the case—since his own wedding vows hadn't stopped him from pursuing the other woman.

"No. She's never been married."

But she had a five-year-old son. Kirk's son. She wondered what kind of custody agreement they had come to. Biting the inside of her lip, Lillie hitched the big bag she carried with her "doctor's kit"—items designed to divert children of varying ages from whatever immediate trauma they might be facing—farther up on her shoulder and hugged her arms around her waist.

"She's been expecting me to marry her since our divorce was final."

"Because you told her you would." The point was pertinent. Kirk lied.

"I meant to. I thought I wanted to." She'd never heard that insecure tone in his voice. Kirk was *the man*. Always had been. She'd been fool enough to be attracted to his confidence when she'd been too young to recognize the difference between ego and a healthy self-image.

A car drove slowly past the parking lot. Becca Parsons, the mayor, probably on her way home from the city offices just down the street from the clinic. She waved. Lillie waved back.

Shelter Valley sign language for "Yes, I'm fine."

"The truth is, Lil, I kept putting the wedding off because I just didn't feel ready. At first I thought it was too soon." He shrugged, looked down at his casual designer leather shoes that probably cost him a couple hundred bucks. At least. "You know, I felt I had to be divorced long enough to let the end of our marriage sink in...."

He stopped as she flinched, as though realizing that he'd misspoken.

"It took me a while to figure out the truth," he said, scuffing the toe of his shoe as he kicked a small rock a couple of inches in front of him.

He was silent, as though waiting for her to ask about the truth. She wasn't *that* tired.

"The truth is, I couldn't marry her, or anyone, because I'm still in love with you. I told her so the night I left."

Lillie's jaw dropped.

WOULDN'T YOU KNOW it, the boxes of farina were all gone. Staring at the bottom shelf in the grocery store with a hungry boy kicking his feet back and forth in the cart after work on Thursday, Jon considered his options. He'd used up the last of their hot cereal that morning. He and Abe lived on the stuff. Mostly because it was Abe's favorite.

He glanced at his watch. Six-thirty. He had to be at Lillie's at seven to measure for the tile backdrop she wanted along the counter in her bathroom. And to install the second safety catch he'd picked up during lunch that day to install on her sliding glass door.

No time to get to the store outside of town for cereal.

"Eat!" Abe's voice was loud, even for him.

"I know, son," Jon said, smiling at the pudgy-cheeked little boy. Abe's hair was getting a little long, curling along his forehead. He liked it. "We'll splurge on a grilled chicken sandwich at the drive-through just as soon as we're done here. We're going to see Lillie tonight."

"Illeee," Abe said, kicking his feet harder against the cart. Leaning over, he reached for the colorful box of breakfast treats closest to his line of vision.

There'd been another break-in the night before, which made Jon tense as hell. He'd been a thief once. And if people knew that…

If Lillie knew that…

She wouldn't let him in her home to measure her backdrop. He had to get over there to ease his mind.

"Daddy just has to find some cereal for us to have in the morning," Jon said, confident that Abe's reach wouldn't quite make his target. He and Abe were experienced shoppers. Jon had learned the hard way how to measure shelf and cart distances.

"And then we'll go see Lillie." He used the mention of the name shamelessly. Sometimes a guy had to do what a guy had to do.

"Illeee," the boy said with another, harder kick.

Abe had it bad for Lillie.

Bending down again to the yellow "on sale" ticket sticking out from the empty shelf space, Jon continued, "Let's just hope there's some farina hidden in the back."

Abe had had two tantrums at day care that week. Jon wasn't going to risk having the boy be upset before he even left the house in the morning.

Even if it meant he was coping, rather than teaching his son to cope. A guy walking a tightrope could only do so much teaching.

Score. One lone box of farina lay on its side in the very back of the bottom shelf, one corner of the box a little bashed in. He'd take it.

"Good news, buddy." He talked to his son as the top half of his body disappeared under the shelf above the cereal. "Daddy found a box of cerea—"

"Nooooo!" The shriek was unmistakable. Jon still had a foot in front of the cart. He knew it hadn't moved. No one had come near his son.

Hitting his head as he jerked out from underneath the shelf, he stood in one motion, reaching for Abe with both hands. "It's okay, Abraham," he said firmly, right in the boy's face, as Lillie had taught him to do. Get Abe's attention, she'd told him that morning when, after dropping Abe off for day care, the boy had lost it in the reception room again.

Lillie had been in the back room, waiting for a little girl whose father had just left her mother and would be attending day care for the first time.

"Nooo!" Abe's screams pierced the entire store as the boy expressed his displeasure, apparently because he'd been unable to reach the box of breakfast cereal. A woman at the end of the aisle stood, cart in front of her, staring at them. People wheeled past the aisle, no doubt on purpose, just so they could see what was going on.

He recognized a girl from one of his classes.

He leaned down to stick his face nose to nose with his screaming toddler. "Abe, use your words," he said, enunciating clearly.

It's my fault, he wanted to announce over the store's loudspeaker. His son had a problem because he *had* avoided exposing Abraham to crowds. Too many people around meant too many opportunities for someone to snatch, or otherwise hurt, his son.

People equaled danger.

"Abraham, Daddy can't help you if you don't speak to me."

Maybe this was a normal temper tantrum. He was in his terrible twos, after all. "Use your words, son," he said, touching his nose to Abraham's.

The boy stopped crying and gave Jon a wet-eyed stare. "Use your words." Jon took the opportunity to remind Abe before the child started to scream again. "Daddy can't help you if he doesn't know what's wrong."

"Daddeee." Abe's voice wavered, as though he was about to cry again. "Daddee, go."

"You want to go?"

Abe nodded.

"Tell me."

"Go." The word shot out.

"Okay, we can go, but Daddy has to reach under that shelf and get our box of cereal first, okay?" he said, praying that they wouldn't be putting on another show for the citizens of Shelter Valley. "Okay?"

Abe nodded, his chin still quivering. Those big brown eyes watched him as he bent down—he knew because he kept eye contact as long as he could. And his heart broke a little bit as a leftover tear dropped off one of those baby-long lashes.

His son was not a bad or spoiled kid. He just had some things to learn.

And so did his dad.

CHAPTER TWELVE

"CAN WE GO somewhere we can talk?" Kirk had walked with her to her car. Lillie wanted him to leave. Jon and Abe were due at her house soon, and though she'd lent Jon a key to her place, she still wanted to be there when they arrived.

She wanted to see them.

Just to make certain that Abe had fully recovered from his upset that morning.

Or so she told herself.

"We have nothing to talk about."

"How about we go to that little pub on campus? Remember all the nights we hung out there? In that little booth in the back? I stole my first kiss from you there on our second date."

She tried not to think about such things, thinking instead about having dinner with Jon in that very same booth.

Jon. A client. Because her life was about work.

"I'm tired, Kirk. I just want to go home, get out of these clothes and relax."

She recognized her mistake the second she saw the slow sexy grin begin to cross his face. "Sounds good to me."

"Fine, we'll go to the pub." She had to eat. And it wasn't as if she was apt to see anyone she knew there. The class she'd graduated with had all moved on to the rest of their lives.

But Lillie gave the room a once-over, anyway, before

she took a seat at a table around the corner from the booths when she arrived there a minute or two ahead of Kirk. She'd told him she had an errand to run and that she'd meet him at the pub. And then she'd swung by her house, just in case Jon and Abe were early, but Jon's truck wasn't in her driveway. Or parked out front, either.

"What, our booth wasn't empty?" Kirk asked as he slid into the seat across from her, bumping his knees with hers under the table.

"Can it, Kirk, or I'm leaving."

"Sorry."

Lillie glanced up from the menu she'd once known by heart. "What did you say?"

"I'm sorry, Lil. So sorry. About everything."

Her throat tight, Lillie tried to swallow. And to look away. "I don't think I've ever heard you say that."

"I was a damned fool," he said now. "So full of myself."

It was a line. Had to be. He'd matured, she'd give him that. He'd learned humility—or at least how to feign it. But…

Kirk was looking her straight in the eye. His blue gaze was open in a way she'd never seen before.

She didn't want to care.

About him. Or Jon. Or the fact that Papa and Gayle thought that something was wrong with her because she was too closed off.

"I agreed to have dinner with you," she said. Because she hadn't wanted to take a chance that he'd follow her home, or show up five minutes after she got there, and see Jon or Abe.

More to the point, she didn't want Jon to see him.

There was no way she was going to let the past taint her life in Shelter Valley. She'd healed. Moved on.

Even if Kirk's parents didn't think so.

"I didn't agree to revisit the past."

"Fair enough."

"Tell me why you're really here."

"You just said you didn't want to revisit the past."

"If that's why you're here then…" She gathered her purse.

Holding up his hand, Kirk said, "No, please, stay, Lil. That can wait. I really was concerned about you. I've been trying to work up the courage to make the drive out here to see you, and when I read about the break-ins I knew that I couldn't put it off any longer."

Because he couldn't call.

If he'd been anyone else, if she hadn't seen him in action so many times, manipulating people, saying just the right things so they'd think he was giving them what they needed rather than getting them to buy what he wanted them to have, she might have softened.

But she doubted it.

"I'm sorry, but I find it hard to believe that you're suddenly so concerned about my safety."

"My concern isn't sudden." He didn't back down. Or look away.

"What can I get you two to drink?" The server's arrival startled her. Lil hadn't seen the girl approaching. Still, she welcomed her. And, when Kirk deferred to her first, she ordered a soda and the same type of salad she'd had the week before with Jon.

"Make that two." Kirk smiled at the girl. When Lillie and Kirk had been in college, dating, inseparable, they'd eaten off the same plate.

"I'm serious, Lil," Kirk said as soon as the girl turned away. "I've always thanked God that you moved back to Shelter Valley. I lived here, too, remember? If there's a town in this country that's safe for a young woman to live in alone, it's this place. Not only because everyone here knows everyone, but the people in this town are rabid about their public safety."

It was true. And a big part of the reason she'd chosen to settle in the town where she'd met the man who'd crushed her heart. That, and the fact that the job offer had been perfect—and that Shelter Valley was close enough for her to still see Papa and Gayle on a regular basis.

And visit Bray's grave when she needed to.

"But these break-ins..." Leaning forward, he lowered his voice as he moved his face closer to hers. "From what I heard, they've been going on for a couple of weeks and the sheriff is no closer to finding out who's behind them."

Lillie didn't say a word. Didn't acknowledge the fact that he was right.

"You aren't safe here by yourself, Lillie."

"Don't be ridiculous! You think I'm the only single woman in this town?"

"Of course not, but—"

"I'm perfectly safe," she said, although, if she was honest, she had to admit that she was a bit uneasy about facing the night alone.

"Tell me you don't have a sliding glass door."

"I do. But it's got a safety catch on it that prevents it from being lifted off the tracks."

Thanks to Jon.

Who was probably at her house right now.

And Abraham, too.

A little boy in her home.

She wanted to be there....

"That's good, at least."

"Sheriff Richards has increased night patrol," she said. "He's got a posse of volunteers, and they have a list of streets to pay extra attention to. My street is on that list."

"Are you sure?"

"Positive."

Bonnie had told her. Having the inside scoop was one of the perks of working part-time for the sheriff's sister.

Their waitress returned, placing their food and drinks in front of them. Feeling hungrier than she'd realized, Lillie started right in on her salad, paying more attention to the vegetables in her bowl than to her dinner companion.

Kirk asked her about her job. She gave him a brief rundown. He wanted to know if she was happy.

She assured him she was. Unequivocally.

"You practically radiate when you talk about what you do," he said, watching her cut a cucumber in half.

"I told you how much I loved it when I first started working in the field," she reminded him.

"I know. But a lot of jobs seem great in the beginning. To still love your career almost seven years into it—you're lucky, Lil."

Had he lost interest in advertising? She didn't care one way or the other.

Kirk was her past. Period. "So, now that you've satisfied yourself that I'm safe, you can go back to Phoenix with a clear conscience," she said as they finished their salads almost simultaneously.

"I'm clearly being put in my place," he said, his gaze serious.

"You have no place in my life."

"That's the problem."

He hadn't just said that. He wasn't looking at her like that.

Lillie's heart sped up. And stopped. Sped up. And stopped.

She couldn't do this again.

He was the father of her precious, precious boy. The other half of Braydon.

With a lump in her throat, she asked one more time, "What do you want, Kirk?"

"Just to have a chance to be in touch with you," he said. "Take my calls, Lil. That's all I ask."

She didn't believe him.

"I won't call often," he said. "Once a week if you'll let me."

"And then what?"

"And then…who knows? I swear to you. I know what I want, but I also know that I can't make it happen."

Wow. He *had* changed.

"I need your help, Lil. Just until I can get my footing again. You understood me like no one ever had. I know I blew it with you. I understand that you hate me. If it's any consolation, I hate me, too. But I'm lost here. I want to make my life right. Just talk to me now and then."

There were parts of Lillie that were dead forever. But not as dead as she'd thought.

"I need you to understand, in no uncertain terms, that there is no hope for us as a couple. Ever."

His nostrils flared and he sucked in his lip, as though he was physically preventing himself from saying whatever sprang to his lips. And still, he was one of the most handsome men she'd ever known.

But not the manliest. Or the sexiest.

A picture of Jon in her house, among her things, with Abraham on his hip, sprang to mind. She'd have liked to have been there with them.

She pushed the thought away.

"I understand," Kirk said. "And I want you to know that if you ever change your mind—"

"I won't. And if you think you're going to convince me otherwise, then this conversation is over." She picked up her purse and stood, thought about digging for money to pay the bill and decided against it.

Let Kirk pay.

"I swear, Lil…" He hurriedly stood beside her, pulling a wad of bills from his pocket, rolling off a few and dropping them to the table as though if he didn't pay fast enough she'd get out the door ahead of him. "I won't bring it up again. Not unless you do, first."

Without saying a word, Lillie made her way to the door and out into the cool October darkness. Kirk kept up.

"I am not out to convince you of anything, Lil," he said. "To be honest, I don't know what I hope to achieve by talking with you. I just…I have a feeling that what I need to know can only be found in you. And that if I don't find it, I'm never going to amount to anything."

He was Papa's son.

And Papa was one of the greatest men she'd ever known. Some of that had to have rubbed off on Kirk.

"Okay," she said. For Papa's and Gayle's sake. They still cared about Kirk—needed him to amount to something. "Phone calls. Once a week. Nothing more. And when I say the conversation is over, it's over."

"Okay."

He was quiet as he walked her to her car and waited for her to unlock the door and climb inside.

With one hand on top of the frame, he closed the door behind her. But not before she heard his final words.

"Thank you, Lil."

After watching him in the rearview mirror as she pulled away, she cried all the way home.

CHAPTER THIRTEEN

HE'D BEEN LOOKING forward to seeing her all day. With Abe sound asleep in the next room, Jon lay in bed Thursday night with pillows propped up behind him and his laptop computer across his thighs.

He had a paper due the following Wednesday in his freshman English class. A five-hundred-word "how to" piece. He'd been halfway through detailing a French door installation before he admitted that he was working up a plan specific to Lillie's kitchen—in effect, killing two birds with one stone. She hadn't called. He'd left a note—had even had Abraham scribble a few marks at the bottom of it. And while he hadn't specifically asked for a call-back, he'd kind of expected one. They'd talked a couple of times since their trip to the zoo the previous weekend. She'd called him on Monday to discuss Abe's first day care tantrum of the week and he'd called her Wednesday night to arrange a time to measure her countertop.

And then there'd been the second day care tantrum of the week. Just that morning. They'd both been there when it happened and had dealt with it as a team. Like coworkers. Or parents.

Looking down at his computer, Jon reassessed his situation. According to his word-processing program he'd used up 248 of his 500 words. He still didn't have the sliding glass door frame removed and disposed of. Hadn't even placed the frame for the French doors, let alone leveled, squared and shimmed it.

His mind kept going back to Lillie. He wondered if she was at home. Lillie worked all hours of the day and night, which was why he hadn't been surprised when he and Abe had shown up to an empty house earlier that evening. She'd told him she'd be there unless she got called in to work. Had told him to use his key if she didn't answer his knock.

He pushed the backspace key, deleting the notation about reciprocating-saw safety. If the existing sliding glass door was affixed with nails instead of screws, the job would require the use of a reciprocating saw to cut through the metal. This was a French door installation how-to paper, not an essay on tool safety.

Abe coughed—the sound traveling through the speaker on his nightstand as clearly as if the toddler was in the room with him. Jon got out of bed to check on him and—satisfied that his son was doing fine—wandered out to the kitchen for a glass of milk. Finishing it in one chug, he rinsed the cup and returned to bed. To his paper.

There had been another break-in the night before. Everyone had been talking about it at the plant that morning. And at school, too. Each time it happened, Jon started to sweat more. He had nothing to do with the crimes, but he knew damned well that if anyone found out about his past... His lungs tightened inside his chest.

His records were sealed.

But they could be viewed by law enforcement in the investigation of a crime.

Clara Abrams knew about his past. Kate had made certain of that. Back before she'd become pregnant with Abe. Back when the only reason she'd started dating Jon was to convince her parents she'd be better off living somewhere else. To convince them to let her move to New York.

He picked up his cell phone. No missed calls or new messages.

Lillie hadn't called and it depressed him.

What the hell? He was a grown man, not a young kid with unrealistic dreams about a pretty girl.

Scoffing at himself, Jon pushed the speed-dial button temporarily assigned to Lillie.

"Hello, Jon." She picked up on the first ring, as though she'd been waiting for his call.

"I hope it's not too late." If she'd been working, it shouldn't be. He figured her for a night person.

"No, it's fine. I got your note but didn't want to call and risk waking Abe. I know he goes down at eight."

"He'd sleep through a hurricane," he told her, not quite buying her excuse.

She didn't say how long she'd been home. Or where she'd been.

"So you saw my estimate for the tiles?"

"Yes, it's lower than I expected. You're sure you figured in the cost of the grout and everything else you'll need?"

"I've got the tools and the grout," he told her, wishing he didn't even have to charge for the tile.

"Well, if you're sure you want to take this on, then yes, I say let's do it. I'll leave a check for you in an envelope at the day care," she told him.

"As long as you're sure you want to continue helping me with Abe."

"Of course I'm sure." Her voice took on a tone of urgency.

"Are you all right?" he asked.

"Yes."

"You sound…off."

"I'm fine."

He was a business acquaintance. He didn't have the right to push any further into her life.

"I put a second safety catch on your back door," he told her. "It's a blocker in the track itself. You'll need to lower it to open the door."

"I've already checked it out. Thanks."

She'd been checking out her doors? "Are you nervous, staying there alone?"

"A little uneasy, I guess. Just the idea that there's some creep slinking around at night…"

"Do you have someplace else you can stay?"

From what he'd seen and heard, she seemed to know every person in town.

Chuckling, Lillie said, "Lots of places. But I'm where I want to be."

The chuckle, the confidence, had him guessing just where in her house she might be. Which led to wondering about her state of dress. Or undress…

Pushing the covers into a ball at the end of the mattress, Jon focused on his computer screen for a couple of seconds. Got himself under control. The hard-on her words had triggered was going to take a bit longer to subside, but he could ignore it. Move on.

"I have a suggestion," he said, thinking of his paper. And of the time the week before when she'd used the very same words to suggest that he and Abe go to the zoo with her. "I think you should let me replace your sliding glass door with French doors."

"You can do that?"

"Yeah. And I really think that it would be a good idea," he continued. "Not only would it increase the resale value of your home, but they'd be a hell of a lot safer. We could install a dead bolt just like we did on your front door."

"I love French doors," Lillie said, her voice growing

in energy again. "And at this point, I'd just as soon never have sliding glass doors in my home again. But wouldn't the transition take a lot of work?"

"It'd be a breeze," he said. "I could have it done in one evening. The big deal is the cost. French doors don't come cheap. We're talking anywhere from $350 to $4,000, depending on your taste."

"My safety is worth the cost." Her answer was immediate. Which it had been every time he'd discussed costs with her. She was obviously well compensated for what she did. And the piddly few hours he was putting in for improvements around her house couldn't possibly be paying for the time she was spending with his son.

They were supposed to be going on another outing on Sunday. Unless something had changed with her plans.

"Are your friends keeping Abe again tomorrow night?"

"Yes." He had some research to do for the chemistry experiment he and Mark were planning for the following week. A chapter to get through in Trig. And a shitload of paintings to memorize for a quiz in Art History.

"Do you have plans?"

"No," he said.

"Maybe we could shop for doors together," she said. "I'll need you to show me what my choices are. Will we have to order them?"

"Not if you like something they have in stock."

"How soon can they have them delivered?"

He had a hunch she was more than a little uneasy about the break-ins. And admired the hell out of her. The woman had strength. And grit.

"If you buy something in stock, I can load it up in the back of the truck," he told her. "And if you're quick about making up your mind, we might even have time left for me to install them before I have to pick up Abe tomorrow night."

He'd give up a little extra sleep that week to get his schoolwork done.

Abe came first.

And Lillie was his best hope for helping Abe with his anxiety.

"It won't take me long," Lillie assured him. "I know what I like."

Was she talking about him?

"You're sounding better." He hadn't really meant to say that out loud, but it was better than telling her that his body was seriously feeling her. Which was the thought at the forefront of his mind at the moment.

Get control of yourself, man.

"I am feeling better. Thank you."

Loosening the drawstring at the waist of his thin cotton pajama bottoms, Jon looked at the garish cartoon faces splashed in all directions across his legs. Abe had grabbed at the tacky pajamas with chocolate-smeared hands when they'd been at the big-box store, and Jon had felt he had to buy them.

"I didn't do anything," he told her. And if she knew what he wanted to do, she'd probably be calling her sheriff friend instead of thanking Jon.

"Yeah, you did. I can't really explain it, but...I'm in a better mood now than before you called."

The damned waistband across his hips got tighter.

"I'm sorry." Lillie's voice faded a bit. "I shouldn't have said that."

He couldn't go backward. He should. But he couldn't.

"I'm not sorry," he said, giving up on pretending that Lillie Henderson only mattered because of Abe. "It's the same way with me. Pretty much every time we talk."

"It is?"

"Yes."

"So what does this mean?"

"That we're friends," he said. And then added, "I hope."

"I hope so, too."

"Good." Closing his laptop he settled back into his pillows and grinned at the ceiling. "So, now that we're officially friends, can you tell me what had you so down earlier?"

Her silence stretched long enough to risk ruining the moment.

"I'm not asking you to compromise client privilege or anything," he assured her. "I just…care…if you've had a bad day."

"I'm mostly just tired," she said. "And tonight I found myself dealing with a situation that took me back down memory lane."

"A good lane or a bad one?"

"I'm not sure," she said, sounding far away. "Maybe both. Crazy, huh?"

"Not at all."

"You ever feel that way? Like you miss what once was, but don't ever want to go back? And then you find yourself wondering if this or that had been different, if you'd feel differently about going back?"

"It's natural to feel nostalgic about things." There wasn't much about his past that he missed. But she was obviously feeling nostalgic and this wasn't about him. "Tell me one thing you'd go back to if something had been different."

The request met with total silence.

Because he was beginning to suspect that, with Lillie, reticence didn't necessarily mean that her reply was none of his business, Jon said, "Okay, tell me something you miss."

"Spending time with my parents." Her response was immediate. And reality bore down on him again.

Lillie wasn't like him—or the kids he'd grown up with. She had family. People who'd ask questions about her choices. Give opinions on decisions.

Judge him.

People who, like Kate's family, found his "kind" something to avoid. At least in the close relationship sense. He was considered good enough to work for them, though.

And that was what he was doing for Lillie....

His mind spun with thoughts, taking him down and then back up.

Her end of the line was still silent.

"You said you went to college in Shelter Valley," he said, having himself firmly in check again. "Did you grow up here?"

"No." She sighed as if she was settling back—against a chair? In bed? "I'm a California girl. Inland, though, not a beach baby. My father was an engineer. He worked for the government doing different testing things in the desert. I was never really sure what it was all about."

His chest tightened. A guy with government clearance. A man like that would never accept a man like Jon in his daughter's life.

"What about your mother?"

"She taught school when I was little and was an elementary school principal by the time I was in junior high. It was nice because she always had the summers off."

"What about siblings?"

"Nope. My folks talked about having another baby sometimes, but they never did have one. We were good together, just the three of us. Happy."

Reveling for the moment in the picture she painted, Jon laid back in his bed, and shut off the light, figuring there was no harm in living vicariously for the duration of the conversation.

"What about grandparents?"

"My father's folks were in Florida. We saw them several times a year. They were both older, though. Had him when they were in their forties. They passed away when I was still a kid."

He had no idea if he'd had living grandparents. "And your mother's parents?"

"My grandfather died of a heart attack my first year of high school. Gram didn't last long after that. Mom said Gram died of a broken heart. They were fairly young, both in their seventies."

"That must have been rough."

"Yeah, they lived down the road from us. I used to stop in at Gram's after school, to wait for Mom to get home, and she always had a snack waiting for me. More often than not, it was homemade cookies."

It was his dream. The "real family" dream. He could almost taste the cookies and smiled. It was good to know that the ideals he'd conjured in his head really did exist.

Sliding his heels along cool sheets, Jon asked, "So where are your folks, now? Still in California?" With the lights off he could see it all so clearly: the home she'd grown up in, with an afghan her mother had made on the back of the family room couch. A nice sofa in the formal living room. A cherrywood dining table with matching chairs. Hardwood floors and plenty of windows letting in light.

Flowers everywhere. He could almost smell them....

Lillie's thick silence imposed itself over the image. Something had gone wrong with his picture.

He heard her sniffle and sat straight up. "Lillie?"

"I'm sorry..." She was crying. And he couldn't do a

damned thing about it. Why in the hell had he started in on the questions? He had no business.

"Don't be," he said. "I'm sorry for prying. I—"

"No. It's not you, Jon. I just…it's been a long day and…I don't know, I guess I needed a good cry."

Was this a female thing, then? For a second he hoped it might be, but he didn't really think it was.

"I'm… It… I actually feel better talking to you. Really."

He had to believe her. Wanted to believe her. And he wasn't going to ask any more questions.

"I'm here for you anytime," he said. "You can talk to me day or night. That's what friends are for, right?"

She chuckled. Sniffed. "Yeah."

He tried to think of something to say to change the subject, to ease the tension.

"They're dead, Jon."

Her words cut through the silence with the sharpness of a blade.

Dead? "Both of them?" Lillie was twenty-eight. Her parents should still be young, living life.

"Yes." She was crying again. "They were killed in a car accident when I was a junior in college."

Swallowing, Jon stared into the darkness. Not sure which was worse, to have had the dream and had it snatched so cruelly away. Or to have never had it at all.

"God, Lillie. I'm so sorry."

"Me, too. I don't dwell on it much. I miss them every single day, but I have a good life and I'm happy. It's just today, I don't know…anyway, thanks for asking. It means a lot."

If she didn't stop, he was going to do something stupid, like cry with her. "It means a lot to me, too."

He took a deep breath. The emotion pushing up inside his chest subsided. He was fine. Chances were, after about two decades without shedding a tear, his tear ducts were dried up, anyway.

But the close call was a warning. Lillie Henderson meant more to him than anyone else he'd known in his adult life.

Other than Abe, of course.

He just wasn't sure if his meeting Lillie was going to be the best thing that ever happened to him, or the worst.

CHAPTER FOURTEEN

LILLIE HAD HERSELF firmly in check by the time she climbed into Jon's truck the following afternoon, a comment about Abe ready and waiting on her tongue.

"Abe didn't cry this morning," he said before she could speak.

Nodding, she noticed the chest hair visible in the V at the top of the oxford shirt he'd tucked into formfitting blue jeans. And looked away.

"I know," she said. "I talked to Bonnie about him when I stopped in this afternoon. She's been trying to provide some one-on-one companionship to him while integrating him into bigger playgroups. With some success, I might add."

"She told me." Jon's voice wasn't warm and intimate like it had been the night before on the phone. He was Abe's father again. Still nice, but more like a stranger than a friend. And Lillie, glad for the distance, relaxed back into her seat and thought about French doors.

HER HOME WASN'T overly large, but it had never seemed small, either. Until that Friday night, standing in her kitchen while Jon expertly and seemingly easily removed her sliding glass door from its track with big suction cups, unscrewed the metal frame that had been holding the panels in place and carried the entire fixture out to his truck.

"Do you want to try to sell these doors?" he asked her

as he wrapped the glass in furniture-moving pads that he'd carried in from the back of his truck. "You could probably get seventy-five dollars."

Immediately seeing a way she could pay him the money he needed without damaging his pride, she said, "No, if you wouldn't mind disposing of them, I'd appreciate it. If you can make any money doing it, it's yours."

Without saying another word on the subject, Jon carried them out, one at a time, coming back a couple of minutes later with the wooden frame they'd just purchased balanced on a homemade dolly.

It wasn't yet seven o'clock. He didn't pick up Abe until ten. Wiping her sweaty palms on the sides of the jeans she'd pulled on during the ten minutes she'd had between arriving home from work and Jon's arrival earlier that afternoon, Lillie couldn't calm the sexual jitters gathering force inside her. She was a healthy woman. She got urges.

But never like what she was feeling every time Jon Swartz was around. Maybe it was his cologne messing with her pheromones. A scientific explanation.

Except he didn't seem to be wearing any cologne.

Holding the door frame with both arms spread wide, he braced the wood with his head and one thigh and reached for the tape measure clipped to the front pocket of his jeans.

Reached, and missed.

"Let me get that." Lillie jumped forward, before the precariously balanced frame could come down on him, and removed the heavy aluminum tape measure from its resting place.

It came loose easily. And she refused to acknowledge where the backs of her fingers had brushed. Stepping through the wooden frame, she opened the tape and, facing Jon, held it up. "It's seventy-two inches."

"I know." His face was inches away. His gaze directly on her. Intense. "They come in standard sizes." He licked his lips. Swallowed.

"Oh." She meant to move. His big brown eyes compelled her to stay, to come closer, as though the door frame were some kind of bizarre magnetic field. "I thought you were reaching for the tape measure," she said.

"I was," he said, still staring straight at her. "I have to square it up." He was still holding the door frame balanced with his hands and one thigh.

"I have no idea how to do that."

He said something about measuring from the corners.

"Give me the edge of the tape." Jon's voice sounded dry. Maybe holding the frame so long was hurting him. Maybe she'd imagined the whole episode between them. "I can hold it up here while you take it down to the bottom left." Placing the bent metal edge of the measuring tape in his fingers, Lillie pulled the tape with her toward the bottom left corner of the frame.

What in the hell was the matter with her? She was ready to strip off her clothes and have sex with the father of one of her clients.

She worked in the health field. And didn't ever have unprotected sex. Nor did she have any condoms hanging around.

"One hundred and nine inches," she said from below. If her face was red, he could put the heated look down to her bent position.

"Okay, hold on." Jon's voice was easy, granting her a few more seconds to get her bearings. His jeans met the laces of his leather shoes perfectly.

The frame tilted a fraction, changing the angle slightly. "Try it now."

His thighs were right there, an inch from her face. If she wasn't careful, her shoulder was going to brush his knee.

Twenty-eight was too young for hot flashes.

She looked down. "One hundred and ten point five."

"Fine. Now let's try the other side and make certain that we're even."

She was glad that he was thorough. Not the least bit surprised that he'd do the job exactly right. Knew he was conscientious. She just wasn't sure she had what it took to see this task through.

"I WAS GOING to have a steak salad for dinner. Would you like to join me?"

Jon was kneeling in front of her newly installed French doors, picking up his tools and returning them to the proper compartments in his toolbox. He reached for the piece of plastic coating that he'd peeled off one of the new door-knobs. So did Lillie.

"I owe you dinner, remember?" she went on. "You paid at the pub."

Fighting the instinct to snatch his hand back, he remained still. Outwardly calm. Waiting for her hand to drop away. "I'd like dinner," he said, willing to give up the clandestine fast-food trip he'd promised himself earlier that day if it meant spending more time with her.

"Good." She held on to the plastic. And licked her lips as she looked over at him. They were both still on their knees. "I've got some French bread I can heat up." The plastic was slipping. Jon held on. She chuckled, sounding more like a schoolgirl than the medical professional he knew her to be. "French bread to celebrate my new French doors. Seems appropriate…"

A shadow passed over her face. And just before he dropped the plastic, he reached for her hand, catching both the plastic and her fingers in his grasp. "French bread is completely appropriate," he said, the husky tone to his voice barely recognizable to him.

His grasp was loose. She could easily pull away. Jon leaned forward. Without making a conscious choice or giving any thought to the consequences, he moved until his lips were touching hers. Lightly. Gently.

Sitting back on his heels, he looked at her, while taking her other hand in his. "I've been needing to do that," he said.

She squeezed his fingers, let go of the plastic and pulled free from him, running her right hand along the side of his face as she stood.

A brush-off. His emotions froze, sliding quickly and quietly back inside whatever hole they'd sprung from.

Packing up the rest of his tools, he turned around, facing the kitchen where he'd heard the refrigerator open and close, a drawer open and close, the sink go on and off.

"I hope that you won't let this get in the way of our arrangement," he said forthrightly because that was the only way he knew how to do things. "Abe needs you. And I can't accept your help without paying my way."

The shock on her face as she looked up confused the hell out of him. "I thought you were staying for dinner."

Jon, never more unsure in his life, set the bucket of tools down at his feet. "I was," he said, looking her straight in the eye. "And then I kissed you."

She nodded. Expressions chased across her face, and he wasn't sure what any of them meant. "One kiss scared you off?" she finally said with a chuckle that sounded slightly forced.

The woman was an enigma. And he was drawn to her, compellingly so, in spite of all of the reasons why he shouldn't be. He had no proof that she wasn't working for Clara.

He needed her help.

She'd already indicated, the night they went out for burgers, that she didn't want an intimate relationship with him. And he had no time, or energy, for an intimate relationship.

At least that was what he'd been telling himself over the past two years, that he'd been celibate by choice. And Lillie was definitely not the type of woman a guy took for a one-night stand. Not that he'd been into that, ever. And most definitely wasn't now that he had an impressionable boy in his life.

Had the one kiss scared him off?

"No, the kiss didn't scare me." He took his time to answer, trying to figure out where he stood with her. "I assumed that I offended you."

Turning back to her salad, she chuckled again. More naturally. But still with little humor. "No, Jon, offending me isn't the problem."

So there was a problem. He'd been right.

"What is?"

"I'm too embarrassed to tell you." Her hands moved quickly, shredding, mixing and chopping. All without missing a beat.

Her head was bent over her task. Hiding her face.

"We're friends. You don't need to be embarrassed."

The assurance earned him a shake of her head. So maybe they weren't friends now? Or being friends wasn't enough to grant him access to her personal business.

"You witnessed me standing in a room full of gawking women while my son screamed bloody murder, indicating to everyone there that I had no control over him." He said the first thing that came to his mind. "It doesn't get much more embarrassing than that."

"No one was thinking that you couldn't control your son. Only that he was experiencing acute distress. You actually had him under control. He wasn't hitting and kicking and pushing you away or running around throwing magazines all over the floor."

Jon stared at her. "You've witnessed that?"

"More than once. Some kids panic when they're faced with a medical procedure that frightens them. They lash out. Sometimes uncontrollably."

Amazing. She always had a way to make him feel like a winner.

She was chopping a cooked steak into small pieces with her delicate hands. And he found himself turned on once again.

"You still haven't told me why you were embarrassed," he said. Things had to be set straight between them or he couldn't stay.

"And your example was not a personal embarrassment."

He'd damn sure felt personally embarrassed. "What was it, then?"

"A public one."

Oh. "Well, how about this? My pajama bottoms have Abe's favorite cartoon character all over them." Now *that* was personal. And embarrassing.

Her knife slipped. Luckily onto the cutting board and not her finger. Other than that, Lillie didn't miss a beat. Sliding the steak into the salad bowl, she mixed the ingredients one more time and, with a professional-looking flip, tossed in the salad dressing. Pulling a half loaf of presliced French bread from the toaster oven, she carried everything over to the table, set out a couple of plates, added silverware and napkins, grabbed a couple of bottles of water and sat down at the table.

"Sit," she said, indicating the seat across from her—not the one that was perpendicular and might result in their knees bumping. "Eat."

Jon sat.

But if she thought he was just going to eat, that the conversation was over, she was wrong.

He needed answers.

CHAPTER FIFTEEN

SHE COULDN'T STOP thinking about his pajama bottoms. Who was the character?

The thoughts brought another X-rated image to her mind—Jon's oh-so-manly part pushing at the front fly of thin cotton pants....

And the knot in her stomach wasn't leaving a lot of room for her dinner.

Both hands resting on the table on either side of his untouched bowl, Jon said, "I'm sorry that it embarrasses you, but I either need to know what's going on or I need to get the hell out of Dodge."

Pushing her salad bowl away, Lillie longed for a glass of the pinot grigio in her fridge.

Get the hell out of Dodge. Jon was a man's man. No one had ever talked to her like that before.

And it turned her on.

Putting her napkin on her lap, she faced her guest. "I'll tell you what embarrasses me, but I want your word that it won't change anything. I still get to help you with Abe."

"I still get your invaluable assistance with my son's adjustment issues," Jon said, nodding.

"And I get my backsplash."

"We've already purchased the tile." Jon would pick it up in the next day or two.

"So I have your word?"

"Yeah."

Butterflies swarmed in her stomach. She couldn't do it. "How can you give me your word when you don't even know what I'm going to say?"

"Because I know myself. Whatever is going on, as long as you want to help me with my son, I will do whatever it takes to see that Abraham gets the benefit of your services."

"That kiss was not your fault," Lillie blurted.

He sat back, his delicious maleness filling her chair. Her kitchen.

"I take full responsibility," she managed to get out with a fair amount of professional distance.

Crossing his arms, Jon cocked his head. "I kissed you. How can you take responsibility for that?"

Was he laughing at her? His face was straight. Lillie didn't get flustered anymore. Not since she'd first found out Kirk was having an affair. But she wasn't entirely sure she could trust herself here.

"I…subconsciously asked for it."

He tilted his head slightly and studied her. Lillie swore she glimpsed a certain…satisfied?…glint in his eyes.

"If you did it subconsciously, how do you know?"

Resisting the urge to kick him under the table, she told herself she'd brought this on herself. She should never have mentioned a problem. Or created one, either. She had no business being turned on by this man. Or even thinking about him at all.

"You said there's a problem." Jon spoke up when she couldn't. "Until I know what it is, I can't help you out. Or know how to fix it."

Just like a man—always wanting to fix the problem. Sometimes there was no fix. Sometimes you just had to let it sit. Learn to live with it. Wait for it to go away.

And then she saw the heat in his eyes when his gaze moved to her lips and quickly back to her face.

And she knew. He was enjoying this. At her expense.

That glint gave her the strength to stand up to him— and turn the tables on him, too. If he was trying to make her squirm, she'd just see how well he could take his own medicine.

"You turn me on."

She had to hand it to the guy. If there were emotions sizzling inside him, he hid them well.

"And?"

"And? And what?" A note of tension entered her voice in spite of her mental demand that it not.

Frowning, Jon dropped his hands back to the table. "I thought there was more."

"What more could there be?"

"You could be getting ready to blame me for taking advantage of the situation. Or getting ready to tell me that the problem is that you're afraid I'm going to take advantage of the situation."

"I just told you the problem. You turn me on. It's inappropriate. And embarrassing. We're working together. Not dating."

"Oh." He didn't quite smile, but there was something there. A slight movement at the corner of his mouth. "Well, if it makes you feel any better, you turn me on, too."

Thank God. *No!* That wasn't what she meant to think.

"It doesn't change anything. We aren't... You and I can't be—"

"Agreed," he interrupted her, nodding. "Completely."

"Good, then." She wanted him to kiss her again. And touch her. In intimate, aching places. "So...are we still on for the children's museum on Sunday?"

"Yep."

"It's only open until four so we'll probably want to leave a little earlier than noon. If that works for you."

She'd rescheduled breakfast with Papa and Gayle for seven in the morning at a little café by Camelback Mountain where they lived.

"Abe and I are up at dawn. And Sunday's cleaning day. You won't get any argument out of either one of us for having to cut that short."

"We don't want to overtire him, though, or we risk doing more damage than good with our crowd introduction therapy."

There, she'd described their activity as "therapy." Put them right back on professional ground.

"I can pick you up around eleven," he offered.

"Sounds good. We can leave whenever he starts to wear out and what we don't see of the museum this week we can get to next time."

"Okay."

It was eight-thirty. Still an hour and a half to go before he had to collect his son. So much could happen in that time. People could do things. Lives could change.

Pushing back from the table, he stood. To come closer? Just get the inevitable over with? They'd acknowledged their mutual attraction....

"I'll stop by to see if the tile's in on my way home from work tomorrow," he said, gathering her plate and his, and heading to the sink.

"Great." She stood, too. Afraid to follow him to the sink. To get any closer. Afraid of herself. "You don't have to do those," she said.

"Are you kidding?" Ignoring her protest, he proceeded to locate her scrubber on the inside cupboard door in front of the sink, rinsed the dishes and loaded them with precision into the dishwasher. "I learned early on that if you don't help prepare the meal, you help with the dishes."

"You've never mentioned your folks," she said. "Abe's mom isn't in his life, but what about his grandparents?"

Good, Lil. Much better. Kinda hard to think about sex when moms and dads were the topic of conversation.

But there was that gorgeous butt again. The opposite side of the groin pressing up against her kitchen sink.

She had never cared much for butts before. Why now? Why his?

Breaking out of her musings, she realized he hadn't answered her.

He finished the dishes. Wiped the table, rinsed her cloth and hung it back up on the bar inside the cupboard door. Closed the cupboard with what seemed like finality.

"Jon?"

"It's just Abe and me." He leaned his sexy backside against the counter and faced her.

"You sound defensive." He studied her. She wasn't sure what he was expecting to find.

Eventually, he moved back to the table and dropped into the chair he'd occupied earlier. Joining him, she felt like she'd passed some kind of test.

And was leery to speak for fear of saying the wrong thing.

"I'm sorry." They weren't the words she'd expected.

"For what?"

"I just… I know I have an attitude when it comes to… some things. I'm working on it."

Not sure where they were heading, Lillie just nodded. Did his folks blame him for having a child out of wedlock? In this day and age that was a little hard to believe.

"You want to talk about it?" she finally asked.

"Not really. But if you're going to help Abe, I suppose you should probably know a little bit more about him."

"It might help," she said. "Was there some trauma in his life? Something to do with your folks?"

Maybe his loss was still new...raw. It had taken her a couple of years before she could talk about her parents without breaking into tears.

"I have no folks," Jon said.

She waited.

His elbows on his knees, he stared at the floor. "As in, I've never had folks."

"Oh."

"I was born—full-term, amazingly—to a user."

"Drugs?"

"Yeah." He nodded, focused on her ceramic tile.

"I was taken away from her at birth by the child welfare people, with the caveat that I would be returned to her as soon as she was clean."

"And that didn't happen."

He shook his head. "But she never gave up hoping, apparently, because she wouldn't release me for adoption, either."

Lillie knew how that worked. A lot of her patients during her rotation in the neonatal intensive care unit at the children's hospital in Phoenix had been drug babies. The ones who didn't make it to term in their mothers' wombs. "You grew up in foster care?"

"Yeah."

"Did you ever meet her?"

"Nope. Not that I remember, at any rate." He didn't sound sorry. Or even sad.

Her heart broke for him, anyway.

"Did you suffer any residual effects from the drugs?"

"No. Incredibly, she managed to stay clean during the

majority of her pregnancy. I came out completely healthy. She'd just started using again right before I was born. And from what I heard, she never stopped."

"Do you know if she's still alive?"

"Nope."

He could have checked. If he'd wanted to know. Surely he'd know that.

"What about your father?" Lillie hated to ask, but figured they might as well get it all over with at once.

"I have no idea who he is. She listed 'unknown' on my birth certificate."

"What about her family?"

"Again, I have no idea. Just that they weren't in the picture. No one stepped forward to take me when it was time for me to be released from the hospital. That much I know."

And, obviously, they hadn't stepped forward since, either, or he wouldn't have grown up in foster care.

Jon looked tired. Far more tired than a day's worth of hard work merited. Lillie had a feeling she was witnessing a side of him few people ever saw.

"You have no reason to be ashamed," she said softly, wishing she had the nerve to reach over and run her fingers along his neck—to massage away the tension of a lifetime of having to be tough.

She understood so much more now. And was drawn to him more than ever. A dangerous combination.

"I'm not ashamed," Jon said after a long moment.

But as he stood, gathered his things and wished her good-night, his shame hung between them.

CHAPTER SIXTEEN

AT WORK ON Saturday, Jon got a call from Mark. A floating shift supervisor, Mark worked different areas as needed.

"Cooker seven is down," Mark said without preamble.

"On my way." Already jumping on his cart to head toward the area where the 500 gallon tank would be filled with raw juice squeezed from the prickly pear cactus fruit and heated to a boiling point of 221 degrees, Jon pictured the tubular, gas-fired cylinders beneath the vat.

If one of them was out, a safety valve would shut off the gas supply to the entire vat. And if allowed to cool, not only would 500 gallons of product be lost, the vat would be contaminated and have to be shut down for cleaning, which would take the entire line out of production—and cost the company more money than Jon could afford to contemplate.

"I cleared the premises," Mark said, meeting Jon as he entered the area in the middle of the several acre plant. "Temp's down to 219," he said. "Larry called me as soon as he noticed the drop."

"Still well above boiling point," Jon said. Two degrees down. He had a window of another six to eight. He had to work fast.

"Gas is off." First things first. Sliding under the vat, Jon saw the problem at once. "There's a hairline crack in the main line," he said. Not good news. The line had been down for what was only supposed to be occasional cleaning the month before. It wasn't due to be down again for quite a while.

Sliding out from under the vat, Jon wiped his hands on the brown cotton pants he'd bought from a surplus store and grabbed a roll of heavy-duty duct tape off his cart.

"Wait a minute, what are you doing with that?" Mark asked.

"Taping the line."

"No way, man. There'll be gas left in the line. Static electricity could cause a spark and then—"

"It's a minor crack. Just enough to throw the safety valve. We cover the crack, get the vat back online for the few minutes it still has to boil. We can shut down the gas as soon as it tips for pouring into the cooler." The juice would sit in another vat to cool before traveling through a series of pipes into a vat where it would be sugared.

"At least that way we save the product," Jon said, already heading back under the vat.

Mark was right beside him with a gas detector in his hand. "If this shows no gas leak, then fine," he said.

Jon pointed to the damage. Mark checked the damaged spot for leakage and then proceeded to make his way around the other cylinders.

"We're wasting time, man." Jon didn't want lost product on his watch. He couldn't afford the write-up on his file.

"Lives are more important than money." While frustrating, Mark's reply wasn't completely unexpected. Or completely unwelcome, either.

A couple of hours later, as Jon was once again under the now-empty-and-cooled vat, cutting out the damaged piece of line to replace it with a new section, Mark was right under there with him.

"Aren't there some other folks who could use your eagle eye?" Jon asked, only half teasing. "If you're not careful, you're going to make me think that you don't trust my work."

"Has nothing to do with your work," Mark said. "This is a gas line. A fire hazard. You work, I monitor, and we both go home tonight."

Remembering Mark's past, Jon understood. Mark had lost a close friend to an explosion on a line under his supervision. Back East, in the little town where he'd grown up.

Bearing down on his cutters with enough force to make it through the piping with one thrust, Jon recognized the warning signs of trouble.

Internal trouble.

Emotional attachment, whether it be friendship with Mark or something different with Lillie, brought risk. Especially, it seemed, for him. Once he started to care about someone, he got careless, quit watching his back so much, did things to please that person, lost his good judgment.

Threading new pipe into the coupler joining it to the existing gas line, he checked his work.

And double-checked. Mark slid out from under the vat after him and waited while he turned the gas back on.

"Let's give it five and check for leaks," Mark said, which left them standing there with nothing to do while they waited.

"How much do you think we lost today?" he asked his superior. Work was about dollars and cents for the company. Losing too much would cost him his job.

"Not much," Mark told him. "Cleaning was already completed on nine. The switchover only took a few minutes. In the long run, we'll show profit," he added. "With nine done early, both will be back up before projected."

Jon nodded, more relieved than he'd ever admit. He needed this job if he was going to stay in school. His scholarship covered his living expenses, but only his. And if he dropped out he'd have to pay back what he'd already spent: a semester's tuition, rent, books and other expenses.

"I didn't get a chance to ask when you picked up Abe last night, but how was your evening?"

"I put the doors in, no problem." Jon had mentioned Lillie to Mark, but so far, Mark hadn't asked any questions.

Leaning against a metal column, his head covered in the safety helmet everyone in the plant wore anytime they were on the floor, Mark crossed his feet at the ankles and grinned at Jon. "I knew you'd have no problem getting the doors in," Mark said. "I wasn't sure you'd actually been able to meet up with Lillie and get it done. So how'd it go?" Mark asked again. "Did you have dinner with her again?"

He never should have told Mark about the trip to the pub the week before. "Yeah. She made a salad."

"You stayed home?"

"We were at her place, yes."

Glancing at his watch, Jon was dismayed to see that only two minutes had passed. It was turning out to be a damned long five minutes.

"And?"

"And nothing." He turned her on. Didn't mean she cared. "I'm way out of her league."

"Bullshit." Mark's vehemence was surprising, until Jon thought about his friend's situation. Mark, a blue-collar guy like Jon who'd also grown up without a mom, was engaged to a lawyer.

"You've got the world's greatest grandmother," Jon said. "My mom was a druggie."

"Mine was a drunk. Wrapped her car around a tree when I was twelve."

"That when Nonnie took you in?"

"Nope. I was with her from birth."

"Well, there you go, then. I was in foster care."

But it wasn't being a ward of the state that was the real cause of his shame and Jon knew that. Being an ex-con was.

He'd gone with his foster brothers of his own free will. He'd known they were going to rob the convenience store. He'd taken the goods from the site. He'd made the choices—damned stupid choices—because he'd wanted to be one of them. He'd wanted to belong.

"From what I hear—and living with Nonnie I hear everything—Lillie Henderson wouldn't care if you were raised in a sewer."

Mark wasn't telling Jon something he didn't already know. But…

Four minutes had passed. Mark didn't seem to be in a hurry to get the test done and move on.

"It's obvious you've got a thing for her." Mark passed the gas monitor he was holding back and forth between his hands.

"I do not have a thing for her." The words were unequivocal. They had to be. Jon was not going to screw up again. Not this time. Because his son would pay. He needed Lillie Henderson to help him—with Abe's stress issues, and with Clara Abrams, too, if the older woman ever decided to check up on him.

His friend sobered. "Sorry, man. It's just that…Addy and I had a bet about how long it would take for you two to—"

"Hold it right there." Jon straightened. Grabbed another gas monitor out of his cart. "There's absolutely nothing going on…like that…between Lillie Henderson and me. She's Abe's child life specialist. She's just helping me out with this tantrum thing."

"The Parsons family has known Lillie for years."

Mark's voice was low, and dead serious. "She's had more clients than anyone can count. And they say that she's never shown as much interest in anyone as she has in you and Abe. Truth be known, the whole town's watching you two."

He felt sick.

Will Parsons was president of the university. His wife, Becca, was Shelter Valley's mayor. They were both close family friends of Addy's—Mark's fiancée.

"Lillie's been alone a long time. No one thinks it's good for her," Mark said.

Finally, someplace Jon was in agreement with the rest of the world.

Not that he could have anyone watching him. Or looking too closely. Not with Clara Abrams's interest in Abe. Not with the break-ins happening in town. And not with a son who had adjustment issues, either. Still, he said, "They think she's interested in me?"

"It seems pretty obvious."

Good God, could it be true? Could he really have finally met *the one?* Could his dreams really become reality? Could Abe one day have a mother?

"I gotta warn you, though," Mark said, pushing back from the column and heading back to the underbelly of the vat. "If you do anything with her, you'd best be serious about it." The warning tone allowed for no misunderstanding. "Because I can assure you, if you break that woman's heart this entire town will lynch you."

Even though Mark's warning brought him back down a couple of notches, ex-con Jon Swartz still left work that afternoon floating with the knowledge that the people of Shelter Valley thought Lillie Henderson was falling for him.

"KIRK TOLD US he came to see you." Papa waited until they'd ordered breakfast—Lillie was just having oatmeal and fruit because she didn't know if Jon and Abe would want an early lunch—before bringing up the subject Lillie had feared would arise.

Sipping her Diet Coke, she said, "He did," as if Kirk's visit was no more of a news item than traffic on the freeway. It really hadn't been anything more than that. An irritant that put you in a bad mood and then was over.

"If he did anything…"

Reaching across the table in the booth she shared with the two people she loved most in the world, Lillie patted Papa's hand. "He didn't do anything, Papa. I promise. He was a perfect gentleman. You'd have been proud."

"I can't imagine being proud of that boy."

Not anymore. There'd been a day—many of them—when Papa and Kirk had been closer than most fathers and sons.

"Give him a chance, Jerry," Gayle told Kirk's father.

"I just don't want *you* giving him any chances," Papa was looking straight at Lillie. "After what he did to you…"

She gave his hand a squeeze. "It's okay, Papa. I'm okay. I wish you'd believe I really am happy."

"I'll believe it when I see you marrying and having a family of your own. You were born to be a mother, Lillie."

"Or to support children in another way," Lillie said, looking to Gayle for help.

Her ex-stepmother-in-law was frowning, too.

"Look, you guys. Kirk's affair, leaving me like he did, even abandoning Braydon, weren't the worst things I've ever suffered," she reminded them. "Losing Bray…that would have happened no matter what Kirk did. And if anything keeps me tied up inside, it's that."

"If you'd had your husband beside you, grieving with

you, you wouldn't have been able to retreat so deep inside yourself," Gayle said. She'd been a schoolteacher, once upon a time. Before she'd met and fallen in love with Jerry Henderson.

"I lost my parents, too," she reminded them. "Life goes on. We don't forget, but we move on, right? And where Kirk's concerned, I've moved on."

"I wish I could be sure of that." Jerry's shrewd gaze was turned fully on her.

"Besides," Lillie added, hoping only to reassure him, "I think Kirk really might have done some growing up since the last time I saw him. He seemed more mellow."

A little disconcerted by the glance Papa and Gayle shared, Lillie wasn't as hungry as she'd been moments before.

And, of course, the waitress appeared right then to deliver their food. Oatmeal for Lillie and broccoli quiche for Papa and Gayle. Leaving a basket of fresh-baked goods in the center of the table, she offered to refill their drinks and left.

Papa's silverware remained on the table in front of him. Stopping with her second spoonful of oatmeal almost to her mouth, Lillie asked, "What's wrong?"

"I'm sorry, Lil. I just can't allow... My son's a smooth talker. It's my fault. I taught him how to sell to people. But I meant him to use the skill to sell valuable products to people who needed them. Or to sell things to people with too much money on their hands."

Papa's honesty was one of the first things that had endeared him to her. She didn't know how he was with his clients, but in his private life, he told it like it was.

"Kirk's one of the top advertising executives in the company. But as a man, he's a lowlife."

"No, he's not." Lillie couldn't stop the words from escaping her lips. "He's weak. Selfish. But he has boundaries. He wouldn't ever do anything illegal."

"Just immoral," Jerry said.

"He wouldn't harm a child, or steal from old people or leave the scene of an accident." She knew that firsthand. Once, when they'd been out clubbing in college, Kirk had rear-ended a car as he'd been attempting to get his car out of a tight parking spot. He'd found the owner of the damaged car and made amends.

"He wouldn't kick a dog," Lillie added, trying only to ease the pain she read in Papa's eyes.

"He also turned his back on his firstborn because he was ill," Jerry said softly, leaning forward. "And he's missed every single major event in Ely's life."

Gayle wasn't eating, either. With her eyebrows drawn in worry over dark, compassion-filled eyes, she watched the exchange between Lillie and Papa.

"I won't be able to live with myself if my son marches back into your life and somehow convinces you to give him another shot." Papa's eyes glistened.

"No worries there," Lillie assured him.

"A woman's heart is a funny thing." Gayle spoke softly, too, but no less emphatically. "And I agree with Jerry in that Kirk is very convincing. Especially where you're concerned." With a compassionate tilt of her head she added, "You're right, Kirk seems to have changed some, seems to be more aware…"

"…and truly contrite," Lillie added, more to see if they agreed with her assessment, or if Kirk had managed to pull the wool over her eyes already.

"He's sorry," Jerry said. "I know that for a fact. But sorry doesn't make up for what he did. Nor does it mean he wouldn't break your heart again in the future."

"There is no future between us."

"He told us he's going to do whatever it takes to win you back," Gayle said.

And Lillie finally understood why they were having this conversation.

"If Kirk was truly sorry, if he really wanted to make his life right, the first place he'd start would be with Ely," Jerry said. "That young boy loves his daddy. He's hurt every single time Kirk misses an event."

Papa and Gayle had made their bimonthly visits with their grandson no secret. But they didn't usually talk about him, either.

"Papa?" She took his hand, held on. "There's no way Kirk is going to hurt me. He's never going to get that close to my heart again. I promise."

He studied her and she let him, meeting his gaze head-on for as long as it took for him to believe her.

"But I need something from you," she added after he finally nodded.

"Anything. You know all you ever have to do is ask."

"I need you to forgive him, Papa. I have."

"I—"

"He's your son. You love him. He loves you. And he needs you."

Glancing at Gayle, she saw the other woman nodding. "I've been trying to tell him the same thing."

"Kirk looks up to you." Lillie couldn't believe she was pleading her ex-husband's cause. Never thought the day would come that she could. "He listens to you," she said, and added, "Most of the time."

Lord knew that Kirk hadn't listened—at all—when it came to Lillie and his marriage.

"Talk to him about Ely. Help him."

"And if I do this, you'll stay away from him?"

"I'll make certain that he doesn't get close enough to touch my heart."

"You want me to have a heart-to-heart with my son?" Jerry shook his head. "I may need a stiff drink first."

With a chuckle bearing little humor, Gayle cut into her quiche. Took a bite, chewing slowly.

Lillie tried again. "He needs your influence, Papa. And you need your son back."

Papa had aged twenty years in a five-year span.

"I'm not suggesting you condone what he did, only that you move past it. I have."

It was the healthy thing to do. And exactly what she'd tell the family of a child as they helped the child get past a trauma.

Although they changed the subject and focused on enjoying breakfast and easier topics from there on out, neither Papa nor Gayle seemed convinced by her assurances.

As she drove home, with their looks of concern seared on her heart, she told herself that she wasn't damaged, or in any way less whole because she chose to live life alone. Her goals did not include marriage. She'd made that mistake—trying to replace what she'd lost—after her parents were killed, and she knew that it was not the answer to living a joyful life.

Finding a man was not critical to her.

Loving and being loved, in whatever capacity, was her key to joy.

As Shelter Valley loomed closer, she thought of the day ahead. She'd show everyone. She could enjoy her friendship with Jon Swartz and not hold back when it came to the things she did feel. She wanted to make love with him. In the worst way. If he needed a bit of intimate adult companionship, maybe she could help him out. And prove that she was as normal, as capable of interacting on an intimate level, as she thought she was.

And afterward?

There didn't need to be one, did there? As long as she and Jon both knew, going in, that they were just doing each other a service. In the same way she was helping him with Abe and he was helping her with her house. Shelter Valley was a small town. Even after Abe was adjusted and didn't need her anymore, she and Jon were bound to run into each other.

Could she handle that if they had sex?

Lillie didn't know.

CHAPTER SEVENTEEN

ABE SLEPT THE whole hour and fifteen minute drive to the Phoenix Children's Museum. Jon had kept the boy active all morning so that the two-year-old would nod off in his car seat and thus be fully rested and ready to go when they got to their destination.

Ten minutes inside the place and he knew that it didn't matter if Abe had just woken from a ten-hour sleep— he wasn't going to last long in the place. Bright colors were everywhere, hands-on exhibits, things to explore and climb on.

"This is pretty spectacular," he told Lillie as he took in their surroundings with Abe straddling his hip. Passing the gift shop off to the right of the entrance, they headed down the hall.

"Doin'?" Abe's voice sounded in Jon's ear. He almost stumbled. *Doing?*

"Did you hear that?" He turned to Lillie, who was looking where Abe was pointing his finger. He'd been working with Abe for over a week on the word and, out of the blue, there it was.

Nodding, Lillie smiled, and told the boy about the exhibit. "We need to go up to the third floor," she said, leading them back toward the elevator. "The exhibits up there are specifically designed for imaginative play for toddlers."

"You've been here before."

"Many times," she told him. "First when I was taking

my child development classes when I was an undergrad at Montford, then during my practicum and internships, and later, with various patients. The exhibits are geared to different levels of developmental appropriateness."

Where was their friend Lillie? This woman, spouting developmental appropriateness sounded like a health care professional.

Which was why she was with him, he reminded himself.

She'd been a bit distant on the drive, too, after giving him an initial, blood-warming smile when she'd climbed into the truck. But no more distant than he'd been, he acknowledged. They'd talked about Abe. And work—she'd been inordinately interested in the story about the cracked gas line from the day before and he'd been happy to give her a play-by-play, tacking on a crash course in jelly making to pass the time.

They entered the elevator and rode silently up to the third floor.

"Let's take him to Ian's Corner," Lillie said as soon as they'd exited the elevator. "It's just inside the pit stop exhibit."

A pit stop. Someplace to sit and get their bearings. He liked the sound of that. "What's Ian's Corner?" he asked.

"You'll see, Abe will love it."

"Doin'?" the boy asked again, pointing to an area filled with long noodles suspended from the ceiling. *Oh, man.* Abe could get knocked over. Or lost. And if he panicked in there...

"That's Noodle Forest," Lillie said. "Do you want to go to Noodle Forest?"

Before Jon could express his doubts, Abe said, "No!" quite clearly, wrapping his hands around Jon's neck.

With a smile for the boy, Lillie rubbed the top of Abe's small hand and moved on. Jon's gut tensed. He felt as if he'd just failed some professional child-rearing test. He needed to quit being so overprotective. If Abe fell, he'd stand back up. If he screamed, he'd stop eventually.

As soon as they entered Ian's Corner, Abe was pushing his feet against Jon's thigh. "Down, down!" he said.

His second new word that week.

With trepidation, Jon put the boy on the ground and watched as he tripped over himself on his way to a toddler-size car shaped like a tube of toothpaste. Abe was wearing a bright yellow shirt and Jon's gaze remained glued to the color.

"He loves the plastic-wheeled scooter in the playroom at Little Spirits," Lillie said as she stood next to Jon, watching Abe climb aboard the car.

Without taking his eye off his son, Jon figured out what had just happened. "You were going to make sure I put him down, huh?" He grinned.

Because she'd been right. And she cared.

"Something like that." He didn't even have to look at her to get turned on. The saucy tone to her voice was enough.

Going from the toothpaste car to a pickle car, Abe pretended to drive it for a bit and then ran to a real motorcycle, demanding, "Up."

"Let me take a picture of you two," Jon said, taking his phone out of its holster as Lillie stood holding on to Abe on the other side of the motorcycle. Jon snapped several shots with the camera on his phone, knowing that one of them was going to be his new screen saver at home.

Next, Abe wanted to launch a race car down a track and watch its progress. At one point, Abe held up his hand like a traffic cop to get another little boy to stop his car. He was using his words, interacting with other kids, and laughing so hard he farted.

That was his boy—just putting it all out there. Healthy, well adjusted and apparently a future NASCAR driver.

The day was good. Great. And through it all, Lillie was right beside him, cheering Abe on, intervening when necessary, playing with him, watching over him as though he was her own son.

THEY TALKED ABOUT the day, reliving Abe's breakthroughs all the way home.

"All those people and not one tantrum," Jon said again as they neared Shelter Valley. Since it was at least the fifth time she'd heard the comment, Lillie just smiled.

They'd only stayed in the museum for a couple of hours, but she agreed that Abe had done well. Of course, they'd both been standing over him nonstop the entire time. But they'd made certain that his focus had remained on his activities first and them second.

The day could have been perfect—except that several times she'd seen Abe give that hand signal. The stop sign. Holding his hand straight up and out as a way to tell someone to stop. Something kids did. Adults, too.

And when added to the rest of the behaviors and anxieties Abe had exhibited since she'd started watching him—his fear of crowds, panicking for seemingly no reason...

"Have you had Abe's hearing checked?" she asked Jon as they approached her neighborhood. It was Sunday afternoon and people were out and about. Caro waved at them from the sidewalk as they drove by.

Lillie waved back.

"Of course, he's had all of his checks," Jon said. "Passed with flying colors in every way. You know my landlord, Caroline?"

Abe's hearing was fine. He wasn't Braydon. He wasn't hers at all. And there was nothing wrong with him.

"Caroline Strickland?" she asked.

"Yeah, she just waved to you."

"She waved to us," Lillie said, "but yes, she's a friend of mine." She told him about her early-morning bike rides with Caro, leaving out the part about how they met—the medical emergency that had brought Caro to the clinic with a traumatized child.

She told him that Caro knew about her new doors and faucets.

He nodded.

It was all very casual and friendly and nice. And Lillie was on edge. They were almost at her house. He'd drop her off, say good-night, take his son home to bed and get on with the rest of his life.

She should leave it at that.

She'd just proved that she was in over her head with the Swartz men with her irrational concerns over Abe's well-being. Her overreaction to his simple hand movements. He'd been acting normal and she was seeing hearing loss. Imagining that Abe's panic was due to not being able to hear. Fearing that the little boy was going deaf.

There was no way she could pretend to herself that Jon and Abe were simply a job to her. She cared deeply about all of her patients, but her feelings toward Jon and Abe were…personal.

And when it got personal, she feared the worst. Because she'd lived through the worst and couldn't go through it a second time.

Stopping the truck in her driveway, Jon shut off the engine and turned to her. "Caroline knows that I'm helping at your house. What else did you tell her?"

"Nothing about Abe's issues, if that's what you're wondering. I don't—"

"I wasn't worried about that," Jon interrupted. "I meant

about our…friendship. Won't she find it odd that we're in the car together on a Sunday afternoon?"

She hadn't thought about that. Or cared. Nodding, she said, "I'll tell her that…"

She couldn't think. Not with his arm on the back of the seat so close to touching her.

"Just tell her you were working. You have my permission to mention Abe's crowd issue if you want to. If that's what this is about."

He'd given her the easy way out. Take it. Take it. Take it.

"It's not."

Frowning, Jon glanced at his son still asleep in the backseat and said, "Look, Lillie, you have no worries where I'm concerned. I know I screwed up the other night, but you don't have to worry that it's going to happen again."

He was so close. And his distance was driving her to craziness. "I think part of what worries me is that it might not."

His breathing seemed to stop. And she turned hot. And then cold. She'd make a mistake.

"Are you coming on to me?" The question was soft, intimate.

There was a two-year-old sleeping a couple of feet away. One she couldn't take any further into her heart.

"No." Was she? "At least I don't think I am. I'm just… The other night, you said we both acknowledged…" For someone whose entire life was dedicated to finding the right words to soothe people she was failing miserably. "But I really don't want anything more than friendship."

She couldn't take on Jon's son. Not as her own. She'd smother him. Worry herself sick over every little hiccup. Or hand signal.

She honestly did not want to marry again. Ever.

"I'd like to tell Caroline that we're friends. If she asks. Which I know she will."

"That's fine."

But that wasn't all she wanted.

"You do realize how a small town works, don't you?"

"I've never lived in one—at least, not long enough to become part of the gossip mill, but I've heard about them. From what I understand, Shelter Valley is a pretty tight-knit community."

"That's right."

He studied her and she could see something going on in his eyes.

"What?"

"I was told, I'm not saying by who, that you're in pretty tight with a lot of folks here."

"They're like family to me." Where was this leading? Her heart racing, libido pounding at her core, Lillie admonished herself for behaving like a teenager. Jon was just a man.

"I was...warned."

"Warned off?" It was her turn to frown. Who would want her to not be friends with Jon? And why?

"No." The shake of his head was easy, as was the hint of a grin at the corner of his mouth. "Just warned that if I hurt you, I'd best leave town before anyone got wind of it."

"Oh." She was hot again. "They watch out for me."

In the five years she'd been in Shelter Valley, she'd never done anything worthy of the gossip mill. She liked it that way.

"I got that."

"I'm just surprised...other than at the day care, I didn't think we'd been seen together." She thought back over the past couple of weeks, and added, "I told Bonnie and Caro what a great job you did on my French doors...."

"I… Just someone who knew I'd been to your house mentioned that I should be careful not to…toy…with you."

The care with which he chose his words was endearing. And maddening, too.

"Toy with me?"

"I think I got the go-ahead to see you, just not to break your heart."

Oh, well, then. "No worries there. My heart's not available for breaking."

"I'm aware of that."

"I know yours isn't, either," Lillie assured him quickly, lest he think she considered her feelings more important than his—or that she was only looking out for herself. "I fully realize that Abraham has your whole heart right now."

Right now. Why had she tacked on the qualifier? Like, maybe, sometime in the distant future, he might be available to her?

Because, sometime in the future, she might want that?

She didn't want that—and couldn't lead him to believe she did. "Look, I'm making a mess of this whole thing. Let's just agree to tread carefully, shall we?"

"Of course."

Jon nodded. Stared at her lips as though he wanted to kiss them, and then started his truck.

Taking the cue, Lillie leaned over, planted a lightning-quick peck on his cheek and ran up to her door without looking back.

CHAPTER EIGHTEEN

ALL THOSE CROWDS and not one tantrum. New words every day. Abraham was on track and as normal as any other two-year-old. They weren't going to need Lillie's help much longer.

But they needed her.

Jon sat in class on Monday, stared at photos of art in places he'd probably never see, talked to Mark about chemical compounds, figured out a calculus problem before the professor had it solved on the screen—and daydreamed about Lillie Henderson.

She thought her heart was inaccessible. He knew better. He could feel it every single time she was anywhere near Abe.

And even if she'd never love Jon, it was pretty clear she liked him. A lot.

He could settle for that.

At work that afternoon, he heard about yet another break-in. Closer to town. At the home of another woman living on her own. She wasn't home when it happened. But more stuff had been taken from her house than the previous homes. The word was that the sheriff was on a mission to find the guy responsible. He had a posse of volunteers 24/7 helping him now, and anyone walking alone at night was subject to suspicion.

Which meant Jon wouldn't be doing any walking at all, except from his truck to wherever he was going. And he had to dispose of some of his tools—the ones he'd used to remove Lillie's sliding glass door—no matter how much of a waste it was. He couldn't afford to come under suspicion. If they arrested him, Abe would be put in foster care, at least until he could prove his innocence. And he'd have to drop out of school, which would mean he'd not only lose the scholarship, he'd have to pay back the thousands of dollars he'd already spent.

Sweating, and working himself up to panic mode, Jon reminded himself he'd done nothing wrong.

This time.

But if he was the sheriff, and he knew about Jon's past, he'd suspect himself.

He had to find out more about what was going on. If they were going to be pulling people's records, it might be time to grab his packed duffel and head out.

They'd have to leave Lillie.

He had a life here.

But he'd have no life if he was arrested.

And there was Clara…always the threat of Clara…in the background.

"Addy has an in with the sheriff," Jon said to Mark as they shared a late lunch perched on the rocks outside the plant. "Have you guys heard anything about this guy doing all the break-ins? Do they have anything to go on yet?"

"Just that he wears a size-ten shoe. And they figure from the indention of the footprint in the dirt that he weighs about 180. They also think he's a student at Montford," he said.

Jon's sandwich stuck in his throat.

"Why do they think that?"

"They found a token from the cafeteria on the ground outside one of the homes that they suspect fell out of his pocket."

The tokens were given as change when students used dining passes. Jon had a bowl full of them on his dresser at home. He didn't eat at campus much because of Abe, but a dining hall pass came with his scholarship and he used it for the occasional lunch when he was on campus. And he sometimes used it to pick up fruit and packaged items, like microwavable macaroni and cheese, that he could bring home.

He wore a size ten and weighed 175.

As, he was sure, did many other average guys on campus.

But how many of them had confessed to breaking and entering? Or done time for being caught red-handed with the things he helped steal?

Hell, he'd had stolen beer in his belly, and on his lips, at the time of his arrest.

Stuffing the remainder of his lunch in the trash, Jon swallowed, and said, "Well, I hope they catch the guy soon."

Mark nodded, chewing on the same type of bread and peanut butter he carried to work almost every day. "They will. You can count on that. Sheriff Richards is smart and determined. He'll get the guy."

"So what's up with you and Lillie? I heard you two were driving through town together yesterday."

Mark's knowing glance gave Jon more pause. This thing with Lillie... They'd agreed to be careful.

"It was strictly business," he said. "That stuff with Abe I told you about. We took him to a museum for kids in Phoenix yesterday."

Mark asked about the museum, how Abe had liked it, what he'd done. He'd allowed Jon to distract him from his real question.

Turning, Jon headed back toward the plant. Mark caught

up with him as he slid his badge in the slot and reached for the door.

"Funny," Mark said, just behind him. "I heard that she said you two were 'friends.'" Mark's emphasis on the word was too obvious to miss.

Lillie was talking about him. Them.

Jon's gut leaped. And his tension dissipated. Everything would be okay if he had Lillie by his side. Abe would be fine. And Jon...that dream of having a woman to look after, to protect. To look after him. Fight for him...

Rein it in, dude.

Mark was paged. And, with a teasing nudge to Jon's shoulder and some pithy words that Jon didn't catch, he was off.

Jon got back to work, too.

Lillie might like him fine now. Chances were good she didn't have any idea about his past. His guilt. And if she got too close, she'd be bound to find out.

And to have second thoughts.

Kate had known. He'd been released from detention shortly after his eighteenth birthday. He'd had no family to turn to. No real friends.

He'd called Barbara. She hadn't wanted anything to do with him—not since he'd turned "bad," as she'd called it.

It was bad enough coming from juvie, but coming out after growing up as a ward of the state—no one believed he'd amount to anything.

He'd been labeled. By everyone but himself.

His foster brothers were already serving time again for other crimes. Jon was determined not to be like them.

He'd needed a fresh start, and so he'd taken his parole officer's suggestion and sought help from Kate's uncle—a man who helped released prisoners start new lives.

Kate knew that. Knew what jobs and housing her uncle reserved for the men he "rescued."

Jon's ex-con status had been the reason Kate had come on to him to begin with. And, in the end, the reason why she'd left. He was convinced of that.

If he'd been different—up-and-coming with a pressed white shirt and a trendy tie—they'd have moved to New York together. Abe, too.

With the mental reminder, Jon tried to stop thinking about everything but that which was under his control, which, at the moment, meant conductors and production times.

LUNCH ON MONDAY was a brief affair for Lillie—a quick snack cup of pears and some crackers with cheese. After a busy morning at the day care—which included another surprising tantrum from Abraham while he was standing in a circle holding hands with a group of kids for movement class—she'd rushed to the clinic to assist with a four-year-old who'd split his chin open, and then supported a couple of children through radiology procedures.

The worst was yet to come: a two-year-old with a bowel condition, requiring several surgeries that mandated tube feeding. The good news was that the condition wasn't permanent. Little Manny's prognosis pointed to full recovery and normal life span.

Sadly, the toddler required a kind of semipermanent IV line that had to be exchanged. As she was already in radiology, Lillie made it to the room in plenty of time to get things ready for Manny. This was their second time together for this particular procedure. The first had been as close to a nightmare as Lillie could remember. The procedure, which consisted of inserting a thin catheter in the arm just above the elbow and guiding it by X-ray close to the heart, could be completed in a matter of minutes. Manny's had taken an hour and a half. Partly because, after forty-five minutes of unsuccessful attempts to get his soft little veins to cooperate, Lillie had called for a break to let the little guy recover a bit.

With the lights down low, music playing softly in the background and a plastic console that she could hold in front of the boy as he lay on his side on the table, she was ready. Manny liked to press buttons.

He was crying as his distraught mother—a young woman who lived with her family on a cotton farm ten miles outside of Shelter Valley—brought him into the clinic.

"Manny, sweetie, what's wrong?" Lillie asked. Taking the toddler from his mother's arms, acknowledging the grateful smile on the worried woman's lips, she settled Manny on her hip, held the hot and sweaty little head against her chest and rubbed his scalp, talking softly to him as she carried him through the doors leading out of the waiting room.

Not waiting for the boy to answer her, Lillie kept up a steady stream of quiet chatter, keeping her voice light, nonthreatening, as she told him that they were going to have a much better time together than the last time they'd seen each other. She told him about the box they were going to play with. The lights and buttons he would get to push.

Thankfully, there were a couple of radiology rooms at the clinic. Lillie had purposely requested the one Manny hadn't been in the last time for today's procedure. She'd taken care to decorate the room with colorful stuffed animals and plastic wall hangings. An overabundance of them. Visual stimulation that would help distract the boy if his veins refused to cooperate again.

"Look!" she said, picking up the console box at the

same time that she set the boy down on the procedure table, intending for him to begin playing and not pay attention to where he was sitting. She'd scheduled fifteen minutes of alone time with the boy before his procedure was due to begin.

Michael, the radiologist on duty, came in with his support staff right on schedule.

"Look, Manny, it's Michael! Do you know who Michael is?" she asked the little boy.

Manny wasn't crying, but there was mistrust in his eyes as he stared up at the short-haired man wearing scrubs with cars all over them.

"Michael's the zoom-zoom guy!" she said. "He can make everything go zoom! You want to watch how fast he is?" she asked, handing Michael a big plastic car and pointing to the ramp she'd pulled in from the playroom down the hall.

Michael shot the car down the ramp a few times and let Manny play, too.

"Okay, big guy," Lillie said, scooping the child up with one arm while keeping the car in his toddler hands with the other. "You hold on to the car while we make you go zoom-zoom," she said, glancing to make certain the technician had a papoose—a special cloth apparatus that would hold the boy still during the procedure—open on the table.

"You're going to go zoom," she told Manny, not asking him if he wanted to so he didn't have a chance to say no and then be ignored. He had no choice in this matter so she wasn't going to feed his distrust by pretending like she was giving him one.

With a few quick motions, she had the car on the table beside Manny's head and the little boy was wrapped firmly in the papoose, with both arms free.

Free because they might need both and didn't want to

have to fight to get Manny back in the papoose a second time. And because she hoped to distract him from the arm Michael needed by engaging his right hand.

With the little boy lying on the table, Lillie moved the toy cars as Michael situated him, keeping Manny engaged. The old line was out and the new one in before Lillie had a chance to move on to another distraction.

"All done!" Michael smiled and mouthed a silent "thank you" in her direction.

"Zoom!" Manny said, dry-eyed and ready to roll over the table some more as they released him from the papoose.

With an ear-to-ear grin, Lillie returned the little boy to his relieved mother. Disaster averted.

She'd distracted Manny—and herself, too. Her concerns about Abraham, her feelings for his father—those were distant.

This was her life.

Helping other people's children.

And she was good at it.

WHEN HE GOT off work a couple of hours early on Monday, Jon didn't head straight to the day care as he would normally have done. After calling Little Spirits to check up on Abe, he turned the truck toward Phoenix and a drugstore where he could buy some personal items without anyone in Shelter Valley finding out about it.

The existence of his sex life was none of their business. As it stood, he didn't have a sex life. Might not have one ever again. But he'd already gone and created one child to the dismay of the child's mother. He wasn't going to risk a replay.

With the condoms safely hidden in his backpack, waiting to be transferred to his nightstand drawer, Jon stopped at a busy construction site trash compactor and reached for his expensive glass suction cups. He'd left them right where he always did. In the bucket with his furniture movers. They weren't there. And then he noticed that the bucket had tipped over. The cups had fallen out. Grabbing them, he tossed them, pushed the button to destroy the evidence and drove away as quickly as the speed limit allowed to pick up his son.

Dinner that night was a messy affair. Jon made spaghetti that Abe insisted on feeding himself. After dinner, Jon took his son on a trip straight from the booster seat to the bathtub. After Abe's bath, they retired to Abe's playroom. Jon set himself up on the floor with his tablet and his laptop and Abe played happily—a normal, self-directed little man who was going to grow up to be president.

With or without a mama.

Life was good.

LILLIE WAS STILL working in her office Monday evening when her phone rang.

Jon. She should tell him about Abe's tantrum that day—although it had been the shortest one yet.

It took her two rings to find the thing in the pocket of her big leather satchel.

The phone sounded a third time as she read the caller display.

Kirk.

Her heart sank to her stomach.

"Is this a bad time?" her ex-husband asked when she picked up.

Glancing out to the quiet hallway beyond her office door, Lillie bit back her initial reaction and said, "No. What's up?"

"I need to talk to you, Lillie."

They'd already been through this. "So talk."

"I...just... Don't hang up, okay? At least, not without...
I'm breaking the rules already, aren't I? Trying to tell you
what you can and can't do."

He sounded odd.

"Where are you?"

"Home."

Papa and Gayle had said he still lived in Scottsdale.

"Are you drinking?"

He'd never been a particularly heavy drinker.

"No. Though it would probably be better if I was. Help
take the edge off."

"What edge?"

"Tell me about him."

Jon? How had he found out?

Jumping up from her chair, Lillie held the phone to her
ear with one hand and packed up the last of her things with
the other. It was time to go home. She could finish charting in the morning.

"Please, Lil. I know I'm scum for asking, but I have
to know."

Jon was the first man she'd been seriously interested in
since the divorce. Had her failure to replace Kirk kept him
secure? Was that what his recent change of heart was all
about? Not an internal struggle, a coming to terms with
who he was as a person, but a need to know that Lillie
hadn't replaced him?

"What do you want to know?" She wanted to know how
Kirk had found out about Jon.

If he was spying on her, having her followed...

"Everything. I wasn't there for any of our baby's short
life. It's gotten to the point where I can't even spend time
with Ely because he's such an acute reminder."

Outside, alone in the dark, Lillie walked briskly toward her car.

Noticing a movement in the shadows, Lillie said, "Keep talking, Kirk. Just until I get to the car."

There was movement again. Maybe just a tree, its branches rustling in the breeze.

There'd been another break-in the night before.

"Where are you?"

"Leaving work."

"Is anyone else there?"

"Just the nurses and technicians on the night shift. No patients so far tonight, so no docs." She was only a few yards from her car. And she knew that Kirk would call 9-1-1 immediately if—

"You shouldn't be out alone this late. Especially not with those break-ins. It's pitch-black outside. I heard there was just another one. They still haven't caught the guy."

Had the latest break-in made the Phoenix news? Or did he have an "in'" in Shelter Valley?

Her key fob in hand, Lillie pushed the automatic unlock and dived for the car handle. "I'm alone at night all the time," she said, sliding onto her front seat, pulling the door shut behind her and hitting the automatic lock.

She was safe.

"If that was a barb aimed at me, it hit its mark." Kirk's voice had dropped another octave. "And was well deserved."

That hadn't been her intention. She didn't have the energy to blast him.

"Okay, we've had a conversation. Are we done now?" Lillie asked, ready to put the car in gear and head... She hadn't decided where yet. Probably home. Maybe to stop someplace for a salad. Or to deliver the zipper-and-button toddler pillow she'd asked Bonnie to order for her and that had come in that day.

"I need to know about him. Please, Lil." His voice broke.

And she caved. Pulling around to the front of the clinic where the lights were bright and she could be seen from the reception area, Lillie parked again.

"I don't have any idea what to say." She didn't know how much he'd been told. And she wasn't about to give him any information he didn't already have. She was sorry that he was suffering, but whatever he was feeling couldn't come close to the devastating betrayal and heartbreak he'd put her through.

"Maybe just little bits at a time," he said. "Tell me about that last month. Did you feel him move? Remember that first time you felt him move? We were out to dinner with clients. I can't remember where. But you jumped and spilled my water glass...."

"It was at the Phoenician." An upscale resort.

She'd said the words without thinking—had traveled back in time with him without realizing where he was taking her.

And...

He was asking about Braydon. Not about Jon. Heat rising beneath her skin, Lillie realized something else. He'd just admitted to her that he couldn't relate to his son, his living flesh and blood, because of unresolved issues regarding his dead one.

Papa and Gayle had told her how Kirk's lack of involvement hurt the little boy.

Ely was paying for his father's mistakes.

And that wasn't right.

So she did what she could. Granted Kirk ten minutes of question-and-answer time. And then, when she'd had enough, when she'd actually started to feel his pain, she cut the call off, put her car in Drive and turned it toward home.

No matter what kind of transformation Kirk was making, or what kind of regret he was feeling, he was no longer Lillie's business. Or concern.

She'd do what she could to help him, for Ely's sake, but she couldn't take Kirk on again. Couldn't afford to lose any more of her to a man who only thought of himself.

Still, she felt his pain. They'd lost a son. Their son.

After picking up the phone to call Kirk back, she dropped it again.

She didn't love him. She was absolutely certain of that. Please, God, don't let her be so weak that she'd fall under Kirk's spell again.

Lillie made a U-turn.

It wasn't Kirk she wanted. She knew that without a doubt.

CHAPTER NINETEEN

JON HAD JUST put Abraham down for the night when he saw headlights shining in their living room window. He could close the blinds, block the regular passing of headlights up and down his street all night, but he preferred the company as he sat in the living room alone doing his homework.

His rented condominium had an adjoining unit. And the complex contained forty-six other units that shared a total of twelve driveways with four parking spots in each. One of his neighbors must have just arrived home.

He'd met the two young men who lived in the adjoining unit the day he'd moved in. He'd introduced them to Abraham, apologizing ahead of time if the toddler cried and disturbed them, and promised to do his utmost to keep the little boy happy. In return, he'd asked if it would be a problem for them to keep noise at a minimum after eight o'clock.

He hadn't seen or heard them since—except coming and going, usually as shadows in the night. They kept different hours than he did.

But they were quiet. Which was all he cared about.

A knock on his door had him jumping out of his seat.

Not convinced that Abraham was fully asleep yet, he didn't want whoever it was to knock again.

Barefoot and shirtless, dressed only in the cartoon character pants he'd pulled on after bathing Abraham, Jon pulled the door open. His body sprang to instant attention when he saw who was on his doorstep. Staring at his naked chest.

"Lillie! Come in."

Stepping back into the shadows behind the door, he pushed the screen door outward.

She looked incredible in her tight jeans and a white, formfitting long-sleeved T-shirt.

He didn't ask why she'd come. Wasn't sure he wanted to know.

He'd bought the condoms. And there she was.

Not that he really believed he was going to have sex with her that night.

"I brought this for you," she said, holding out a plastic bag.

A gift. He didn't receive many. Wasn't particularly good at accepting them.

Embarrassed, he pulled open the bag and glanced awkwardly inside. And then he recognized the softly padded cushion, the big zippers and buttons.

The gift wasn't for him. He grinned.

"You ordered one for us?" he asked, glancing over at her. He'd checked with the day care owner about the educational tool, planning to order one, until he'd found out the cost.

He and Abraham would have had to give up fast food for three months. At least.

At the moment, he didn't care. He'd sacrifice a year's worth, a lifetime's worth, of greasy burgers, if it brought Lillie Henderson to his door.

"Abe loves it and doesn't get enough chances to play with it," she said. "He's good about sharing, and that's important, too, but I thought—"

"It's great!" Jon jumped in. "Really, this means a lot. Thank you."

He was staring at her now, not at the toy in his hand.

"You're welcome." Her smile grew. And she wavered.

"Uh…how much do I owe you?" He knew the ballpark amount. Not exact. And hoped she'd take a check because he didn't keep much cash on him—other than what he'd stashed in the emergency bag that he never touched.

"You don't owe me anything." Still standing in his doorway, her hair coming out of the ponytail he now knew she wore to work every day, Lillie shrugged.

"No way. I'm already so far in your debt I'm going to end up remodeling your entire house to get myself back in the black. Tell me how much I owe you."

"It's a gift, Jon. From me to Abraham. You don't pay someone back for a gift."

"A rubber ball—that would be a gift. This…"

He didn't have to make it an issue. But it kept her standing there. He'd write a check later, for more than Bonnie had quoted.

And learn how to make hamburgers and French fries at home as well as the fast-food restaurant did.

"Bonnie gets things donated from wholesalers," Lillie said. "And she also gets things at a huge discount. She shares with me."

"Does she know you're giving this to me? For Abraham?"

"Yes."

He tried to come up with another argument, but failed.

"Cute pants." She was staring at his cartoon characters.

"I told you about them." About the sticky fingers that had taught him to always keep a safe distance between strollers, shopping carts and goods that he didn't want to buy.

"Yeah, they look a lot better on you than I imagined."

Hoping she couldn't make out particulars in the dim

light, he stepped farther back and said, "You want to stay for a bit? Have some tea or something? I'd offer you wine, but I don't have any."

He'd done his share of drinking as a teen. Hadn't had more than a beer or two at a time since he'd been let out of the prison for juveniles.

"I really have to get going," she said, but she didn't move toward the door. "I haven't been home from work yet."

He knew by now that when she was planning to stop anywhere on her way home, she changed out of her scrubs at the clinic. The jeans and T-shirt were telling him something.

"Have you eaten dinner?"

"Not yet."

"I made spaghetti." He heard the words coming out of his mouth and was proud of himself for thinking of them. "Homemade sauce. I'd be happy to heat up the leftovers. It's not enough for another meal for Abe and me."

"But you saved them."

He shrugged.

"I do that, too," she said, not moving from her spot just inside the doorway. "It's my job to keep all leftovers until they start growing things. Then I can throw them away," she said with a grin.

"So you'll save me from having to be host to the container in the refrigerator until it grows things?" he asked.

"I guess." She glanced around. "As long as I'm not disturbing anything." Her gaze landed on the computer and tablet on the couch where he'd left them.

"Homework," he said. "I'm pretty well caught up."

He'd actually been reading ahead, in case he got offered extra hours at work in the coming days.

"I like your sofa."

It was dark plaid. "It's washable," he offered. "The place came furnished."

"I know. I helped Caroline a bit this summer with re-painting some of her student rentals."

"Was this one of them?"

"No. It wasn't this complex. But she described the various decorating schemes she'd applied to make each of her properties a little different from the others."

Lillie followed him into the kitchen and told him about some of Caroline's experiences as a landlord while he heated the spaghetti. When it was ready, he sat with her at his little table for four and watched her eat.

"Caro is a firm believer in environment as a contributor to success. If she can offer students a nice place to live, she believes they'll have a better chance at succeeding."

Her plate almost empty, she was staring at the booster seat. Jon looked, too, expecting to see splotches of spaghetti sauce he'd missed. Toddlers had a way of leaving things in the most inconspicuous places.

"He had another tantrum today," she said slowly.

Jon straightened. "Bonnie said he'd had a good day." He'd asked her when he'd called. And again when he'd picked up his son.

"She wasn't there when it happened. And it ended so fast we decided not to chart it."

"Was he in a big group when it happened?"

"Yes, but the crying didn't start until the kids all started to move."

Disappointment hit him, although he tried to hold it at bay. They'd had such a good experience at the museum the day before. All those crowds, the hoards of unfamiliar kids, and Abe had held his own like a champ. A NASCAR driver and president all rolled into one.

Give him a year to develop some coordination and he'd be a professional ball player, too.

He'd thought they were through the worst of it.

"They were in movement class, learning to play ring-around-the-rosy, and when the kids started to walk around in a circle, he lost it for a bit."

"A normal two-year-old tantrum because he liked the spot where he was standing?" Jon asked hopefully.

"I'm not sure." She was frowning. "The good news is that it was over almost as soon as it had begun. All of Abe's instructors know to kneel in front of him to get his focus and then ask him to use his words. As soon as the movement instructor did that, he stopped crying and responded to her. He was fine afterward."

"Did he play ring-around-the-rosy?"

"Yep. And he laughed like crazy when they all fell down."

So, a minor setback. They weren't out of the woods, but they could see the clearing. "I love that laugh," Jon said, grinning. Who'd ever have thought such a little thing—his kid's laugh—could make him feel so good?

"Don't you ever get the least bit resentful of having to do it all alone?" Lillie's gaze was clear, direct.

"Nope." She could report anything he said or did....

Jon stopped himself.

She was his friend. And his answer was still the same.

Lillie's face had cleared and she was staring at him again. In that way.

"Did Caroline ask about us today?" He didn't know where the words had come from. He hadn't been thinking about them in that moment. At least not consciously.

"Yes."

"And?"

"I told her that we were friends," she said, like the topic

was no big deal. But there was something slightly whimsical in her tone, too. Something he could barely capture but wanted to hold.

"Did she let it go at that?"

"Pretty much." She licked her lips.

He slid his lightly covered hips a little bit farther under the table. "So we have nothing to worry about?"

Except that the news had traveled all the way to Mark Heber by lunchtime.

"I wasn't worried to begin with."

"These people are your friends."

"I don't ask them about their sex lives—" Eyes wide, mouth open, she broke off.

Jon leaned his elbows on the table. "Is that what we're talking about? Our sex life?"

He was a man. With a woman who turned him on. And God knew, he wasn't perfect.

"No! Of course not."

Her face was red. And he was hotter than hell.

"Are we going to have one?"

"I...don't know."

"We need to find out what it's like," he said out loud. But not loudly. "Sex. Between us. To put an end to this constant wondering."

She nodded.

"It's just a physical thing."

She nodded again.

"Want to get it over with?" He did. Now before it was too late. Before the sheriff came knocking on his door with a copy of his criminal record in hand, asking questions. Before Lillie found out about his past.

Or turned him over to Clara. He needed her to know the real Jon Swartz. The man inside who would love and protect for as long as she'd let him.

After her third nod, Jon stood in front of her.

Taking her hand, he led her to the living room and the couch she'd admired, but didn't sit down. Pulling her against him, he let her feel the extent of his arousal and gave himself the heavenly relief of pressing himself into her sweet body. Then he dropped his mouth to hers.

The kiss wasn't "hello." Or "I want to get to know you." It wasn't even "I want to taste you." Jon, a man who generally held back in deference to his overzealousness, took Lillie in his arms and went straight for "I have to have you."

Her response was better than anything he could have imagined.

LILLIE ENJOYED SEX. She felt the usual things in the usual ways. But Jon's touch ignited feelings she didn't know existed. A hunger and aggressiveness she'd never have believed possible of herself.

Like a stranger at her own party, she moved and reacted, and didn't recognize herself at all.

And all they'd done was stand in Jon's living room and kiss.

"Who am I?" she murmured aloud as Jon lifted his lips and stared down at her. Her only consolation was that his breathing was as ragged as hers.

"My dream come true."

The words should have been corny. The sincerity shining from his eyes melted her.

Melted any last speck of her that his body hadn't already incinerated.

Her hands moved of their own accord as they stood there staring at each other. Her palms had already traversed every inch of his smooth and muscled back. His shoulders.

Now, as they separated an inch, she slid her fingers

around to the front of him, burying them in the mass of dark hair covering his chest. His nipples were there, waiting for her, but she avoided them for the moment—almost afraid of what that next step would bring.

"I've wanted to do this since that first walk we took on campus." She couldn't believe she'd told him that.

"You have?"

"Uh-huh." The roughness of his hair tickled her palms as she lightly massaged his pecs. "You had your shirt unbuttoned and your hair was peeking through and…I noticed it."

"You want to know what I noticed about you?"

She hadn't thought she could get any more turned on. Any more needy. "Yes."

"Your hands."

"What?"

"Your hands. They're slender and soft and feminine and so…capable."

His hips, still pressing against her, shifted, drawing her attention to his very erect penis. She pushed her pelvis against him.

"You're turned on by my hands?" It was different. But nice.

"Yeah…" The word was as much a groan as a verbalization. "And your legs and your butt. The slenderness of your waist. The way your hair falls out of your ponytail. But your breasts really do it for me.…"

He pushed against her again with his lower half while separating their torsos just a bit as he glanced down at her top.

Could he tell that her nipples were hard and straining for him? "But then, looking at your knees does it for me, too," he added.

She laughed. And stopped. Sex had never been funny

before. Or particularly fun, either. It had felt good, but been focused. Serious.

"Is it always this intense for you?"

"You mean, has the sound of a woman's voice ever made me forget my own name, like yours does?"

His honesty spun her out of control. Jon wasn't only the first man she'd been truly interested in since Kirk, he was a whole new world for her.

"You've got it bad, sir," she told him with newfound freedom, prepared to fly as high as he'd take her.

"Guilty as charged." He didn't seem to mind as he leaned forward and kissed her again, his lips open against hers from the start, his tongue probing the inside of her mouth.

It was just physical, he'd assured her.

But she couldn't take him in far enough, couldn't get far enough into him. Her whole being pushed toward him, needing far more than he was giving her.

Needing him to touch places that hadn't been touched in too many years. And a thought struck her....

She hadn't had sex since Braydon. She'd given birth to him naturally and things had...changed. Would sex hurt?

Would Jon be able to tell that she'd given birth?

She should know these things, but she didn't.

There'd been no reason for her to ask her doctor about postnatal intercourse when she'd had Braydon.

"What's wrong?" Jon had stopped kissing her.

She panicked. And still wanted him. "Abraham," she managed to get out. "What about Abraham?"

"He's sound asleep."

"What if he wakes up?"

Frowning, Jon held her shoulders, gently rubbing them. "I'm not sure," he said. "You'd know better than I would about something like that. What do parents do if their kids wake up while they're having sex?"

"Best-case scenario is that they're in their bedroom with the door locked so there are no surprises." She could breathe again and was feeling better.

"I have a lock on my door."

Okay. Good.

No one in Shelter Valley knew about Braydon. She'd lost him in her old life. "I don't have any birth control. Do you?" she asked.

She was a professional who worked in the medical field.

And her body had been inhabited by a wanton woman who was taking her places she wasn't sure she was ready to go.

But she *wanted* to go.

God, how she wanted to.

CHAPTER TWENTY

"I HAVE CONDOMS."

Jon answered Lillie's birth control question. But they weren't going to have sex. At least, not that night. The shadows in her eyes made that clear, even if her questions did not.

Taking her hand, he led her to the couch, relieved to see that she followed him easily.

"Look," he said right off. "I don't want you to feel pressured at all. If this isn't right for you, that's okay. We don't have to sleep together." He meant every word.

"But—"

"No," he interrupted her. "We can be as close as you're comfortable with. Physically or not. We're friends either way."

"I want to have sex." Her smile was tinged with sadness as she ran her fingers gently across his face. Jon turned and kissed them. "I guess I'm just not as ready as I thought I was."

"Then we'll wait."

"Not too long," she said, her eyes getting that hungry look again, confusing him with her mixed messages. "I'm… I just wasn't prepared tonight and—"

Remembering the months he'd spent with Kate, prior to the pregnancy, he wondered if she was having that time of the month.

"I don't want you to think I'm rushing things," he told

her again in case his first impression was accurate and she just wasn't ready.

He could manage fine without sex.

At least, he'd been doing all right without it before she'd come waltzing into his life, a human aphrodisiac that just didn't quit.

"I also want you to know that I just bought the condoms today. I haven't had sex since before Abe was born," he continued, holding her hand and hating that his body was still begging him to do so much more.

"I got them in Phoenix," he added. "So no one here could see me buying them and draw conclusions about us."

Lillie leaned into him and pressed her lips to his. "I wasn't worried," she said. "I trust you, Jon. Implicitly. And if people think we're having sex, that's okay, too."

The rush those words brought was almost better than sex itself.

IN BETWEEN HER early-morning bike ride and work, Lillie managed to make a phone call to her doctor on Tuesday morning. She reassured Lillie that while the first time she and Jon made love might be a little uncomfortable for her, she would be just fine.

And while it was possible to tell if a woman had given birth—more so if the man in question had been versed in the physical intimacies of a particular woman's body before the baby—it was unlikely in her case, as she and Jon had never made love before.

Dr. Jordon had also suggested, not lightly, that if Lillie were embarking on a serious relationship, she should tell the man that she'd had a son. And lost him just days after his birth.

Assuring the doctor that if she was seriously considering a long-term relationship, she would do so, Lillie hung up, relieved. And almost called Jon to tell him the good news.

Then she remembered that he hadn't known there'd been a problem.

She hadn't, either, until the night before, when they'd been seconds away from taking off their clothes.

When he called her later that afternoon, offering to get started on the tiling that evening—with Abraham in tow—she agreed immediately.

That night, as well as the two nights after that, she spent the early part of the evening looking after the little boy who was quickly tunneling his way into her heart, and then, after eight when she'd settled him into her bed, she spent the rest of the time working beside Jon.

By ten o'clock on Thursday night, Lillie was pretty well tied up in knots.

"Do you like it?" In his old work jeans and a T-shirt, with grout dust covering his hands and a portion of his cheek, Jon surveyed the new backsplash in her bathroom—the last of his tiling projects.

"I love it!" The glossy beige and tan and crystal squares looked even better than she'd hoped against the off-white walls and beige granite sinks. She was covered in grout, too, although she'd washed her hands.

"Good." Putting the lid back on the almost-empty container of grout, he dropped his dirty trowels in the bucket of warm water he'd brought in with him and put the lid on that, too. "I'll get this stuff out to the truck and be right back for Abe," he said.

Reaching out a hand, Lillie grabbed his arm. "Don't go."

He froze, the few inches he had on her seeming more like ten as he looked down at her. "Don't go?" he repeated.

Lillie nodded.

And because she'd been a little unclear the other night at his house, she added, "I'd like you to stay. To…hold me."

"Lady, I am willing to do many things for you, pretty much anything you ask, but I do not believe I'm capable of simply holding you right now. Or anytime soon, for that matter."

The intensity in his gaze went straight to her heart. "What if I'm not asking you to 'simply' hold me?"

He frowned and she rushed on. "I was hoping we could finish what we started the other night. You told me to tell you when I was ready."

His gaze changed yet again, consuming her. "You're ready?"

"Uh-huh." Whether her grin was due to nerves or her surging homones, she wasn't sure. She just knew she couldn't stop herself from smiling up at him.

"Right now?"

"Yeah."

Glancing around them, he dropped his bucket and took her hand, pulling her into her bedroom where his son lay sleeping on her bed. Still holding her, he scooped up the sleeping toddler with his free hand, settled him on his shoulder and hauled her gently down the hall, stopping where she'd dropped her purse on the counter when she'd come in that evening.

"You'll probably want to grab that," he said softly, leaning away from his son's ear.

"We're leaving?"

"I'm not going to blow this opportunity," he said. "And the crib where Abe is safe, the monitor that keeps him that way, the shower I desperately need and the condoms I bought are all at my place. Not to mention a bed that isn't occupied."

Still grinning, Lillie grabbed her purse, laced her fingers through his, locked up as they left her house and said, "I do have a spare bed, you know."

JON'S BED HAD come with the apartment. The sheets were his own. They were his one extravagance—a gift to himself after years spent sleeping on a bare cot with only a horsehair blanket to cover him.

That night, he and Lillie marked those sheets with their wet soapy bodies because they hadn't been able to wait until they'd finished their shower and dried off. He'd intended to be slow and deliberate with every touch. To frame each moment in his memory. But he'd no sooner shoved his drawers to the floor of his bathroom and stepped into the shower, before she was in there with him—completely naked and slick with water.

"I was too impatient to wait my turn," she said, reaching up to stick her tongue in his mouth. "I swear to you," she said as she licked water off his chin, "I'm not a wild woman." Her tongue dipped to his nipple. "This thing that you do to me…"

He would have asked what thing if he could get air out of his lungs. Just because he wanted to hear her talk about it. She was traveling lower and Jon knew that it would all be over before it began if he let her dip any farther.

Grabbing the bar of soap, he rubbed her back first, and then her arms, pulling her upright and moving on to her hands, her quads and knees and calves and toes. By that time she'd finished soaping up his back and backside and was sliding around to the front.

Choking, he grabbed her hand and made a beeline to the bed, tumbling their wet bodies down. He donned the condom in record time and sank himself into her waiting warmth.

"Can you stay?" Jon asked now, holding Lillie's body

against him as the aftermath of the most exquisite moment he'd ever known slowly faded and he settled back onto wet sheets.

"I don't have much choice, do I? Since you're my ride home and Abe's fast asleep."

He didn't even glance at the computer he'd still had the mind to set up on its pad on his nightstand, so that he could hear his son and see his room, as well.

"I could get him up. He'd never know the difference."

"I'll stay."

That was all Jon had needed to hear. "Stay right here a second," he said, sliding out from beneath her and covering her with his robe as he strode buck naked out of the room. His bathroom had come with a separate shower and tub.

The tub, while apparently standard in this part of the country, was unlike anything he'd ever had at his disposal before. Double-wide and deep, he'd never used it, preferring the more standard, shallower tub in the bathroom across the hall from Abe's room to bathe his son.

Filling the thing now, he added a dab of shampoo to the water gushing from the faucet, tested the temperature once more and went back to the gorgeous woman who was lounging back on his pillows watching him approach.

"How about we get this dried soap off our skin?" he asked. "Then we can raid the kitchen for some lemonade or tea and see what we can do to a second set of sheets."

"You have a second set of sheets?"

"Five of them," he told her, standing there, letting her look him over. Letting her see the obvious effect her unabashed perusal was having on him. "Abe was sick a couple of months ago. Kept throwing up. I couldn't care for him and worry about laundry, too, so I took some money out of my savings and bought new sheets."

She was staring at his penis. And swallowed. He watched her.

And when she lifted her arms, he bent and picked her up and carried her into the tub with him where he didn't think about sheets at all.

CHAPTER TWENTY-ONE

LILLIE WENT TO the day care on Saturday specifically to see Abraham. She didn't pretend, even to herself, that she had a legitimate reason for being there. After Jon had dropped her off early that morning, on his way to take Abraham to Little Spirits and then to work at the cactus jelly plant, she'd showered, put on a clean pair of scrubs in case she was called into work, stopped for a bagel at the diner and ended up in the Little Spirits parking lot.

Her phone rang as she was heading in the back door. Seeing the name of her caller, she answered immediately.

"Papa? Is everything okay?"

"I just saw my son."

Dropping her purse off in the locker she'd been assigned, Lillie closed the small staff room door, poured herself a cup of coffee and sat down on the small, faux-leather couch.

"He said you two are talking."

"We've had two conversations," Lillie told him. "You have nothing to worry about, Papa. I'm a big girl. And I won't make the same mistake twice."

"My son seems to think that there's something still there between you two."

Kirk was Braydon's father. There would always be something there. But not in the way Papa meant.

"I've made it clear to him that there isn't."

"Apparently not clear enough."

Looking at the colorful collage of photos on the wall in front of her, Lillie said, "You want me to call him?"

"No!" Jerry's voice was unusually sharp. "Exactly the opposite. I know my son, Lil. When he wants something he gets it. At any cost. And right now he's convinced himself that he's going to win you back. I won't have him hurting you again."

"No worries, Papa." And before she could talk herself out of it, she added, "I'm not available."

"What?" His voice took on a confused tone. "You've met someone?"

"Lillie has a boyfriend?" Gayle's squeal in the background sounded clearly over the line.

They were going to make far too much of this, which was why she hadn't intended to mention her friendship with Jon. But if it put their minds at ease...

It wasn't as though they'd ever have occasion to meet Jon. He wasn't free on Sunday mornings when they met for breakfast. And Papa and Gayle rarely visited Shelter Valley. Never without first letting her know.

"His name's Jon, Papa." Kirk's father would tell Kirk. And put an immediate end to any plans Kirk had, too. This was all good. "He's twenty-seven."

"Who is he?" Gayle's voice again. "Where's he from? What does he do?"

"When can we meet him?" Jerry asked.

This was all good, Lillie reminded herself as she took a deep breath and said, "His son was a client of mine."

"He's divorced?" Jerry's tone sharpened again.

"No. Never married. Abraham's mother had him and left him at the hospital."

"This is the guy you told us about at breakfast—that single dad you were helping out in exchange for renovation work."

"Yes," Lillie admitted.

"So…does he know…about Braydon?" Papa's question was uttered softly.

"No, Papa."

"Don't you think you should tell him?"

She and Jon were just friends. With benefits. Jon wasn't ready for more. And neither was Lillie. "I'll tell him," she said because she knew that Papa and Gayle would make way too much of things if she didn't agree. "When the time's right."

"Tell her to bring him and Abraham to breakfast in the morning," Gayle's could be heard saying.

"Jon's really busy," Lillie said before Papa could ask, wondering if she'd made the best choice in telling them about him.

And then she thought of Kirk. And knew that his knowing about Jon was the best thing. Especially now that she knew he'd told Papa that he was going to win Lillie back—in spite of his promises to her that he accepted that they were through. Kirk was too smart to let his prey know that he was preying on them. He was a master at finding entry where there were no doors or windows. Why Kirk was doing this, she didn't know. Because he was bored? Because she was the one thing he couldn't have? Because he really had experienced some kind of life change and wanted to right his wrongs?

Whatever Kirk's reason was for wanting to get back together with her, she wasn't going to be his victim.

Not ever again.

LILLIE SPENT THE night at Jon's again. Waking at dawn on Sunday morning with her lying naked beside him, her head resting on his shoulder, Jon knew that he was going to ask her to marry him.

Clearly this was more than just sex. She was the one. And now that he'd finally found her—after a lifetime of searching—he saw no point in wasting any more time.

Until he thought about the truths he'd have to tell her—things she deserved to know before she bound herself to him for the rest of her life.

Maybe he'd wait a bit. Enjoy the moment. At least until the sheriff caught whoever was behind the Shelter Valley break-ins.

Until he was a little more certain that Lillie loved him for more than just his body. And his son.

Still, as he lay there, unable to fall back to sleep, he imagined what it would be like, lying in bed with her as his wife.

And he smiled.

THE FIRST THING Lillie saw when she opened her eyes was the pair of pudgy hands on the edge of the mattress.

"Illie! Ake!" Abraham's smiling face peering over the top of the bed was only inches from hers and she leaned forward to give him a kiss.

"Illie! Ake!"

"Abraham!" Jon's voice didn't sound nearly as pleased as his son's as he strode into the room dressed in a pair of black sweatpants and nothing else. "I'm so sorry," he said, his tone dropping to a dangerously sexy tone as he turned his attention on her. "I told him not to bother you. He's got the doorknob thing down pat, unfortunately, and I can't lock the bedroom from the outside."

"No worries," she said, wishing she wasn't naked under the covers and could lift the toddler into the bed with her.

Note to self: next time bring a nightie to store over here.

As Jon came close to pick up his son, she got a whiff of him, and wanted to make love again.

They'd already done it more than half a dozen times in two days. She was beginning to think something was wrong with her. A hormone imbalance, or something.

And then she saw the clock on Jon's nightstand. "Is it really seven?"

She never slept past five.

"Yeah, I was just waiting for you to wake up to make breakfast."

Her eyes wide, she sat up, pulling the sheet with her. "I can't stay, Jon! I have to go."

And she couldn't get up with Abraham right there. It just didn't feel right. She wasn't the boy's mother.

Couldn't be a mother. Couldn't be waking up to pudgy hands and wet kisses.

"I have to be... I have something I have to do and I'm going to be late," she said. If she told him about breakfast with Papa and Gayle he'd want to know who there were. How she knew them.

And if she told him they were Kirk's parents, he'd want to know why she was still in touch with them.

"Illie! Ake!"

"Yes, Abie, Lillie's awake!" she praised as thoughts flew through her mind.

"You're working on a Sunday morning?" Jon asked, still standing there, the delicious glint in his eyes distracting her.

How could a man look so sexy while he was holding a toddler with his fist in his mouth?

"No...it's...no, I'm not working." Her business was her business. She and Jon were just friends—their no-commitment agreement had been very clear—but she couldn't lie to him.

"Oh. Okay, maybe next time." Something changed in the air. With him. "We'll be in the other room," he said.

Turning his back, he picked up his robe off a chair and laid it on the foot of the bed before leaving the room with Abe.

Lillie didn't use the robe. She stepped into the scrubs she'd had on when Jon picked up Abraham the previous afternoon and asked her to join them for take-out burgers and a Disney movie at his place.

Thinking about the day before, the different activities she'd done with Abe to see if she could detect anything of concern regarding his hearing, she joined the Swartz men in the living room.

"You okay?" she asked Jon, who'd been standing by the front window when she walked in. Abraham was playing with his zipper pillow, sitting in the middle of a sea of little cars.

"Fine." He turned, smiled that hungry smile that captivated her every time and moved over to plant a very thorough kiss on her lips.

Tempted to call Papa and postpone breakfast, Lillie thought of Abraham on the floor beside them, and pulled away, saying, "I have to go, but…what are you doing tonight?"

The toddler was holding two cars, one in each hand.

"Making macaroni and cheese. From scratch. As of this week, Abraham won't eat the boxed kind anymore. You want to join us?"

Nodding, Lillie said, "How many cars, Abraham?" He knew his numbers. Bonnie had moved him up to the three-year-olds' class as soon as she'd tested his cognitive development. And maybe because there was a bit less chaos with the older age group.

"Vroom, vroom," Abraham said, ignoring her question. Not unusual for a toddler engaged in play. She leaned down, put her face in front of his to ensure she had his attention and asked him again, "How many cars do you have in your hands, Abe?"

The little boy looked at his hands, as if seeing them for the first time. And then, dropping a car, he worked hard to get two pudgy little fingers to stand out from the rest and held the result up to her.

"That's right, son!" Jon grinned. "He knows two, all right. It wasn't just a fluke!" They'd shown Jon the boy's progress the day before.

Lillie was having a hard time keeping her thoughts to herself. Was she being paranoid? Or did she have to have a serious talk with Jon?

She knew the answer.

She couldn't risk the chance that she was right.

"I'd love to have dinner with you," she said. "And, if you don't mind, once Abraham goes down for the night, I need to talk to you about something."

Jon's grin faded. "Did I do something wrong?"

"Of course not!" Seeing the sudden distance in his eyes, Lillie leaned into him and gave him another kiss, one that included a lot of tongue. "You, sir, are perfect."

It was his son she was worried about.

But now wasn't the time to tell him about it.

WITH ABRAHAM'S HELP, Jon did laundry, cleaned the bathrooms, vacuumed, made an afternoon run to the store and refused to let himself dwell on where Lillie might be and with whom. He had the mac and cheese warming in the oven by the time Lillie rang their bell just after six.

"I blocked you in again," she told him. Guest parking spots were nonexistent on their little driveway and the night before he'd had her pull in behind him. The two guys next door could back out from their assigned spots on either side of Jon's truck, but just barely. At some point, they'd have to move their little party to her house. Maybe put a portable crib in her spare room…

Slow down, bucko.

It wasn't just with women that Jon barreled ahead. He'd learned young that if he was going to have anything in life he had to snatch it the second the opportunity presented itself.

Foster care, juvenile detention, they were all the same in terms of too many bodies and not enough of anything to go around.

But he had a normal life now. He could afford to take his time.

He wanted to kiss Lillie hello. It had been hours since he'd tasted her lips. But he didn't. She didn't kiss him, either. And he wondered if there was significance in that.

She kissed Abraham, though. And gave all of her attention to the toddler as they sat at the table and shared a real, homemade family dinner. Jon might have been jealous of all the attention his son was receiving if he hadn't been so damned grateful for it.

And turned on, too. Those hands again, lithe and long fingered and soft as they helped his son's short fingers wrap around his fork or hold his sippy cup. As they cut the hot dog Jon had heated to go with Abe's mac and cheese. And handed tomatoes and cucumbers to the little boy.

She'd remembered which fresh vegetables Abe would eat and which he wouldn't.

Later, Jon did the dishes while Lillie gave Abraham his bath, at Jon's suggestion. He wanted her to have time with Abe, to know exactly what it took to care for him at home—not just at the day care where she could do her job and walk away.

If Abraham was going to be too much for her, they needed to know now.

Besides, he'd needed a break. She'd been pointedly not engaging with him all night.

She'd said they needed to talk. All guys knew those words were the kiss of death.

He'd been rushing things. Taking her to bed two nights in a row. Not that she'd done any complaining.

"Did you have a good day?" he asked, following her into the living room and dropping down on one end of the couch as soon as Abe was asleep in his crib. If she thought he was going to give her hassles about who she'd been with that day, then she was wrong. They hadn't agreed to any kind of commitment. She owed him nothing. But he couldn't keep sleeping with her if she was seeing someone else.

"It was a busy day," she said. "I spent a lot of it at the office, catching up on charting and doing some research."

The office? "I thought... I assumed... You'd said you had a non-work-related thing."

"Breakfast," Lillie said. "After that, I worked all day."

There was no reason for the heady relief that surged through him. To the contrary, he needed to be concerned that her lack of a day-long date with someone else affected him so severely.

"You said you wanted to talk." Get straight to the point. Good or bad, that was his way.

Sitting close, but not touching, Lillie clasped her hands in her lap and studied him.

It was going to be bad. He'd been through this enough times to know. First, the state telling him his mother wasn't coming for him. Or letting him be adopted, either. Barbara, bailing on him when he was twelve. His court-appointed advocate telling him that he was going to juvenile detention for the rest of his high school years. And then Kate...

Mustering his best rendition of an encouraging smile,

he waited for the boot, betting that Lillie would give him the best one yet. She was too sweet to do otherwise.

"I'm concerned about Abraham."

Not sure what that meant, Jon nodded and waited for her to say more. If she was about to tell him that she'd been working for Clara, after all, he'd deal with it.

If she didn't want to take on the full-time responsibility of helping raise a two-year-old, he could understand. He'd deal with that, too.

She took his hand. Yep, this was going to be the best one yet.

"Jon, I think Abraham has a hearing problem."

Jon heard her words, but it took his mind a few seconds to process them. At first he thought he was the one with a hearing problem.

"I think he's losing his hearing."

"That's ridiculous," he said, remembering with acute clarity that she'd asked him the week before about Abe's hearing test. They'd been at the museum. Watching Abe interact happily with the other kids. "He was tested over the summer."

"I know." Nodding, Lillie squeezed his hand. He was glad she held on. And wanted to be free, too. "That's why I've been second-guessing myself. But I've been watching him all week, and today I spent a lot of time looking at case studies of two-year-olds with hearing loss and they describe Abe's behavior to a T."

"Behavior? What behavior?" Whatever their problem might be, he'd deal with it. He didn't think, for one second that it had anything to do with his son's ability to hear.

"The tantrums, for one."

"They're virtually gone," he quickly pointed out. "A couple of mini tantrums is all we had this week and they were over almost as soon as they started."

"Because we're tending to the symptoms and, by doing so, putting a bandage on the problem."

"What symptoms?" He was with her all the way. Just had to hear her facts so he could help her see where she erred on this one.

"I think I was wrong about Abe's aversion to crowds."

See, she got things wrong. Crowds. Hearing. It happened. No big deal.

"Or rather, I wasn't wrong. He does have problems in crowds, but not for the reason I thought."

Uh-huh.

"Crowds were a problem because they create confusion, because he can't hear what's going on, and he gets scared. It's the fear that causes the tantrum."

It was a good theory, but it didn't apply. "He hears fine, Lil. He didn't pick up a gazillion new words in just a few weeks by reading lips." He kept his tone gentle. He wasn't upset with her. He knew she just wanted to help.

"I agree, he hears. For now. But I think something's going on in his ear canal. He's losing his hearing."

The worry in her eyes wrenched his heart. He wanted to hug her. "He just had his hearing checked," he reminded her. "They looked in his ear canals."

"And that's why I think something's going on. He shouldn't be exhibiting so many signs of hearing loss this quickly unless something changed in the few months between summer and now."

"What signs is he exhibiting?" Tantrums? He'd asked his doctor about them. A medical professional. The pediatrician hadn't mentioned anything about hearing loss attributing to tantrums.

"Visual cues," she said. "Things a developmental specialist would look for."

Giving her the benefit of the doubt because he trusted her overall, he asked, "What visual cues?"

"Last week at the museum, he held up his hand to tell another child to stop, rather than saying the word."

"One hand gesture is a sign of hearing loss?"

"He did it four times. With different kids."

"He doesn't know the word *stop* yet."

"He knows numbers. He can count to three."

"I know," Jon grinned. "Pretty amazing, isn't it?" Bonnie had given him the good news on Thursday afternoon—Abe had only been with the three-year-olds since Monday and already he'd been picking up new things.

"This morning, when I asked how many cars he had, he held up his fingers."

"He just learned how to do that this week. It's a new trick. He's proud of himself. Kids repeat new tricks." She should know that. She knew all about the developmental stages of kids.

She wasn't a medical doctor. She didn't have ear canal training.

"He's been using visual cues more increasingly for a while now."

He wasn't convinced. At all. He knew his son—he was with Abe every day. He'd have noticed if there'd been some change in him. Or if his son was going deaf.

"He answers when we speak to him."

"Yes, he does. I didn't say he was deaf, only that he's exhibiting signs of losing his hearing. But think about it, Jon…" Her gaze was so sincere, so filled with compassion, he knew he was in grave danger of falling in love with this woman.

Not just in love and if you leave me, fine. But in love and if you leave me it's going to be horrible.

The kind of in love he should be with his wife. The kind he'd always dreamed about.

"One of the practices we instigated to help minimize the tantrums was to get right up in Abe's face when we talk to him."

"To get him to focus," Jon agreed. "When he focuses, he uses his words and communicates his wants and needs instead of freaking out. We put him in control of his own destiny so he doesn't have to panic."

He'd listened well. And her idea had worked.

"That's right." She let go of his hand. Jon left it where it was on his thigh. "The teachers at Little Spirits have been told to do the same."

He knew that.

"I've been noticing that Abe focuses on our mouths every time we talk to him, not just when we're right in his face. My professional opinion is that he's learning to figure out what we're saying by using a combination of skills, his limited hearing and lipreading."

"He's always had that look of concentration about him when he looks at you," Jon said. Abe's six-week-old pictures included a shot of him with that same frown on his face, as if he was trying to solve a calculus problem or something. It had always been Jon's favorite of Abe's baby pictures.

"I think he throws tantrums because he can't hear, and when something sudden happens that he doesn't expect, it scares him. As soon as we get in front of him and he can see that we're talking to him, can hear us in the midst of all the white noise around him, he calms down."

She was digging deep. And he loved her for it. For caring about them that much.

Okay, he was admitting it. In a few short weeks, he'd

fallen in love. Professional caring didn't mean she loved him back. She'd said she was only after the sex.

Fine.

He'd deal with it.

CHAPTER TWENTY-TWO

"IT WAS JUST a weekend of great sex." Lillie pedaled hard, putting herself almost a full bike length in front of Caro as the sun was rising up over the horizon Monday morning.

She'd thought about denying having had sex at all, except that she'd left her car parked outside of Jon's duplex—which Caro owned—overnight. She'd known someone would see it and comment. Saturday night she hadn't cared.

"I know you better than that," Caro said, not the least bit winded as she caught up. Of the two of them, Caro was the better athlete. She was also two decades older and had given birth three times. Lillie should be able to outride her. "What really happened?"

"Why did something have to happen?"

"Because Friday morning you were as jittery as popcorn in hot oil and this morning you're trying to pretend that you don't feel anything at all."

She wasn't pretending. Mostly. Pedaling more steadily, she turned a corner and glanced at her friend as they fell in line next to each other for the long empty strip of road in front of them.

There were very few cars out on the roads at this time of the morning. And the nip in the early-morning air kept the wildlife quiet, too.

"I told him that I think his son has a hearing problem."

"In the middle of sex?"

"No! Of course not." Focusing on the vivid fuchsia color

of a bougainvillea plant in the landscaped front yard they were passing, Lillie thought of her conversation with Jon the night before.

Of the way he'd brushed off everything she had to tell him—shrugged aside all of the signs she'd laid so plainly in front of him. Abe's focus, he'd said, was just something he'd been born with.

Maybe that was what had made him so adept at lipreading at the age of two.

"I take it he took the news badly?"

"Not really."

"Then what's the problem?"

"He didn't believe me." Glancing at her friend, Lillie looked for Caro's reaction. Did her friend think she was overreacting, too? Was this really not about Abraham at all?

But about Braydon?

About loving a child. And fearing the worst?

After one weekend in bed with Jon, she was already making Abraham out to be sick. Because she was never going to be able to have another child—love another child—without the constant fear of losing him riding on her back.

Which was why she was never going to have another child. Or marry again, either. Her job was to care for other people's children so she could keep breathing when diagnoses came back bad.

She pedaled hard.

Caro kept up.

"I spent yesterday afternoon poring over case studies of two-year-olds with hearing loss and Abe has every single one of the symptoms." As they rode, turned a corner and headed up the opposite block, Lillie listed off the same signs she'd told Jon about the night before.

"Sounds to me like you're spot-on…" Caro said, drawing out the last word.

"But?"

"It sounds like he could be, too," she said. "When you put all those things together, they do paint the picture of a child with hearing loss. But, at the same time, each one of those behaviors, by itself, isn't all that unusual. They could all be explained by the things Jon said."

"You think I'm wrong, too?"

Coming to a stop sign, Caroline put her foot down to the ground and sat on her bike, waiting for Lillie to do the same. "What's all this about right and wrong, Lil? I've never known you to second-guess yourself where your work is concerned."

"No one's right all the time."

"Of course they aren't. You're reminded of that every single day when you go into a room with a sick child."

They'd had that talk before—about the potential for people who spent their days with sick children to get burned out.

"So why are you beating yourself up over this one? Seems pretty simple to me. Jon gets Abe's ears tested and you deal with the results."

"I told you he didn't believe me."

"He's not going to have Abe's ears tested," Caroline surmised.

"He just did this summer. He sees no point in putting Abe through the procedure again."

"And you're afraid that in the meantime the little guy's going to lose hearing that he might not be able to regain."

"Right."

And she was worried that she was losing her professional grip completely. That she was seeing potential illness where there was none.

Lillie pushed off and Caroline followed her up the street.

Maybe Lillie was seeing a father who couldn't deal with the fact that his son might not be perfect.

The thought hit her like a tree limb falling from the sky. Was Jon in denial? Like Kirk had been? Jon didn't have Kirk's ego, by any stretch, but he did seem overly obsessed with how perfectly he was raising his son—going on the defensive anytime he perceived she was criticizing his parenting skills. Or Abe.

"I can see where it's hard, Lil." Caro was beside her again, speaking loud enough that she could hear her as they rode. "Especially considering the fact that you're involved with Abe's father and are growing to care for the boy on a more personal level."

The words struck instant fear inside her. Caro was validating her own conclusion—she was in too deep.

"...can do is keep a close watch on Abe and if you continue to see signs, if you continue to be convinced there's hearing loss, have another talk with his father. I've only met them a couple of times, but it's pretty clear how much that man loves his son. He'll do the right thing."

Kirk had loved his unborn son, too. Braydon's conception had had a profound effect on her ex-husband, one that had gone deeper than anything she'd ever seen with Kirk. He'd been in awe, and humbled. The first time he'd heard Braydon's heartbeat it had been as if Kirk had been reborn. He'd apologized for Leah. And others. Swore to Lillie that she and the baby would be it for the rest of his life. The baby had brought out the very best in the man she'd married but begun to doubt in so many ways.

And then they'd found out how imperfect their unborn son actually was.

At first, like Jon, Kirk had been in denial. And later... she'd never seen a man change so quickly.

Or so cruelly.

She absolutely could not go through that again.

But it didn't stop there. As Lillie showered half an hour later, donned scrubs and drove herself to the clinic, by-passing the day care completely, she knew that even if Jon came around and did the right thing where Abe's hearing was concerned, even if Jon was absolutely nothing like Kirk, she still had to cut short her involvement with the Swartz men.

Because if it wasn't Abe's hearing, it would be some-thing else. She'd be watching for potential problems every step of every day. He'd get a cold, she'd see lung disease. Have a dizzy spell, she'd see heart failure. Fail a test, she'd see a brain tumor.

She'd drive herself and Jon crazy imagining symptoms, and suffocate the boy in the process, running him off to the doctor far too often.

She was not and never would be a mother.

JON DIDN'T HEAR from Lillie on Monday or Tuesday. On Wednesday, after hearing in lab about another break-in, he called her.

This one had been slightly different. The sliding glass door had been broken. Either the thief was getting care-less, or desperate, or both.

Lillie didn't answer his call. He tried again when he parked his truck in the employee parking lot at the cactus jelly plant before going in to work. Again, no answer. He called the day care, to check on Abe, of course, but intend-ing to ask if anyone had seen or heard from Lillie. He was probably overreacting. Lillie was busy.

Or possibly not wanting to take his calls. Chances were she was just fine.

It never hurt to check.

"Abe's doing fine now, Jon," Bonnie Nielson said as soon as he identified himself.

"Now?"

"He'd been crying, not a tantrum, just crying, which is unusual for him."

Abe didn't cry much—unless he was sick. Wrapping his finger around the keys that were still in the ignition, he started the truck. "Does he feel hot?"

"No, he's fine. He's inside playing ring-around-the-rosy and laughing so hard he's making his teachers laugh."

He turned the ignition back off.

"He was asking for Lillie," Bonnie told him. "She was scheduled to meet with a parent this morning, and as soon as she got here, she went in to see Abe. He ran straight to her and the tears stopped."

That answered one question—Lillie was fine.

"Is she still there?"

"No, she's got a full schedule at the clinic today. She was only with him for a few minutes. Long enough to give him a hug and talk to him a bit. The woman's magic with kids," Bonnie extolled while Jon's thoughts ran way ahead of her. "I'm not sure what she said, but that's all it took."

No, that wasn't all. Where Lillie was concerned, his son had it as badly as he did.

In a short period of time, Lillie had become a part of their small family.

And because Jon had unwittingly exposed Abraham to an overdose of the woman, his son was feeling her absence. Suffering for it.

It was up to Jon to do something about that.

The bottom line was, they needed Lillie.

He just prayed that she needed them, too.

And that, when she found out about Jon's past, if she didn't already know, she'd still want them.

ON WEDNESDAY AFTERNOON, pulling into the parking lot of the funeral home where she was going to be supporting a six-year-old who'd just lost her older brother to a car accident, Lillie heard her phone ring.

She couldn't keep avoiding Jon's calls. She didn't even want to. She just wasn't sure what to do—how to be friends with him and keep her distance, too.

At the third ring, she pulled her phone out of her purse. One thing was clear—they were going to have to work something out where Abe was concerned. The boy needed her. With all the time she'd spent with him, she couldn't just drop him cold turkey because she'd had incredible sex with his dad.

The caller wasn't Jon.

"Hello, Kirk," she answered. Might as well get the weekly call over with now when she had an excuse to let him go quickly.

"It's good to hear your voice, Lil."

"What do you want?" She'd never have believed she could be so mean. Or cold. She didn't like it.

"Are you working?"

"I've been working all day and I'm about to be again."

"Shelter Valley's lucky to have you."

And he wasn't, didn't, and it was going to stay that way.

"I was thinking I'd drive up tonight, maybe we could get some dinner. Go to the pub again. I've got something I'd like to show you."

"What?" She couldn't imagine anything he'd have that she'd want to see.

"I had something made for Braydon's grave." His voice dropped. "It's meant to sit in front of the stone you and Dad chose. It was just something I had to do, Lil." Kirk's voice broke. He tried to speak, and only made sounds.

Unsure of what to do or say, she struggled for words.

He had never cried in front of her. Ever. Not even when the doctor had told them about Braydon's condition.

She heard ragged breathing and then, "I'm...sorry." His voice was weak, but legible. "I don't know what's coming over me. I just... I swear, Lil, I don't want anything from you. I don't mean to put my crap on your shoulders. I just didn't want to put anything on his grave without you seeing it first and approving it. If you don't want it there, I'll take it back."

Tomorrow was the anniversary of the day she'd told Kirk she was pregnant. Could it be that he remembered? And that he had to visit his son's grave on that day? If so, she couldn't deny him. If he was honestly trying to deal with Braydon's loss, which would enable him to be a better father to his living son, she had to help.

"Okay, Kirk. I'll meet you at the store on the Shelter Valley exit at six. No to dinner or the pub or anything else."

"Six? That's good. Okay, I'll be there."

He was remembering Braydon. She was touched. And didn't want to be.

"And, Lil? Thanks."

THE WILLOW FAMILY wasn't there yet. Waiting in her car for them to arrive so she could walk into the funeral home with six-year-old Chloe Willow, Lillie listened to her voice mail.

Jon had left two messages. And deserved a callback.

He didn't pick up. Relieved, she waited for his voice mail to be activated.

"Jon? It's Lillie. Yes, I'm free tonight. I can swing by around seven, if that works for you."

Abe would sleep better having seen her. He'd be more

relaxed at the day care, too, if she didn't go so many days between visits with him.

She and Jon had to talk about a schedule that would meet Abe's needs and their own, too. Maybe she just had to come up with more jobs for him to do at her house. Keep it about work.

With the appointment with Jon scheduled, her meeting with Kirk would have to be brief.

And if Jon wanted more from her? Wanted to discuss their sex life? Or know where they went from here?

She didn't have any answers.

UNWILLING TO SIT home and let that evening's appointment with Lillie gain momentum in his mind, Jon splurged and took Abe for hamburgers and French fries for dinner Wednesday night.

He stopped in at the big-box store out by the freeway because it was in the same parking lot as the fast-food restaurant. He wasn't going to get all sappy and try to woo Lillie with romance, but neither could he just let their conversation that evening pass without some kind of preparation.

It would be a conversation they'd remember for the rest of their lives.

If he did it right—and was reading her right.

"What should we get her, Abie baby?" After a long day at Little Spirits and with his belly full, Abraham was ready for a bath and bed, not using his words. Two of his fingers hung out of his mouth as he pointed to the bags of candy that were left over from Halloween.

"Candy's bad for your teeth," he reminded his son, purposely not putting his face in Abe's as he spoke. The boy seemed satisfied with his answer, anyway.

Brownies were bad for your teeth, too, but Lillie had

mentioned once that they were her vice. She loved them. Plain fudge. Without nuts.

He picked up what he needed to make a batch.

And bought a bottle of sparkling wine, along with two cheap champagne flutes, satisfying himself with the fact that they were at least glass and not plastic.

He didn't think beyond plastic and glass and the fact that he had a nine-by-twelve-inch pan at home for baking. He couldn't dwell on the might-be's. On the possible outcomes of the night ahead. Or run speeches through his mind. He knew what he had to say. The words would come.

What came out of them, he couldn't know.

Whatever happened, he'd deal with it.

KIRK'S SILVER BMW convertible was under a streetlight in the big-box store parking lot outside town when she pulled in on Wednesday precisely at six. The temperature had dropped down to sixty as the sun went down, and he had the top down.

It was so Kirk.

She drove up beside him, rolling down her window.

"Get in." He nodded toward the passenger seat.

The car was newer than the one he'd had when they were married. And almost identical to it. She shook her head.

"Just show me what you want to show me, Kirk." Their deal had been phone calls only—one a week—and already here she was, meeting him.

Either the man was diabolical or truly reaching out....

"It's in the backseat," he said. "I'm not going to be able to hold it up for you."

She studied him for a second, searching for any sign of duplicity. She hadn't been able to detect it when they'd been married, and had no idea why she thought she'd be able to now.

They were talking about something for a grave, she reminded herself. And got out of her car.

She wasn't getting in his, though. Instead, she leaned over the edge of the back passenger's side, peeking at the seat.

And stared.

There really was something there.

The stone was marble. And in the center of it was a photograph of her, holding a perfect-looking Braydon dressed in a baby-blue outfit decorated with bears and hearts. It had been taken just hours before he died. She was wearing jeans and a yellow spandex pullover, sitting in a padded rocker, and could remember the moment as if it was happening right then.

She'd never gone home after having him, but had spent every single night of Braydon's short life in the neonatal intensive care unit, and every day, too, holding her baby. Feeding him. Praying for a miracle that didn't come.

If, after all the tests they'd done, they'd had hope of any kind of treatment for him, she wouldn't have been able to feed him. Or hold him. He'd have been kept sterile and inside a bubble.

"There were no tubes in this picture." Kirk's voice came softly, beside her. She hadn't realized he'd joined her outside the car. Tears were streaming down his cheeks.

"Where did you get this?"

"From my dad. He sent it to me years ago. Like a fool I tucked it away and refused to look at it."

"It was taken that last day." She'd told herself he wouldn't get to her. That she wouldn't feel. And her throat closed with the effort it was taking to hold back tears. "They'd removed all life support."

And then she saw the inscription on the stone.

Braydon Thomas Henderson
In the arms of angels

CHAPTER TWENTY-THREE

LILLIE WAS RIGHT on time. Jon heard her knock and answered the door, trying to read her expression.

She wasn't looking at him.

"Illie! Illie!" Abraham's screams were a gleeful shrill as he jumped up from his cars and hurled himself in her direction.

Picking the toddler up, she hugged him tightly, as though she hadn't seen him in weeks. Or years. And she spent the next hour, until Abe's bedtime, playing with him, singing with him, reading to him—and touching him. Jon had never seen her be so…clingy. A hand on Abe's arm, running her fingers over the soft hair on his scalp, sitting on the floor with him on her lap.

And he took hope.

Lillie talked to Jon, too. Peripherally. If he spoke, or to ask his permission to give Abe a bath.

And she looked at him a time or two, long looks. Personal looks.

It was those looks that had him cutting brownies and putting them on a plate while she used the bathroom after they'd put Abraham down for the night.

Those looks and the seconds when they'd stood together in his son's room, taking turns kissing the toddler goodnight, and Abraham had looked up at them with his blanket in his hand and his thumb in his mouth and said, "Uv you."

The first time ever.

His boy knew how to pick his moments.

"I guess I should be going." Lillie surprised him in the kitchen while he stood at the counter getting all emotional over a toddler's verbalization of words he'd heard over and over again since his birth.

Turning toward her, plate in hand, Jon said, "I made brownies."

Like some kind of little kid, trying to please. The whole time he'd been stirring the brownie batter he'd been fantasizing about smearing it all over her breasts, her nipples and lower. And then licking it off...

"Brownies?"

She was staring at them. Not at him.

"Yeah."

"Homemade?"

That was when he knew for certain that no matter what was going on with her, she would stay. "Yeah."

Setting her purse on the faux-wood table, she sat down, seeming to study the grain in the laminate.

Jon put the brownies in front of her, along with a couple of napkins. And then, because he was a barreler, he opened the sparkling wine and poured some into the newly purchased flutes.

"DID YOU SEE me?" Lillie wanted a brownie. She had to get rid of some of the knots in her stomach to make room.

"See you?" Standing at the counter, his back to her while he poured what she assumed was sparkling water, Jon sounded sincere.

She'd spent the past hour worrying over nothing.

No. That wasn't accurate, either. There was much to worry about. But apparently, having to explain who Kirk was to the man she'd seen come out of the store while she'd been saying goodbye to her ex-husband hadn't been one of them.

"At the store. I was...across the parking lot when you and Abe came out tonight."

"I didn't see you, sorry," he said easily, joining her at the table and setting a flute of sparkling liquid in front of her. "I guess I was too busy getting a limp two-year-old into his car seat and trying not to dump my groceries on the ground." He didn't touch his glass. Or the brownies. "Did you call out?"

"I was too far away." It was technically true, but she wouldn't have called out, anyway.

But...good, her secret was safe. Picking up a brownie, Lillie smiled at her host, thinking about how badly she wanted a sexless night in his bed, with him holding her until she fell asleep.

SHE WAS EATING the brownies. Jon relaxed. It would be okay. Lillie clearly loved Abraham and wanted to be there with them.

Holding up his glass, he said, "I'd like to make a toast."

She lifted her glass, too, looking curious.

"To the future," he said, cutting himself off before adding, "Mrs. Swartz."

"To the future," Lillie said, clinking her glass to his before taking a long sip.

She barely swallowed before starting to choke. "I... thought...that was...water," she gasped in between bouts of coughing. Jon got her a glass of water and she sipped from it. He rubbed her back. The coughing subsided.

"Sorry about that," he said, sitting down again, feeling like a fool. "I thought you'd know from the flutes and the toast that it wasn't water."

"We've never... You don't keep alcohol in the house."

"I just bought it tonight." He was blowing this. Making a memory that would last forever, but not in the way he'd thought. It probably would have been a better idea to give the idea a little more time to percolate.

But then he'd have talked himself out of it. He'd just wanted it to be natural. Nice. A memory she'd cherish in the years to come. Something he'd cherish, too, in the secret recesses of his mind where a guy allowed such things.

"Champagne," Lillie said, sipping again, more slowly this time. "What's the occasion?"

He stared at her.

"What?" She smiled. "Did you get a promotion at work already? I'm not surprised. Come on, tell me. You have no reason to be modest."

"You love my son."

Her smile faded and she took another sip of her champagne. "I care for him a great deal, yes."

"And you and I… It's pretty obvious that we're…compatible."

"I… It's been a long time since I had male companionship," she said, obviously choosing her words with care. Jon read between the lines. She was hot for him. "I'd be lying if I said that I wasn't enjoying your company. Very much."

It felt right.

"I want to marry you."

"What?"

He'd done it wrong. "What I meant to say was, will you marry me?"

She stared at him wide-eyed. Clearly shocked. And something else, too. He couldn't make it out for sure. Was she scared? "We haven't even said we love each other."

She didn't say, "We don't love each other." The difference was subtle, but Jon clung to it.

"Words don't have to be spoken for feelings to exist," he said. "But just for the record, I know we said what we had was just physical, and I tried to keep it that way, but I do love you, Lillie. I'm not good at it, yet, but I know I can be. I give you my word that I will be."

"But…I don't love you." A sharp intake of breath followed her words.

Okay. Sipping his champagne, he said, "I'm all right with that. You love my son."

"But, Jon…"

"Can you honestly say that you don't care about me?"

"Of course I care about you. I'd never have slept with you otherwise."

Exactly.

"But we said 'no commitments.' No strings attached."

"Neither of us are 'no strings attached' type of people, Lil. We tried. And instead of having a nice romp, we slept together and just kept doing it. The more time we spend together, the more time we seem to want to spend together. Unless I'm getting that wrong."

"No, you aren't. I love being with you and Abe, it's just that…"

She'd used the "L" word. Maybe things would be okay, after all.

"What?" Whatever it was, he could handle it. She had no idea how much he could handle.

But she would find out soon. As soon as she agreed to marry him. Then, when he was certain she cared enough to commit to the long haul, he'd tell her about his past.

"I can't marry you, Jon."

"Why not?"

"I can't marry anyone."

Of course she could. She'd already done it once. She could do it again.

And then something absolutely horrific occurred to him. "You aren't already married, are you?"

She'd said she was divorced. She wouldn't lie about something like that, would she?

She wouldn't let him sleep with another man's wife without letting him make that decision for himself.

"Of course not."

"Then why can't you get married?" The almost-fragile look about her had him wanting to hold her, to soothe away whatever was troubling her. He could be patient. For as long as it took.

Patience was one thing his time being incarcerated had taught him. "Because I'm not ever going to do that again. Not ever."

Apparently it was time for him to know what had happened in her first marriage. He couldn't fix what he didn't understand.

"Because of something your first husband did?"

"Yes." She shook her head. Took another sip of champagne. "But no, not really. He hurt me, of course, but a lot of women get hurt and go through a divorce and still get married again."

Precisely. They just had to work through it all. "What happened? Between you and your ex."

"I don't want to talk about it."

"I know. But I'm asking you to, anyway." Leaning forward, he took her hand in his. "It seems to me that we're at an impasse here, Lil, until we get through this. We can't go back to how it was before we had sex, that's obvious. And we can't really go forward, either, with this…this desire…sitting there between us."

"We could just have sex until the desire goes away."

It happened. A lot. "You really think that will happen here?" he asked. "Because I don't."

She didn't answer.

"You want to take that chance?"

She looked at him then, the first time she'd allowed him to see deeply into her eyes since she'd arrived that evening. And while he saw something there that scared him, he also took heart.

Lillie cared. More than just a little bit. He could see how hard this was for her.

"Was he unfaithful to you?"

It was the obvious conclusion to draw. There wasn't much else a husband could do to his wife to hurt her so deeply, to destroy her trust so completely.

She sipped. Getting up, Jon refilled both of their glasses. She didn't have to drive home that night. He'd gladly have her stay with them.

"Kirk had an affair, yes," Lillie said when he sat back down. Her fingers wrapped around the stem of her glass, she glanced between the cheap flute and Jon and back again. "Actually, more than one."

"He's a fool, Lil. There's not a woman out there with more to offer than you."

Her smile was laced with scorn. "You don't need to flatter me, Jon. I came to terms with Kirk's lack of decency years ago."

"Maybe not, if coming to terms with it means you're robbing yourself, and me and Abe, of the chance to lead a happy, fulfilling life."

"It's not Kirk's infidelity that's the problem."

He'd never liked the name Kirk. He'd known a Kirk once. A simpy guy in lockup. He'd been there for attempted rape. And had cried every single one of the nights that he'd had the cell next to Jon. He'd been released on appeal. And a couple of years later, Jon had read that he'd raped another woman and was now serving life without parole.

"The problem is me, Jon. I just don't have any more to give on anything other than a surface level."

He knew bunk when he heard it.

"Tell that to Abraham." This was their lives they were talking about. He wasn't above pulling out whatever stops it took to make this work for all of them.

The way her mouth started to tremble alarmed him. When, without warning, Lillie bent over at the waist and started to sob as though her heart were shattering into a million pieces, Jon started to get really scared.

He'd done something horrible and he didn't even know what it was. He knew only that, somehow, he was going to have to make this right.

Now.

LEAVING THE CHAMPAGNE and brownies on the table—a memory he'd never forget—Jon lifted Lillie and carried her back to his room. Not because he had any intention of bedding her, but because it was the only room in the house with a lock on the door. He didn't want Abraham to pick tonight as the first time he climbed out of his crib only to find Lillie in such a state. She clung to his neck, digging her fingers into him while sobs continued to rack her body.

The only furniture in his room, other than the bed and nightstand, was a dresser. He gently laid Lillie against the pillows.

"Hold me." She didn't let go of his neck.

"I will, babe. Just give me a second to set up the monitor."

Letting him go immediately, Lillie fell back against the pillows, appearing to calm down a little. And then she started to cry again, more softly.

Those tears trickling slowly down her cheeks bothered

him more than the heaving sobs. They seemed to be coming from a deeper place than the initial gust.

These weren't tears you cried away and then forgot. These were the kind that might stop, but would never end.

Hooking his tablet up to the speaker system on his nightstand and opening the monitoring software, he checked to see that Abraham was sleeping soundly and racked his brain for the right thing to say.

He just didn't have it.

So he climbed onto the bed with her, pulled her against his chest and held on.

Jon lost track of time but he didn't grow tired. Lillie cried some. She slept some, too. And still he sat there, holding on. Because it was what he had to do.

Life wasn't pretty. It wasn't easy. And a man had two choices. To let bitterness grow so big it suffocated every good thing in him. Or to embrace possibility and try to make the right choices.

It had taken him a while to understand but he got it now.

"I can't."

At first he thought she was talking in her sleep. Until Lillie shuddered and pushed up and away from him.

He let her go.

"Can't what?"

She didn't go far. Just sat up next to him, hugging a pillow to her chest.

"I can't marry you, Jon. But more accurately, I can't be a mother to Abraham." She sounded so certain he started to believe her.

"Why?"

Hearing the pain in Jon's voice, Lillie knew she had to tell him. Climbing out from the hell of emotional exhaustion when all she wanted to do was crawl back into his arms and sleep until the world changed, she looked Jon straight in the eye.

"Because I already am a mother." She heard herself and understood what she was doing, but the words sounded completely foreign to her.

And then there was the shocked look in Jon's eyes. His utter disbelief as he stared at her was her doing. How she wished things were different. Wished she was free to love him as he deserved to be loved.

As she wanted to love him.

"You have a child?" Clearly it was the last thing he'd expected to hear.

Swallowing, she saw again the stone Kirk had brought for her approval. A stone for their son's grave.

She'd told him he could have it placed. He was doing so in the morning. Having a little ceremony, just himself and a minister from the church he'd been attending. He'd invited Lillie but she had an appointment at the clinic, an MRI procedure with a four-year-old. Her new life taking precedence over the old.

Jon was still waiting for her answer.

"Had."

He froze. And she could tell the instant that understanding dawned.

"Oh, God, Lil. Oh… I'm sorry. I had no… You didn't… No one said…"

Putting a shaky finger to his lips, she said, "Shhh. It's okay. It's not your fault, Jon." She was tired. Needed to sleep. And get up in the morning to the new life she'd built for herself. "There's no way you could have known," she said, her voice raw from all the crying. "No one here knows."

"No one? Not even Caroline?"

She shook her head and knew she was going to have to explain.

HE HADN'T FIGURED on this. Sitting in his bed with the woman he loved, Jon kept watching her, listening to her.

"I never should have married Kirk." Lillie hung her head, picking at a string on the hem of her jeans, exhibiting none of her usual confidence. Even her mannerisms were different. "I'd just been dating him a short time when my parents were killed. I was all alone in the world and there he was, this larger-than-life popular guy who was certain that he wanted to spend the rest of his life with me. He took me home and introduced me to his parents, who immediately took me in like I was one of their own. Kirk showed me a world where I didn't have to be alone ever again."

He hadn't asked about the guy. Or the guy's perfect family. Something he would never be able to offer her.

He wanted to know about her child.

And he had to know what had driven her to keep such a monumental secret.

Not that he was one to judge on that score. Jon had secrets, too.

"I found out about Kirk's girlfriends about the same time I found out I was pregnant," she continued, still looking down. "He'd told me that there had only been two affairs, that he'd ended both, and that there would never be another. I thought the baby was going to save our marriage."

"You loved him enough to forgive him for being unfaithful to you?" It hadn't sounded that way.

"Kirk and his parents were my family. They were all I had. He was the father of my child. I guess I didn't let myself think beyond that." At that, Lillie glanced over at him, and he wasn't sure what he read in her eyes.

He wasn't sure about anything at the moment. All he knew was that Lillie had made decisions that he and Abe hadn't changed.

"It's understandable, given the circumstances," he said. "You were pregnant with nowhere to turn."

It occurred to him to stop this now. To let her off the hook. He didn't need to know any more. Unless she needed to tell him.

The possibility kept him quiet.

"My being pregnant kept Kirk home," Lillie said. "He'd bring presents almost every day, one for me, one for the baby. Little things. It wasn't unusual for him to leave the office early and have dinner waiting when I got home from work."

Nothing less than she deserved—and Jon had no business wishing he'd been that guy.

Minus the cheating. It wasn't something he would do. Ever. Not to anyone. People had to be able to trust family. There had to be something in the world you could count on.

"He came to all of my doctor's appointments," Lillie continued slowly, a detached, almost unrecognizable tone to her voice. "After our first ultrasound, the doctor called us into her office. I had a feeling something was wrong. Kirk wouldn't hear a word of it. He was certain I was over-reacting. He claimed I had a tendency to look for trouble, to guard against it. He always said it was because of the way I'd lost my parents. I was trying to prepare myself so that, if something like that ever happened again, I could get through it."

It made a frightening kind of sense.

Frightening because if you were trying to prevent further pain, you didn't open yourself up to a level of caring that could cause it.

Sometimes people just couldn't take on any more disappointment. Sometimes they just shut down. He'd seen it happen in detention more than once.

"This time I was right." Lillie's words weren't a surprise. He'd known where this was leading.

"You lost the baby?"

A lot of women did, or so he'd read in the books he'd devoured after he'd first found out Kate was pregnant. And most of the women who miscarried tried again.

Lillie shook her head and looked up at Jon. He understood the resolution in her eyes. The acceptance of powerlessness.

Before Abraham, he'd seen the same look in the mirror every morning when he'd stood in front of it.

"She told us that the baby had a malformed heart."

"Was it a boy or a girl?" he asked, but he already knew. She'd had a son. And she was transposing some of her feelings about the baby to Abraham.

Lillie grabbed her bare toes with both hands. He could see the whites of her knuckles. But her voice was even when she said, "A boy."

"Did you carry him to term?"

"Yes."

Had her son been stillborn? He couldn't imagine the horror-filled months of carrying a baby inside of you, feeling it move and form, bonding with it as it grew, knowing it would not live.

Already grieving the sudden loss of her parents and the infidelity of her husband, she'd also had to endure the hell of growing a child that she knew was going to die.

"Was Kirk with you when you delivered?"

Her expression hardened until she didn't even look like

Lillie. "Kirk hadn't been 'with' me since the day we got the diagnosis. He went back to his girlfriend. Got her pregnant, too. And moved in with her."

Jon scrambled for words. For anything that could make this better.

There just wasn't anything.

"While you were still pregnant?" he asked because, since they'd come this far, he needed to know, to understand the depths of her pain. Because they needed to get this all out now.

She nodded.

"What about his parents?"

"They were at the hospital when Braydon was born."

Braydon. Her tone softened when she said the word. Tears filled her eyes.

And Jon knew that he and Abraham had never really had her heart. Lillie had already given it away. To a little boy named Bray who hadn't lived long enough to call her Mama.

LILLIE STAYED IN Jon's bed for as long as it took her to gather her strength. When she was ready, he let her go without a word.

Just as she'd known he would. He wasn't going to beg.

And she didn't want him to.

She also didn't want to leave.

He followed her to the front door to lock up behind her. The only light in the house was the one they'd left on in the kitchen.

Turning, Lillie looked up at the man who'd come to mean more to her than he'd ever know. His strong, chiseled features would be in every good dream she had from there on out.

"I think it's best that we not see each other socially

anymore." The words hurt, but she knew she was doing the right thing.

His jaw tightening, Jon didn't reply.

"I'll continue to see Abe at the day care, for a time," she assured him. "For as long as he needs me, I'll be there for him. But it won't take long for him to attach to someone else," she added. "Two-year-olds are resilient."

Jon stood unmoving, a stone sculpture in his own living room.

"That's why it's best that we end this now, before he grows even more attached, or gets old enough to remember me."

He didn't argue. He didn't agree. He didn't touch her.

"Say something."

"You're the professional."

Studying his expression, she looked for signs of derision, of sarcasm. There were none.

That was it, then.

Opening the door, Lillie turned her back.

"I'm sorry, Lil. Braydon was a lucky little guy to have you."

Fresh tears filled her eyes as she hurried out into the night.

CHAPTER TWENTY-FOUR

LILLIE RECEIVED A page early the next morning. Having just come in from her bike ride with Caro—and having told her friend nothing about the night before—she read the message before jumping in the shower.

That morning's MRI had been postponed until that afternoon. Which left her with a whole morning to herself.

She could make her normal rounds at the day care, after all. Be on call at the clinic. Work on a papoose design that would allow toddlers' feet to be free, so that they didn't overheat if they were crying while in restraints for procedures. She'd tentatively sold the design to a company she'd worked with at the children's hospital in Phoenix. They'd been expecting a prototype for over a month.

There were any number of things she could be doing that morning, but she was a firm believer in fate. And she knew that there was something else she had to do with her suddenly free morning.

She didn't call ahead. She knew what time and where. She just had to get herself showered. Dressed in a pair of black slacks, a white silk blouse and a black linen jacket, she slipped into her expensive pumps and headed out to her car.

In the beginning, she'd gone every day. Sometimes twice a day. Then once a week. Eventually, at the suggestion of a therapist she'd been seeing since before Braydon was born, she'd only allowed herself monthly visits. For the past two years, it had been only once a year—on the date of his birth.

She went to remember her whole self. And to promise her son that they would be together again someday.

Taking the second driveway in, she turned and turned again until she arrived at the row bearing the Henderson family stone.

Two other cars were there. Kirk's convertible and a nondescript dark-colored sedan, which she assumed was the minister's.

Seeing the middle-aged man standing in a long cloak, she was glad to see that Kirk had been honest with her at least. There was no fanfare. He hadn't brought anyone else with him. This day was between him and the son he'd betrayed.

He introduced Lillie to the minister and, without any small talk at all, the short service was under way. Standing next to her ex-husband, not touching him, Lillie listened to the Scriptures. She bowed her head for a prayer. She heard Kirk's words of sorrow and grief to his dead son and his pleas for forgiveness.

"My promise this day and for every day of my life is to live a life that will honor you, Braydon Thomas. You will be the basis upon which every decision in my life is made from this moment forward."

Her throat caught. She was not going to cry. She had no tears left.

HAVING BEEN UP so late with Lillie Wednesday night, Jon overslept Thursday morning for the first time in the nine years since he'd left prison.

Whether he forgot to set the alarm, or just didn't hear it go off, he didn't know. He was driving Lillie to the hospital to have his baby, and heard sirens coming up behind

him. They got louder and louder but he couldn't see them
in his rearview mirror. Couldn't find them at all.

Until finally they woke him up.

The baby monitor was wailing at him—the siren ring-
tone he'd chosen to indicate movement in Abe's room. A
tone that escalated in volume the longer it played.

Throwing off the covers, his gaze jerked first to the tablet monitor on his nightstand, studying the scene intently,
looking for signs of Abe. Or an intruder.

That was when he realized it was already well into the
morning. The sun was shining through the closed blind in
Abe's room. And through the drapes in his room, as well.

And he realized something else. Abe's crib was empty.

"Abe!" Running to the room next door to his, he looked
around and found nothing.

No sign of the boy. No mess.

"Abraham!" Heart pounding, he ran down the hall.
"Abraham!"

Nothing. No sound. No little boy. Rounding the corner
of the living room, Jon stopped cold. There, sitting in the
middle of the floor, his pudgy fingers carefully lining up
rows of cars, was Abraham. Playing just like he would
have been if Jon had gotten him out of bed and set him
down while he made their breakfast.

Abe was having a regular morning.

With the exception of two things.

He'd climbed out of his crib on his own—something
Jon had known was coming but hadn't yet seen.

And…

"Abe?" He moved close behind the toddler and raised
his voice up another octave.

With a jerk, the little boy turned around.

The monitor, his own calls from down the hall—Abraham hadn't heard them. Or him.

"WALK WITH ME?" His hands in his pockets, Kirk waited for Lillie's nod, for her to fall into step beside him as he started across the crisply manicured cemetery lawn.

His suit jacket was unbuttoned, his red-and-black tie askew, and he didn't seem to notice that the wet ground was marring the tips of his shiny black shoes. He stepped carefully, slowly, making it easy for her to keep up with him unassisted in her high heels.

"I have no excuses, Lil," he said to her. "Over the past couple of years I realized something was drastically wrong with me."

She listened. She couldn't feel. She'd done too much of that. "Actually, I knew before that, but I couldn't believe it. For a long time it was always someone else who just didn't get it. Or something that couldn't be helped and for which I wasn't to blame."

He could have been referring to any number of things. His first affair could have been construed as her fault for not agreeing to be more sexually adventurous with him when he'd asked her to. Braydon's illness had been something that couldn't be helped, and maybe he thought his feelings for Leah fell under that category, too. She didn't know and didn't ask.

"I can't tell you that there was a specific moment, or any one thing that happened, that changed the way I saw things. There were no 'aha' moments or a particular time when the light came on."

They crossed a gravel drive to a paved path that wound around the base of the mountain. A couple of hikers passed them, heading toward the dirt path that led up the mountain. The desert's fall colors were in full bloom: prickly pear cacti with their brightly colored fruit ready to be picked. Saguaro and ocotillo looming along the path and in the distance.

"It's like the knowledge was always there and just took a long time to surface," Kirk was saying.

He needed this. For Braydon's and Ely's sakes, she'd give it to him.

"Leah thought I was losing it. The day I told her I couldn't marry her, that I was moving out, she thought I needed to see a psychiatrist."

Lillie wasn't as willing to go there with him. Her own wound was too raw. Would always be too raw. The way Kirk had summoned her to his office in her advanced state of pregnancy, hearing that he was having a healthy son while she carried the one who would most likely not live to see his childhood…

Her foot came down on a little rock on the path and she stumbled. Kirk grabbed her elbow and steadied her. Held on.

She pulled her arm away.

"The truth is," he continued with a look of sorrow on his face, "I lost it the day I heard about Braydon. I couldn't do it, Lil. I wasn't as strong as you. As good as you. I just didn't have what it took to go through the pregnancy, the birth, only to have him die."

In fairness, she hadn't been sure she had what it took, either, except that she'd had no choice. The baby had been inside of her. Wherever she went, he went.

Until he didn't.

"At first, I was in denial. The doctor was wrong. Or the problem wasn't what they'd first thought. But as your pregnancy progressed, as they did more tests, the situation only got worse and was further confirmed."

"Papa told you that?" Because Kirk had certainly not been there himself. Not since the first day they'd heard there was a problem.

"The doctor told me that. I went to see her after every one of your appointments."

Her head jerking to the side, Lillie stared at him. "She never told me that."

Was this another of Kirk's tricks? A way to insinuate himself back into her heart—her life?

"I told her not to," Kirk said. "At that point I was pretty sure I wasn't going to be the husband you deserved and needed me to be, and I figured the one decent thing I could do, rather than popping in and out of your life, was to leave you alone."

It might have been nice if she'd had a say in that decision. While, ultimately, their marriage would have ended, it still would have been nice to have had Braydon's father around to share the unique burden they'd been given.

At least she would have had someone to talk to who really understood.

Who cared about the baby as much as she did.

"I'm not proud of myself, Lil. At all. But if I'm going to get anything right in my life, I have to be honest with you. After I was sure Bray wasn't going to get any better, I told myself that it was meant to be that way. And that my life would still be just as great as I'd always envisioned. I could move on to have the family I was meant to have."

To Leah. He'd moved on to Leah.

And had Ely.

Lillie had seen pictures of the boy. When she'd visited Papa and Gayle. At first, they'd removed all signs of their grandson whenever they knew she was coming over. But when she'd stopped in unannounced one day and seen the photos, she'd told them they didn't have to hide them.

That, in fact, it was wrong, unfair to an innocent little boy, for them to deny his existence in any way.

"Ely looks like you," she said now. "He's got Leah's

light coloring, but he has your bone structure. Your nose and mouth."

Shoulders hunched, Kirk shook his head. It took a moment for her to realize he was crying again.

"I never saw my son, Lil. He was on this earth for sixteen days, fighting for his life, and I wasn't there. He never heard my voice."

It was something he was going to have to live with for the rest of his life. They both knew that.

"There was nothing you could have done," she had to tell him.

Because the one thing Lillie couldn't bear was to allow someone to suffer if she could help alleviate their distress.

"There were no tough decisions to make, Kirk. No choices. They did everything they could, but he didn't have enough of a heart to sustain him and its absence had already affected his other organs too much to allow for any possibility of a transplant. He arrived. He lived sixteen days. And he left us."

"But you held him."

The picture. The one on the gravestone that Kirk had just minutes ago lifted by himself from his car to place on the ground above their son's tiny casket.

"He was so tiny," she said, daring for once to remember details. "Just under six pounds. And too thin. But they let me feed him. Every time."

She'd had to learn to nurse him surrounded by tubes and monitors, but they'd managed just fine. She'd have continued on forever if Braydon had been able to sustain life.

"My father tells me he had your eyes."

Braydon had had his own eyes. Big and bright and filled with recognition when she talked to him.

Over the next hour she relived those days, sharing memories, things that stood out, with the man who should have been there back then, sharing it all with her.

"I'm so sorry I wasn't there for you, Lil. You had to do all the hard work alone," Kirk said again as they sat down on a bench at the foot of the mountain. The midmorning sun shone brightly down on them, taking the chill off.

Maybe a little piece of Braydon wrapping his parents in his warmth.

"You know," Lillie said softly, giving Kirk a sad smile. "I'm not as sorry as I was," she told him, feeling better, lighter, than she had in forever. "I'm realizing that I was the lucky one of the two of us," she told him. She'd known Braydon. Had held him, smelled his fresh baby scent, even in the midst of all of the medicinal hospital surroundings. She'd seen his gaze as he stared trustingly up at her.

"Thank you for introducing him to me." Rubbing his hands together, Kirk looked over at her. "I didn't deserve it."

Life wasn't about people getting what they deserved. Otherwise, Braydon would be five years old, healthy and happy.

Her parents would still be alive.

And Abraham would have a mother.

CHAPTER TWENTY-FIVE

DR. HILLCREST, ABRAHAM'S pediatrician, had offices at the clinic where Lillie worked, but as it turned out, he only saw patients in Shelter Valley two days a week—Monday and Wednesday. Jon wasn't waiting four days to have his son's hearing checked.

Hanging up the phone half an hour after flying out of bed late Thursday morning, he poured a little more farina in Abe's bowl, made sounds behind the boy's back to see if he'd notice and dialed Mark Heber. Abe didn't notice. Hopefully Mark would find someone to cover Jon's shift at the plant. He could access any schoolwork he missed through his student portal online.

After leaving a message for Mark, Jon washed the pan he used to make Abe's cereal. A voice on the other end of the line, as opposed to a recording, would have been nice.

Assurances that his son was going to be fine would have been better.

Abe going deaf? He couldn't fathom it.

But if it was true, they'd deal with it. Together.

Putting the box of cereal back in the cupboard, he remembered the day he'd purchased it. The way Abe had screamed bloody murder when he'd ducked under the shelf to retrieve that last box in the back. Right after he'd told him what he was going to do.

Abe hadn't heard him. He'd screamed because he'd thought Jon was gone.

Lillie had been right. She'd seen the signs that Abe had been giving them.

He hadn't.

As soon as Abraham finished breakfast, Jon took the boy into the shower with him, cleaned them both up, got them both dressed and carried his son out to the truck.

The doctor would tell him what to do next.

LILLIE HAD JUST come from the MRI and was heading toward her office when she was paged to the clinic's waiting room.

An emergency? Usually they came through the urgent care wing.

Her hair falling out of its ponytail, she pushed through the doors. Jon was standing there, Abraham on his hip.

"Illie! Illie!" The toddler reached out to her and Lillie took him automatically.

Was it only that morning that she and Jon had decided they wouldn't be "friends" anymore?

The little boy placed a wet kiss on her cheek. "Abie baby." She nuzzled her nose against his neck, calling him by his father's pet name before she realized what she'd done. Not that it was the first time. It just seemed too personal now.

Thankfully, that late in the afternoon, the waiting room was empty. There was no one there to notice how long she and Jon stood there, staring at each other.

"Illie eat," Abraham said.

"You can't possibly be hungry," Jon said to the boy. "You just had ice cream an hour ago."

Jon looked directly at Abe, moving in closer to get the boy's attention. He also spoke louder than normal.

"Abe had ice cream in the middle of a Thursday afternoon?" she asked, frowning. Ice-cream day at Little Spirits was on Friday.

For a second, she thought she had her days confused. Was it Friday, not Thursday? Having had so little sleep and after experiencing the emotional hell of the past twenty-four hours, she couldn't be positive.

But...

"You're not at work," she said to Jon. Because of her? Because she'd kept him up half the night? No. Jon would go to work on no sleep at all if he had to.

"Abe and I have just come from Dr. Hillcrest's office in Phoenix," he told her, his face serious, but not grim.

Lillie's heart pounded. "Is something wrong?"

"I had his ears checked."

She wasn't sure she'd heard him correctly, but only because she so badly needed to hear him say what he'd just said.

"And?" she asked. Please, God, let it be something fixable.

"His ear canals have narrowed," he said. "We saw an ear, nose and throat guy in Dr. Hillcrest's office. He spent an hour and a half with Abe. He's not sure what's caused the narrowing, but he assures me that if he puts tubes in Abe's ears, the situation will reverse and correct itself."

"He's not going deaf."

"He could have, if we hadn't caught the situation in time. But no, there's nothing wrong with his eardrums. Once the canals are opened, he'll be fine."

Unprofessional tears sprang to her eyes. *Boundaries,* she reminded herself.

"We're scheduled to have the procedure done here on Monday afternoon," Jon said. "I'd like to ask you to be there, Lil. To support Abe."

For a split second she wondered if this was just an attempt by Jon to get her back into their lives, but she knew better. He wasn't Kirk. Jon was who he was—up front and open. She could trust him.

Which was why she cared so much about him.

"Of course I'll be there," she told him. And with a last hug, she handed Abraham back to his father and retreated to her office to add his procedure to her calendar.

WITH THE CO-PAY of Abe's upcoming procedure and the possibility he would need to take time off from work if there were any complications, Jon picked up extra hours over the weekend. Mark called to say that Addy and Nonnie would be happy to watch Abe so that Jon could go in on Sunday.

They'd had a line go down overnight on Saturday and Mark had been in on Sunday, too, helping to get a conveyer back up and running so they wouldn't miss Monday's shipment.

"Hey, man, long time no see," Jon said, greeting his lab partner at their chemistry lecture on Monday morning.

"Yeah, what's it been, twelve hours?"

He'd picked Abe up at bedtime and their class was at eight in the morning, so that was about right.

"You get the reading done?" he asked Mark as they took their seats in the back row.

"Yeah, you?"

"Not quite, but close." He'd spent a while in Abraham's room, watching the boy sleep. Thinking about how close he'd come to having permanent hearing loss.

Back in his room, he'd had a hard time focusing, thinking of the procedure that afternoon. Needing it to go as well as the doctor predicted.

Needing to see Lillie, too. He hadn't heard a word from her since Thursday. And, other than when he was focused on Abe, he could think of little else.

She'd been through so much. And deserved none of it. He needed to make things better for her somehow.

Lillie cared about them. She was just scared. It was that fear, in fact, that told him how much she cared. She was running away.

And somehow he had to catch her. Which was why he hadn't agreed to not seeing her anymore. He'd just let her go for the moment.

Until he could figure out how to help her.

And then he'd woken up the next morning to the realization that his son was going deaf.

"I heard that that last break-in, the one where the guy broke the glass," Mark was saying as they waited for their professor to appear, "was one street over from you. No one was home, but he found a safe in the bedroom and took some cash. A lot of it. The sheriff called Addy sometime after midnight. Apparently they have a couple of suspects but couldn't get hold of anyone from the county attorney's office and wanted her opinion on something."

Oh, God.

"Did Addy hear from the bar yet?"

Mark's fiancée, licensed to practice law in Colorado, had recently taken the Arizona bar exam to enable her to transfer her practice to Shelter Valley.

"On Friday," Mark said. "She's been official for two days and is already on call."

Mark sounded like he was complaining, but the grin on his face told the truth.

"So they know who's been doing the break-ins?" Jon made himself ask the question. An informed man was an armed man.

Shrugging, Mark shook his head. "She couldn't tell me any more than that," he said, and then nodded toward the front of the room where their chemistry professor had taken the podium—right on time.

LILLIE KEPT BUSY all morning on Monday. Too busy to dwell on that afternoon's procedure.

On Sunday, after having breakfast with Papa and Gayle, she'd driven to the cemetery. Visited with her son and confirmed for herself that, without a doubt, she couldn't risk opening herself up to the possibility of loving—and losing—another child. She was strong but not that strong.

Losing her parents had been hard. Kirk's infidelity had been hard. Losing Braydon had almost killed her.

As she ate her lunch in her office, she dialed her ex-husband.

"Lil?" He picked up on the first ring.

"I've been thinking," she started, and paused. Did she really want to do this? Was it necessary?

"I've been hoping you'd call, Lil," Kirk said. "I promised I'd only call you once a week, but I'd hoped you'd call before then. Something's happening here. Thursday…it was so great being with you—"

"Have you been drinking?" she interrupted. She didn't need to hear any more.

"Only a mimosa with a client over breakfast this morning," Kirk said. "To celebrate the closing of a deal."

It might only have been one. Kirk's newfound humility could be causing him to ramble. Either way, it didn't matter to her.

"I'm calling to tell you that I think it's best that you not call me anymore," she said. Ending things cleanly might seem cruel in the moment, but in the long run it was best for both of them. "If ever I was going to feel something for you, it would have been Thursday," she told him.

"You just need a little time, Lil. Go back to the cemetery again. Without me there to influence you. Just feel Bray. And the family we should have had…"

"If we should have had a family, we would have," she said. "And I've already been back. This isn't about you, Kirk. The things you did don't even come into play here. I simply don't feel a connection to you anymore, other than as someone I once knew." She'd thought of little else all weekend. Braydon. Abe. Kirk. Jon.

She wasn't going to have a life with Jon, but knowing him had changed her. Inexplicably.

He'd shown her her true self.

"I don't feel any butterflies when I'm with you—"

"Of course not, Lillie. We've been married. There's no mystery. No secrets. But that's when real love grows."

Between her and Kirk there was nothing but secrets. Which was part of the problem.

"I don't feel any desire for you, Kirk," she said, knowing that she was going to have to be frank to set him free.

"We were at a cemetery, Lil, mourning our son. Of course you're not going to feel desire."

"I mean period." She had no doubts about this one. Because Jon had taught her what real desire felt like.

"Dad told me you'd met someone. He didn't tell me who, and I figured he was just making it up to keep me away from you. He thinks I'm going to hurt you again, but I'm not, Lil, I swear. I need you to get through this."

"No, you don't. You just want me to make things easier for you." She let his comment about Jon slide away. "And more importantly, I don't need you, Kirk. You're going through a difficult time, and I feel compassion for you, but I can't be the one to help you. Leaning on me, using me, is only going to set you back further in the long run."

Kirk didn't want her. He wanted what he couldn't have. What he'd lost. Maybe because he'd grown up, come face-to-face with his deeper self and found himself lacking. Maybe his need to change was sincere. And maybe he'd even be successful. But if it was going to be real, and long lasting, he had to do it on his own. For himself.

And, she hoped, for Ely, who was still alive and needed him.

But Lillie didn't need him. What was more, she didn't love him.

And that was why she couldn't help him.

LILLIE MET JON and Abraham at the front door of the clinic, dressed in scrubs with her hair pulled back neatly in a ponytail.

"Illie!" Abraham ran to her when he saw his second favorite person in the world.

"Abie baby, how are you?" she asked, taking him into her arms. She barely gave Jon a glance.

And that was just fine with him at the moment. He wanted her focused 100 percent on his son, working her magic so that Abraham would be calm and receptive and have the best chance of success.

From then until they put Abe under, Jon wanted his son relaxed and happy. He didn't want his son resisting the procedure.

"We're going to try laughing gas on him first," Lillie told Jon as she walked them back to a private playroom for children awaiting treatment. The room was deserted.

Setting Abraham down to play with a plastic truck that he could sit on and push with his feet, she kept an eye on him and said to Jon, "Abe has otitis media with effusion, which means that there is inflammation and fluid buildup due to his narrow ear canals, which creates a blockage to his inner ear and results in hearing loss."

He knew most of this. From the doctor. And his own

internet research over the weekend. It still felt good, hearing it from her, and Jon listened carefully.

She wasn't his lover, or even his former lover. She was the expert who was going to help him and Abe through the coming hours.

She was also the woman he loved. And trusted.

And through her, he trusted the rest of the team to do their jobs to the best of their abilities. Lillie would see to that.

"Jon? You're staring at me."

Blinking, he didn't stop looking, he just focused. "I'm a little nervous," he admitted.

The way Lillie's eyes softened reminded him of the time they'd spent in his bed. She could pretend they were beyond it. But it was still there.

"It's understandable that you're nervous," she said with a little less distance. Taking his hand, she led him far enough away that Abe couldn't overhear them. And the fact that they didn't have to go far sent a new wave of near-panic through him.

He could deal with this. With anything. He just didn't want his son to have to face a world he couldn't hear.

"Has Abe ever had anesthesia before?" she asked. Jon shook his head. Lillie was still holding his hand. He wondered if she knew.

"He's a normal healthy little boy and should make it through just fine, but the doctor has to tell you the risks. He's going to tell you that there could be an allergic re-action to the anesthetic, and if there is, they're fully pre-pared to tend to that. There might be breathing difficulties. Again, they'll be watching and take the necessary action if need be. There could be heart irregularities...."

She dropped his hand. Swallowed. And something came over Jon. He was hit with an instinctive sense of Lillie. Of who she was, what she suffered—of her need. And knew that he and Abe could make a difference in her life.

"His heart is fine, Lil. What happened with Braydon was horrific, and also extremely unusual. Most kids are born perfectly normal, grow up perfectly normal."

Lillie squared her shoulders and nodded. He felt like an idiot.

"Illie!" Abe called out. "Dada!" Jon's head swung in his son's direction. Abe was standing by his truck, staring at the two of them, a frown on his face.

"Abie baby." Lillie reached him first, scooping him up in her arms and spinning him around before carrying him over to interest him in some other toys: a swimming mask and a book about diving for treasure. She told Abe a story about diving for his own treasure, about the mask he was going to get to wear and about the dreams he'd have.

Abe looked from her to the oxygen mask she held, and she said, "And when you're all done, you lift your head and I'll be right there waiting to see what you found!"

"Illie," Abe said. And then, "Dada."

"Daddy's right here, son." Jon joined them. "Can Daddy dive for treasure with you and Lillie, too?"

Abraham nodded. And Jon wished he was a religious man.

CHAPTER TWENTY-SIX

ABE WAS PREPPED and ready to go diving for treasure. Lillie stayed by his side every step of the way, doing what prep she could on her own. The fewer strangers who touched the boy, the happier he'd be.

But she didn't kid herself. Ear tubes were common. Almost normal. She was there, touching the boy because it made *her* feel better. Not because the outcome of Abe's procedure depended on his calmness. He'd be asleep for the insertion.

Still, the less trauma he suffered, the less chance there'd be of a raised heart rate and body temperature, and thus less chance of heart irregularities. And the less chance of nausea afterward, too.

Abe went to sleep by the count of three. Waiting until the doctor was ready to start the actual procedure, she slipped out and met Jon in the waiting room, inviting him back to her office. It wasn't regular protocol. While it was her job to support families through their children's procedures, that generally meant checking in with them, not sitting with them in her office.

As soon as Abe was out of surgery she was going to him, to be there when he woke up and sit with him through recovery, as well.

"Any memories he has of today will be with me by his side," she told Jon as she unlocked her office door. "The idea is that he won't have any feelings of being alone or abandoned."

He looked around as he entered, seeming to pay particular attention to the certificates on the wall behind her desk.

And then to the photo of her and her parents, taken the summer before they were killed.

"We went to Europe," she told Jon softly. "To Italy. It was the best."

He nodded, but didn't ask her any questions. She'd wanted him to.

"The doctor's going to speak to you after he's done," she said. She had a job to do. They weren't friends anymore. At her behest.

Taking a seat behind her desk, she motioned to the chairs directly in front of it.

He wandered around the room instead, his hands in the pockets of his jeans. Jon had strong hands. Reliable hands. Gentle hands.

Did he still get turned on at the sight of hers?

Did she want him to?

The chances of her having another child who died were slim to none. Her doctor had told her so years ago. Braydon's malformation had had no basis in genetics. They'd run all the tests.

During her time at the children's hospital in Phoenix she'd helped several families with more than one long-term-care child. Their medical conditions were mostly due to genetics or drugs. But not always.

"The doctor will give you another list of things that could go wrong," she told Jon now. "It will be really important that you keep up with regular checks," she told him. "If the tubes come out too early, or are left in too long, hearing loss could result."

Frowning, Jon sat. "He could still go deaf?"

"Maybe not completely, but he could experience some loss. The chances are slim," she told him, thinking about Bray again. "As long as he has regular checks."

This wasn't about her. "We don't miss his checkups. Ever."

"We'll need to watch for any signs of bleeding or infection, or persistent drainage of fluid," she added. "Blood, mucus and other secretions can block the tubes."

The doctor would tell him all of this but sometimes the information got lost in the telling or seemed overwhelming if you weren't prepared. That was where she came in.

Crossing one leg over his knee, Jon smiled at her.

"What?"

"You said 'we.'"

She had. Subconsciously. "Yes, well…"

Lillie had no idea what she was going to say. And didn't get a chance to say anything, as they were interrupted by a commotion in the hallway outside.

"Lillie?"

Haley, one of the full-time clinic receptionists, poked her head inside Lillie's door. "Oh, I'm sorry, I didn't realize you weren't alone."

Lillie didn't usually have clients in her office. They had their meetings in procedure and exam rooms.

"No problem, Haley. What's up?"

The door opened farther and Sheriff Richards was there. "I'm looking for Jon Swartz, Lil," he said. "I tried him at work, and they said his son was having a procedure here today, but he's not out in the waiting room. Bonnie had mentioned that you and he were friends…."

"He's right here, Sheriff."

Jon wasn't smiling. In fact, the hardened expression on his face made him unrecognizable to her. And she knew, just knew, that he'd kept secrets from her, after all.

JON HAD WOKEN up that morning knowing that it was going to be a hard day. He'd had no idea how hard.

"Jon Swartz?" The uniformed sheriff did not resemble, in any way, the kindly man Jon had heard about.

He was all cop. And Jon knew this drill. Years fell away as his heart froze and he stood, put his hands behind his back.

He'd known this was coming. Some part of him had known.

"I'd like to ask you a few questions." He heard the sheriff's voice, waiting to feel the steel cuffs close around his wrists.

Warm flesh curved around his upper arm instead— the sheriff's hand, not a locking piece of metal. Richards guided Jon back down to the chair and then took the seat beside him.

The sheriff was obviously playing nice for Lillie's sake, but Jon was certain his tight grip hadn't been a mistake.

He needed to tell Lillie his story in his own way.

He should have done it before he slept with her.

He just hadn't wanted to lose her.

Jon started to stand again. He wasn't going to do this here. Not in front of Lillie.

The sheriff was on his feet before Jon was. "Mr. Swartz?" The words were more warning than question.

"We don't need to tie up Ms. Henderson's time with our business," Jon said, his voice and expression giving no hint whatsoever to the turbulence roiling inside him—a skill he'd learned at a young age.

"Agreed," Richards said, "but I'd like you to come with me." Jon hadn't doubted that for a second. By the stoniness of Richards's expression Jon figured the sheriff already had him tried and convicted.

He wasn't in Atlanta anymore. And he wasn't a kid,

either. Wasn't protected by the juvenile court system, or held accountable only until his eighteenth birthday. That had all come and gone.

Lillie's cheeks were white, her eyes wide. And Jon had one thought.

He couldn't let the state take his son.

"Keep Abe for me," he said to her, knowing that she loved his son enough to do as he asked, even if she didn't want to. Knowing that he was manipulating that love to make certain that his wish was granted. "If it comes to it, I'll sign whatever papers I have to sign to give you temporary guardianship."

The sheriff coughed, but he didn't move. Not until he had her promise.

"Lil, please?" He'd beg if he had to. Not for himself. Never for himself, but for his son.

Seeing her nod, Jon set his keys on her desk and, turning, followed the sheriff out to his car.

LILLIE WAS ON the phone before her door was fully shut behind the sheriff and Jon.

"Bonnie? What's going on?" She didn't bother to identify herself.

"I don't know, Lil. All I got out of Greg was that it has something to do with the break-ins."

Greg. Hearing the sheriff referred to by his first name, the name by which Lillie normally addressed him and heard him addressed, took a small bit of the sting out of what had just transpired. But only a small bit. "Greg" had not been present in her office.

Still, she knew him. Knew he was fair. Just.

Jon would be okay.

"Why Jon?"

"I don't know," Bonnie said. "I asked the same thing

and all I got was that Greg just had some questions to ask him. I wanted to wring his neck."

"If he's not saying, it can't be good."

"Don't jump to conclusions yet." Bonnie's tone softened. "Not until we know something for sure."

"Greg would have said if Jon wasn't in trouble."

"I know it's hard, Lil. I'm dying to know, too. Just hold on. You want me to come get Abe? I could take him home with me."

"Of course not!" Lillie's emotions were on overdrive. "Abe's comfortable with me. And…I told Jon I'd keep him. I'm going to take him home to his own house. To his own bed. Jon left his keys. And the little guy has been through too much today. Besides, that way he'll be there when Jon gets back."

Because he was coming back.

And then he had some explaining to do.

A guy didn't just get picked up for questioning for no reason.

"Do you own a set of suction cups used in removing sliding glass doors?"

They were still in the sheriff's car, driving through town. Jon figured everyone they passed was staring at him.

And convicting him, too.

"No, I do not," he said automatically. The sheriff didn't say another word the rest of the trip.

It was like living in the twilight zone. A horribleness she could never have imagined.

Abraham had come through his procedure without any problems and was fine except that he'd probably sleep more than usual over the next couple of days. Lillie made him an early dinner, expecting him to conk out before his usual bedtime.

She heated up some hot dogs. Because all Jon did was boil them so she could fix them exactly the way Abe was used to.

She made a decent homemade macaroni and cheese, too, but it would be different than Jon's. And Abraham might not like it.

The day had been stressful enough for the boy. She didn't need to add to that.

It was the reason she was in Jon's home when she'd rather be anyplace but.

Her phone rang just as she was putting Abe in his crib at a quarter to seven.

"I need access to Jon's house, Lil," Sheriff Richards said. She hadn't known her heart could sink any further. "He said you have the keys."

"Is he in jail?" Her heart pounded.

"Not yet. He's only being held for questioning."

"Here in town?"

"Yes. I've got an interrogation room at the station. He's been there all afternoon."

"Has he said anything?"

After hanging up with Bonnie, Lillie had called Caroline. And then Jon's friend, Mark Heber, whose fiancée was an attorney.

All she got out of anyone was that they were questioning Jon in conjunction with the break-ins. She was trying not to think about it. Not to feel anything at all.

Abraham needed her calm. Cheerful.

And she didn't know for how long.

"He's answered my questions, Lil," Sheriff Richards said. "He says he had nothing to do with the break-ins."

Could he be even better at lying and manipulating than

Kirk was? She just couldn't believe it. Didn't believe it. "Then maybe it's true."

"For your sake and the boy's, I hope so, Lil. But I have to tell you, it doesn't look good. He used suction cups when he replaced your sliding glass door, didn't he?"

Lillie's hesitation scared her. "Yes, why?" Just because a guy had an easy-enough-to-come-by tool didn't make him guilty of a crime. "He used to work in construction, Greg. He's got all kinds of tools in his truck."

"He says he doesn't own suction cups."

"Of course he does. They're in the back of his truck. In a bucket, I think. That's where he put them when he carried them out of my house that night."

Too late, she realized what Greg had just told her—*Jon* had denied owning the cups. He'd lied to the sheriff.

Sweating at the back of her neck, beneath hair that suddenly felt heavy, Lillie shut up.

Things weren't always how they appeared. Bray, the second he'd come out, had looked like a perfectly normal newborn. Until he'd turned blue.

Kirk had seemed like the perfect husband.

"We've already searched his truck," Greg said. "There weren't any suction cups in it."

"But, surely, the fact that he owns suction cups doesn't make him guilty of anything. It's ludicrous, Greg. I know this guy. He's adamant about paying for everything himself. He wouldn't steal anything from anybody."

Greg's foreboding silence made her stomach hurt.

"We'll need to question you, too, Lil." The sheriff's tone was soft. Apologetic.

She felt sick. "You think I had something to do with this?"

"Absolutely not." His tone left no doubt of his sincerity.

"But you spent a lot of time with him. You might inadvertently know something."

"I know he didn't do it. And I can tell you for certain that I haven't noticed anything at all unusual about him or his behavior. Jon's a great guy."

She sounded like a lovesick fool. Blindly standing behind Jon before she heard the evidence.

"There are mitigating factors. And sometimes there are things that don't look suspicious until combined with other facts."

"You said you needed access to his duplex. What do you need?" Did Jon want her to let them in?

If he didn't, he looked guilty. And if he was guilty, she was not going to protect him.

"I have a warrant to search the place."

"Now? I just put Abraham to bed."

"We'll be quiet."

And if Abraham woke up, Lillie would take him to her place. Just until the sheriff was finished.

It shouldn't take long.

Greg Richards and his deputy weren't going to find anything.

"I HAVE FULLY cooperated with you, Sheriff," Jon kept his tone neutral. Doing otherwise served no purpose.

"You lied about owning a pair of suction cups. I just got off the phone with Lillie. She told me where you kept them. Funny, when we searched your truck they weren't there."

"You can't keep me based on a missing set of suction cups." They obviously didn't have much else on him—besides the fact that he was a convicted felon. Which was enough to make everybody believe he was guilty, but not enough to hold him on.

One of the few good things that came out of his time

spent in juvenile detention was a thorough understanding of how the law worked.

Being a ward of the state had taught him not to rely on anyone else to help him. And Jon had had a lot of time to read during his years of incarceration. He knew his rights.

"You admit to having knowledge of how to use suction cups," the sheriff repeated again. He had to hand it to the guy, he seemed to be made of patience. Jon was unfamiliar with the approach.

But maybe that was the difference between being a punk kid the cops knew they could scare and an adult who could hold his own.

Or the difference between being guilty and innocent. Those interrogating him in the past had had him dead to rights. They hadn't needed to finesse one damn thing from him.

"I replaced Lillie's sliding glass door with French doors," Jon said. Lillie had told her friends. They all knew. He added, "I have nothing to hide, Sheriff." He'd already hidden the only thing they could have used to manipulate a case against him. If he'd produced suction cups they could have taken a "print" of the imprint his cups made, compared it to cup imprints left on the doors during the break-ins and manipulated the results to make it look as if he'd done it.

"You also don't have an alibi for a single one of the break-ins."

Not unless you counted a sleeping two-year-old who'd been hard of hearing. But, for that matter, he could have taken Abe with him, left him sleeping in his car seat while he committed the crimes.

His heart lurched as he thought of his son, so he tried not to.

Abe loved Lillie. He'd be fine as long as he was with her.

"And you have very clear motive. I've heard from several sources that in addition to being a single parent and going to school full-time, you work any hours you can get to make ends meet."

"I work the extra hours, Sheriff, so I can make ends meet. I don't have to steal."

"You have a history of breaking and entering. And stealing," Richards said. "You were caught with the goods and confessed."

"I did my time," Jon added. Some things could not be changed. And some could. "I learned my lesson, Sheriff. I am a law-abiding citizen."

Taking the seat across from him, Richards leaned in toward Jon. "I talked to the glass guy at the swap meet earlier today."

The words running through Jon's mind were not ones he ever wanted to hear coming out of his son's mouth.

"He still had the glass doors you sold him. The ones from Lillie's place. And they had suction-cup prints."

Richards was turning up the heat.

"Did you contact Lillie about getting into my place?"

"We're heading over there now."

"She's going to meet you there?"

"She's staying there. Your son is already down for the night. I've promised her that we'll be careful not to wake him." Jon couldn't tell if the man was being sincere or trying to get a rise out of him.

"I appreciate that," Jon said, because he did. And because he knew that the man wouldn't lie to Lillie.

And even if he would, she wouldn't let anyone or anything hurt Abraham.

The sheriff studied him for a moment. "I can tell you this, Swartz—I wish to God I could believe you. Lord knows it would be a hell of a lot easier."

It was a strange thing for a cop to say. Which meant he had an angle. "Why easier?" Jon asked, because he was curious to see what card the man would play next—and to best plan his own next move.

Richards rapped his knuckles against the table a couple of times, stood and made for the door. With his hand on the knob, he turned. "Because I'm catching hell from everyone in this town from the mayor on down. My sister most of all. You've got them all fooled, Swartz, but then a con man like you, that's what you excel at, isn't it?"

Because he was certain that this was just another in a long line of tricks used on him over the years, Jon did what was expected of him. He shrugged.

"I'm surprised at Lillie's support of you, though," the sheriff said, watching him shrewdly as though the mention of her would break him down. If it did, Jon wasn't going to let the other man see.

"If I find that you've taken any money from her…"

Lillie was like him, a working girl. She didn't have money for him to take. Even if he was the taking kind.

"The folks in town might not know about her money, but her ex-father-in-law called me as soon as she moved back here and told me about the settlement so I'd watch out for guys like you—guys who'd steal from innocent young women, old ladies and old store clerks, too."

The slap found its mark. The guy Jon and his foster brothers had ripped off had been close to eighty. Which was why they'd chosen him.

But…Lillie had money?

"Who was she married to?" Jon asked.

"A man with a father with enough money to bury you if you hurt her," the sheriff said. "And I hear—" Richards leaned in again "—that she's quite close with the old man. Has breakfast with him every single Sunday morning."

The sheriff got what he wanted. Jon felt beaten. He remembered Lillie's Sunday morning absences. She'd never told him where she went, or with whom.

Lillie had money? Had lived in the same elite circles Kate came from?

If he'd known that, he would never, ever have trusted her in the first place. "Mark my words, Swartz. I don't just serve this town, I love these people. And I will do whatever it takes to protect them." Jon no longer cared.

"And you have no other suspects." It was a statement, not a question. Because he had to keep up appearances and get out of there.

"One. He had an alibi."

Jon gave one slow nod in acknowledgment. As Richards turned to leave, he said, "Sheriff?"

"Yeah?"

"Did Lillie say how Abraham was doing? If the procedure went as planned?" Abe was all that mattered now. All that would ever matter again.

"She didn't tell me anything that I didn't ask," Richards's answer was about what he'd expected. The man opened the door, stepped through it and ducked his head back in. "But Bonnie threatened me as only a sister can. I'm to tell you that he came through with flying colors. Woke up easily. Ate a good dinner and went to bed an hour early."

The sheriff had to have known that the news would relieve Jon. And he'd given it to him, anyway.

Jon wasn't sure what to make of that.

CHAPTER TWENTY-SEVEN

LILLIE SPENT MUCH of the evening on the phone. She called Becca Parsons, Shelter Valley's mayor, whose children she'd seen a time or two at the clinic. And who, along with her husband, Will, were Caro and John's closest friends. Becca said she'd find out what she could and get back to her. Lillie answered calls from friends like Tory Sanders, Phyllis Sheffield and Ellen Billingsley, who'd called from Phoenix.

Some wanted to know what was going on. Others, those who knew Jon, expressed their shock and supported her standing by him.

All things considered, she was feeling pretty good when she opened the door to Sheriff Richards at a little past eight o'clock that evening.

"We'll be quick and quiet," Bonnie's brother told Lillie as he and a tall, thin, bearded man entered the living room. "You take the kitchen and front half of the place, I'll get the bedrooms," Greg Richards told his deputy.

The officer, a man Lillie had never met, nodded and left, walking softly as he moved across the kitchen to the laundry closet.

Lillie followed Greg down the hall. "This is Abe's room," Lillie said, pointing at the closed door. "That's Jon's."

"Let me do a quick search in here." Pulling back on the door handle, Greg managed to get inside the room without making a sound. He was fairly quiet when it came to opening drawers, the closet and rifling through the toy shelf, too.

His search of Abe's room was over in less than five minutes. And the boy hadn't moved, other than to take long, steady breaths. Natural, normal breaths.

Abe was fine. And probably still feeling some residual from the anesthetic.

Jon's room was next.

Lillie stood in the doorway, taking in Jon's things while trying not to intrude on his privacy. Not an easy feat when a man was going through Jon's underwear drawer.

The briefs and T-shirts and socks were all neatly folded and stacked, the drawers not quite full but well organized. The sight didn't surprise her, but it brought tears to her eyes. Jon was a good man. Careful and honest and hard-working.

"He doesn't deserve this," she said, keeping her voice low.

"He lied during the investigation, Lil. A man doesn't do that unless he has something to hide."

She didn't have a response to that.

"He also doesn't have an alibi for a single one of the break-ins."

"Neither do I, or a lot of people who live alone." They were all alone at night.

Greg Richards had moved to Jon's closet. He emerged carrying a blue duffel, which he set on the bed. Unzipping it, the sheriff grew very still, his hands suspended over the opening, and then he reached inside, pulling out item after carefully packed item.

"He was planning to run," the sheriff said softly, almost to himself. "There's everything he could need here to care for himself and a child—including prepackaged food—for at least forty-eight hours."

Lillie searched for an explanation. Jon was supercareful. He kept a bag packed with baby essentials in the truck, too. But not with clothes or food for himself. Not with a thermometer or syrup of ipecac.

Feeling around in the now-empty bag, the sheriff stopped. His hand was on something. Pulling out the lining, he found a pocket in the bottom left side with a cell phone inside. Pushing buttons, he got no response, and then, flipping the phone over, removed the cover of the battery enclosure.

There were no phone workings inside the case at all. A carefully folded stack of large bills filled the empty metal container. Greg Richards held up the fake phone. "He's got cash stashed away. If he's so hard up that he has to work extra hours just to make ends meet, where'd he get this cash? And why hide it away?"

She had no idea where the cash came from. "He's a careful man. He plans for any emergency. It's because of Abe," she said, defending Jon even while the cash in the sheriff's hand scared her to death. "He's determined to be prepared for anything that could possibly crop up to prove, I think to himself, that he's a good father. That his son is not getting gypped by having only one parent."

"He's got a criminal record, Lillie."

Sick to her stomach, Lillie wanted to grab Abraham and run. Far, far away.

TRAPPED BETWEEN FOUR walls with no freedom to leave weakened a man. Jon knew he'd be fine. He hadn't done anything. They had no concrete evidence to tie him to the thefts. Richards had counted on Jon's confession to seal his deal.

Jon knew he'd be sleeping in his own bed that night.

And the feelings of powerlessness swamped him, anyway. He hated that part the most—the emotions that would not be denied.

It would only be a matter of time before the town pinned something else on him. He was labeled now.

It was going to cost him to leave Shelter Valley. He'd owe the university a full semester's worth of scholarship monies.

He hoped to God that Richards didn't find the cash he'd hidden in the bottom of the duffel. A dead cell phone shouldn't be all that suspicious.

If Richards even found the duffel. As thorough as the guy was, Jon figured he probably would. There wasn't much Jon could do about it if he did. It didn't look good— him having a bag packed as if he was planning to skip town—but it wasn't enough to book him, either.

As he sat there, playing the mental gymnastics that kept him sane, he heard a knock on the door.

Richards must be back.

A head peeked around the door.

Addy?

"Can I come in?"

Jon nodded. "Of course."

Addy placed a thin black portfolio on the table and took the seat opposite Jon. The same seat Greg Richards had occupied for most of the late afternoon and evening.

"Mark's out in the lobby. They wouldn't let him come back here."

"Who's with Nonnie?"

"No one. She's texting Mark every five minutes asking for updates. And we've only been away from the house for ten." Addy smiled.

And surprisingly, so did Jon. He leaned forward. "I'm assuming they let you in because you're an attorney."

Mark had told him that Richards had called Addy the night before. It struck him as odd that she'd be there.

"Right," she said, pulling a pen out of her purse and holding it with both hands. "I'm here to represent you."

"I haven't been charged with anything."

"I know. And they can't keep you here. Which is what I'm going to tell the sheriff as soon as he gets back."

"I can't afford an attorney." The spare cash, if he still had it, was for Abe. Jon had a scholarship to pay back.

And he hoped to God he wasn't going to need representation. Because that would mean that they'd charged him.

"I wouldn't take a fee if you tried to pay me," Addy said. "And before you say anything else, let me just tell you that I don't intend to take no for an answer."

Jon opened his mouth, ready to cut her off. He wasn't a charity case.

"That boy of your needs his father."

He shut his mouth.

"And Mark and I know you didn't do this, Jon." She leaned in. "Please, don't cut off your nose to spite your face here. Let me help you. If not for your sake, then for Abe's."

"You and Richards are friends."

"We know each other," Addy said. "And have mutual friends. I wouldn't say we're friends ourselves. And even if we were, I believe he's wrong. My job is to show him that."

Jon, taking his first easy breath since he'd left Lillie's office, said, "Do you think Richards is fair?"

"I'm certain of it."

"He's on a witch hunt."

"He's very protective of this town, and he's determined to find out who did this. He'd be the first to tell you, if it's not you, he wants to know it. Because if it's not you, then it's someone else who is still out there. He just wants the guy off the streets so the people of Shelter Valley feel safe again."

"I didn't do it."

"I know that."

He wasn't sure whether to believe her or not. Thinking of Addy with Abe in her arms, the way she greeted them at the door each time Jon dropped his son off at Mark's house, he wanted to believe her.

But...

"How do you know?" It didn't make sense to him. He could have done it. Easily. And left no concrete evidence. No way for Richards to pin the thefts on him. He didn't doubt his ability for a moment.

And neither did Richards. He'd seen Jon's record.

"I can't answer that," Addy said with a tilt of her head. "I just get a feeling. But I can tell you I've built my reputation on taking only those cases in which I believed the accused was innocent."

"What's your win ratio?"

"Ninety-eight percent."

Jon gave her a tired grin. "Not bad."

But she didn't know the whole truth. And so Jon gave it to her. Because he had to get to Abe.

"How many times have you committed a crime since you've been on your own?" was Addy's only response.

"None."

"So, are we a team?"

He didn't need a lawyer. Wasn't planning to hang around long enough.

But if she could help him get back to his son any sooner...

"I'd appreciate any help you can give me," Jon told her.

He wasn't a lucky man. But he was a smart one.

THE SHERIFF HADN'T been gone five minutes, taking only the cell phone casing and the roll of cash with him, when Lillie's phone vibrated again.

Who now?

It was nine o'clock and she was exhausted.

Dropping down to the sofa, she glanced at the screen. She almost ended the call, and then didn't.

"Hello."

"Lillie?" Kirk's relief couldn't have been completely feigned. "I wasn't sure you'd take my call."

"I almost didn't."

"Look, Lil, you were right about what you said. Again. I guess I was just using you, taking the easy way out, on my quest for my own salvation."

If this was another ploy she was just too tired to see. Or even to care. Kirk lied. Jon lied.

Greg hadn't been able to give her specifics since Jon's record was sealed, but he'd committed at least one crime in the past, for which he'd been convicted. "I'm glad you're finding yourself, Kirk. I really am. But I meant what I said. I'm done with you."

She was. And it wasn't even hard anymore. She just wanted him gone.

And Jon?

He'd lied to her, too. By omission.

She hadn't actually ever asked if he had a criminal record. And if his record was sealed, chances were whatever he'd done, he'd done as a kid…in foster care.

"My father said he was going to disinherit me if I called you again, Lil, but—"

"Hang up, Kirk. I won't tell him you called."

"I'm not hanging up, Lil, because this call isn't about me."

Her head ached. She just wanted to rest. To escape for a

bit. "For once in my life I'm putting you first, Lil. Thinking about you only, not in terms of what you can do for me, but in terms of you and what you need. My father and I have a long way to go…but we've been talking. And we agree on one thing. The way I treated you, the things I did—they were reprehensible.

"But even worse than the initial betrayals is the consequence of those betrayals. Please, Lil, don't judge other people, other men, by me. I was spoiled and selfish and probably still am, but I mean what I'm saying more than I've ever meant anything in my life. It's not right that you're spending your life alone."

His words poured over her, not really penetrating. Just lying on top of her. Blocking off other sounds.

"Some people are good on their own, maybe even meant to be that way. Maybe I'm one of them, but not you, Lil. You are a natural nurturer. I know what I'm talking about more than anyone else on this earth, Lil, because I lived with you. I'd go days without even being aware of you and yet you'd be there quietly making my day better, easier. You always knew when I had an important meeting and you'd make sure I had a good breakfast before I went, and gave me time to myself to prepare if I needed it. You seemed to know what I wanted without my ever having to say so. You just knew.

"Because you take care of those you love instinctively."

Those she loved?. What did she know about love? She'd thought she was falling for Jon. Had been certain of it, in fact. When he'd been hauled off to the police station that afternoon, and his gaze had met hers with a plea she couldn't decipher, her heart had wrenched so badly she'd actually thought herself in love with him.

She'd thought she'd known him.

Obviously blinded by her affection for Jon's son, she'd made Jon into something he was not.

"I'm going to get on with my life, Lil. I'm going to try to patch things up with Leah. And certainly with Ely. But you, Lil, I can't make right what I did to you. Except to beg you to not let my sins close off that generous heart of yours. Not for my sake but for yours. And for those who need you."

Whether Jon was guilty of the break-ins or not wasn't even the issue anymore. He'd deliberately hidden part of himself from her. Something she'd deserved to know before entering into any kind of intimate relationship with him.

"My father told me that you'd been seeing someone and that, yesterday after seeing you, he had a feeling you'd stopped. Please, Lil, don't stop on my account. I'm not good enough for you and maybe this guy isn't, either, but please don't judge him by me."

Lillie hung up.

She felt like shit.

Like shit, but not shut down. Her heart was raw, aching. Over another man who'd misled her.

CHAPTER TWENTY-EIGHT

THERE WAS STILL a light on in the living room. Sheriff Richards had informed him, as Addy escorted him out of the police station, that Lillie was still at his house with Abraham.

And then warned him not to go anywhere.

They'd sent someone to a lab in Phoenix with the suction-cup print they'd taken from Lillie's sliding glass doors to compare with prints taken after the break-ins. Richards had already made a visual match.

As soon as they had an official match, they'd be pressing charges.

Jon knew they weren't going to have a match—if they ran legitimate tests.

But as long as Richards was trying to pin the thefts on him, the real thief was not going to be caught.

Not that he had to concern himself with anything except leaving town.

The lights from Mark's truck had long since faded away but Jon still stood on the sidewalk leading up to his place, eager to get inside to Abraham, to hear his son breathe and see for himself that he was okay.

But he wasn't ready to face Lillie.

He had to go in.

To be who he really was, not the man he'd tried so hard to be. The front door opened. "Jon?" Her voice was soft as she called out to him.

By college standards it was still early—just past ten. Lights were on in the units on either side of his. He remembered asking the guys who shared the other side of his duplex to be quiet after eight at night.

"Yeah." His hands in his pockets, he took a step forward.

"You coming in? It's cold out there and you don't have a jacket."

He hadn't needed one when the sun had been up, warming the desert.

"Yeah." He didn't want to leave the cool night air and sucked in another huge breath as he crossed the threshold into his temporary home.

"I'll need a ride to the truck," he said. "You've got the keys."

He'd need them back, too.

She nodded but didn't move to get them. "I don't think we should disturb Abraham right now," she said, sounding as if they were back at the clinic and she knew what she was talking about.

"Because of his tubes?" He'd missed the doctor's debrief. Was Abe supposed to lie still for a period of time after the procedure to cut down on drainage? Or to keep the tubes from slipping?

"No, I just don't think it would be good for him to wake up. It's been a weird day and he's still coming down from anesthesia. He might cry. Or even have a tantrum and the pressure in his head wouldn't be good for him."

Jon studied her, found it curious that she wouldn't meet his gaze.

Maybe she was just afraid of him now that he was the main suspect in a string of burglaries.

"I'd have thought you'd have been ready to get out of here as quickly as possible," he told her.

She shook her head. "I need an explanation and now's as good a time as any."

He shrugged. It wasn't as if he was going to sleep. "I need one, too."

He saw her shocked look, as if she found it incredulous that he figured he deserved something from her, and he turned away. "You planning to stay the night?" Because he wasn't going to be trapped there without a vehicle.

"I didn't know when you'd be back so I stopped at my place for some things. I can sleep on the couch."

He glanced over at her. She looked away.

Had the sheriff asked her to stay to keep an eye on him?

He knew full well that Sheriff Richards would have a volunteer posse keeping an eye on his every move until those prints came back from Phoenix. Jon was certain of that.

And considering that he thought Jon guilty, he would not have recommended that a woman spend the night in his home with him.

"I'm going to check on Abe." He had to see his son. Dressed in his favorite pair of race-car pajamas, the little boy was on his side, two fingers hanging out of his mouth.

"I've got the monitor going," Lillie whispered beside him, handing him his tablet. "I've been carrying it with me."

He'd shown her how to turn on the software the first night she'd stayed with him.

He wanted to stay in the quiet room, listening to his son breathe. The small night-light under the crib gave the room an ethereal glow.

Nothing bad was going to happen in that room.

Unless he woke Abraham. He could have a tantrum like Lillie said. Or Abe might not want to go back to sleep.

Jon could go to bed, too. Wish Lillie good-night and

lock himself in his room. It was clear he wasn't going anywhere that night. He'd have to make his move early in the morning—when it would be safer to wake Abe.

But he wanted answers. Had she known all along he was a convict? Was that why she'd hidden her fortune from him?

Was she another Kate, toying with him?

Try as he might, he couldn't make the puzzle piece fit.

He went to the kitchen. He still had more than half a bottle of the sparkling wine he'd bought a few days ago. It seemed like a lifetime had passed since then.

The stuff was flat. Jon didn't really care. "You want a glass?" he asked Lillie, who was leaning against the corner of the wall leading into the kitchen, watching him.

"I guess," she said.

Her hair was down but she hadn't changed out of her scrubs. She always changed after work.

Was she still considering herself on the job, then? Was that what Abe had become to her?

Or was she just that upset?

For a second, he saw Lillie as he'd seen her in the waiting room that afternoon. Saw a woman who was hurt and shy and needing someone to do things for her, instead of always being the one who was taking care of others.

He took a seat at the small kitchen table. "I'm an ex-con."

"Sheriff Richards told me you had a record."

It was sealed. The sheriff had no business telling anyone. He'd probably been protecting Lillie and was willing to take whatever small punishment the court would mete out if Jon found out and pressed charges.

She hadn't accused him of anything. She was giving him this chance to explain. Which confused him.

"I lived in the same foster home from the time I was

born until I was twelve," he said, deciding to give her the whole truth. "My foster mom was not a warm person. She was a decent caregiver, though. There were usually four of us at any given time, though I was the only one she kept long-term. She watched over all of us the same. She taught us values through example and expectation."

He'd been content. Thought he had a good life.

"Just before my thirteenth birthday, she told me that she was getting married. She was already in her forties, and she wanted to try to have a child of her own so she was giving up foster care. The very next week I was gone."

"To another foster home?"

"Three. I finally landed in one that already had two teenage boys—both older than I was. I heard my case-worker say that they thought the boys would take me under their wing. The house was not well supervised and the older guys were thugs."

Which was no excuse. Barbara had taught him well. He'd known the difference between right and wrong.

But being the youngest and the newcomer hadn't boded well for him. Not that the foster parents or his caseworker had noticed.

And by then, after being shuffled around so many times, Jon hadn't thought there was much point in com-plaining.

So he'd done what he had to do to get along. And more, to belong.

"They picked on you, didn't they," Lillie said after he'd told her a little bit about the two older boys, leaving out most of it.

He shrugged. "I learned how to fit in." He should have chosen the beatings. He'd have learned how to fight back.

He'd learned eventually, anyway. In detention.

"By the time I was a freshman in high school they

were seniors, and getting in trouble a lot," Jon said, his jaw tense as he drew his finger back and forth over the grain in the table.

"We were picked up a few times for trespassing, being out after curfew, little things."

"So that was it, then?" Lillie's touch on his hand drew his gaze to hers. Her smile was sad. Compassionate. But growing, including him in a way he didn't recognize.

He wanted to take her to bed, lose himself in her goodness and hold her. He'd probably sleep if she was there in his arms, keeping the world in balance.

"No, that wasn't it," he told her, knowing that she wasn't going to be as sympathetic when he was through.

"One Thursday night, a week before Thanksgiving, they decided to rob a convenience store. It wasn't the first time. Or the first store. This particular one had been family owned since the beginning of time. The proprietors were close to eighty and lived upstairs. They were both half-deaf and the plan was to hit the store as soon as their lights went out upstairs that night. I had to stand outside to watch my brothers' bikes.

"When they came out, they threw a bunch of stuff at me and asked me to shove it into the empty backpack I'd brought. Watches and cigarettes. Candy and cash. A load of cash. And as much alcohol as they could fit in the satchels. They told me to ride to the back lot behind our house and they'd meet me there. They were going in the opposite direction, in case anyone saw them."

He glanced up. Lillie's forehead was creased, her lips tight. But her eyes were still warm.

"I did what I was told, figuring they'd kill me if I didn't, but I swore to myself that that was it. I was getting out even if it meant I had to run away, leave town, make it on my own."

"You were what, fourteen?"

"Yeah. I headed to the back lot but the guys weren't there. It was dark and I was sitting there with all that loot and I got scared. So I opened one of the beers, proving to myself that I was as much of a man as anyone. Drank the whole thing down and opened another. Ten minutes later the cops show up."

Lillie's hand covered his again, picking it up this time, holding on. "Are you about to tell me that your time behind bars started when you were fourteen years old?"

"Yeah."

"And when was the last time you were in jail?" She sounded like it really mattered. But it didn't. Time wasn't the issue. The choices were.

"I was only ever there the one time. Because I didn't get out until I turned eighteen."

"For stealing some stuff from a convenience store and underage drinking?"

Jon shook his head. "I didn't know it, but my foster brothers beat up the old guy. He'd heard them and come downstairs. He almost died. They pinned the whole thing on me and there was no evidence to prove I didn't do it. I'd have been convicted, anyway, just for having been a part of the whole thing and not doing anything to stop them."

"When did you graduate from high school?"

"While I was in detention."

"So you've been out, what, nine years?"

"Yep." It seemed like no time at all. Nothing like the seemingly endless four years he'd spent behind bars.

She knew the rest.

Except that he knew about her money now, too.

"Answer me one thing." Lillie's voice was dead serious as she stared him down.

"What?"

"Did you break into the homes here in Shelter Valley?"

The question was fair. The fact that she was still there, in his home, said a lot.

"No."

"That's what I told the sheriff," she said. "I just needed to hear you confirm it."

She smiled.

And surprisingly, so did he.

But he knew that the moment was just the calm before the storm.

CHAPTER TWENTY-NINE

"I WANT TO HELP."

"Help how?"

"I have no idea," Lillie told the man who'd changed her life. And for that she owed him. "Whatever you need. Money, help with Abe. It doesn't matter."

"Money." He looked over at her. "I hear you have a lot of it."

"What? Who told you that?"

He told her about her father-in-law contacting the sheriff.

"I had no idea."

"I think that was the point."

"And Greg told you about it? But—"

"He was warning me off, Lil. Letting me know that even if I somehow escape this charge, which I will, others will be after me."

Standing, she moved behind him and started kneading the broad shoulders that were, even now, tempting her to lay her head down on them. "Listen to me, Jon. Just listen."

He was silent and she had no words. Nothing made sense. She felt like someone in the vortex of a tornado—the spinning of her own mind making her somewhat sick. Lillie needed to touch Jon to stay grounded.

"I... Oh, my gosh," she said as she watched scenes from her life pass before her mind's eye. Looking different than they had before.

"I've been so selfish." Dropping her hands to her sides, she fell to her chair. "All this time, I've been… I knew about Kate…knew how you felt about being not good enough…and I didn't do anything to reassure you."

"I didn't expect you to."

Of course he hadn't. And that was the point. "Ever since Braydon…maybe even before that…maybe Kirk's infidelity really was my fault…."

It was all making sickening sense. As she'd sat there, listening to Jon, feeling his struggle, she'd been taken wholly out of her own perspective. For the first time since, possibly, ever. Certainly since her parents had died. She'd been removed from herself because she loved Jon. Completely.

He'd become a part of her as much as her own soul—somehow tangling with her most intimate feelings until there was no clear separation between hers and his.

Somehow, Jon had found a way past all of the barriers she'd unknowingly erected—something Kirk had never been able to do.

Barriers that had been shored up by Kirk's infidelity and Braydon's tragic death.

She gave people what she wanted to give them, what made *her* feel good. She gave her time, her knowledge, her compassion.

But not *her.*

Jon had given her everything. Even that which he valued more than himself. He'd given her Abraham. "No one knew about the money, Jon. I didn't want it. Didn't ask for it. I came from a middle-class home and, believe me, we were far happier than Kirk and his family have been with all of their money. I don't use the money. It's in a trust. And the interest it collects is donated to the children's heart foundation."

His eyes flickered, but he didn't speak. "I swear to you,"

she said, taking his hand in both of hers and holding on. "I didn't deliberately not tell *you*. I trust you, Jon."

"Have you ever heard of Clara Abrams?"

"Abrams? Isn't that Kate's last name?"

"Yeah."

"No. Should I have?"

"She didn't hire you to check up on me?"

She dropped his hand. "Of course not."

For the first time since he'd walked in the door, Jon smiled. A real smile. "I didn't think so," he said. And then, after he'd told her about Clara's efforts to take Abraham from him, he added, "We're a pair, aren't we?"

This time he picked up her hand. Held it between both of his. And Lillie felt scared to death again.

But warm, too.

"Two strong people scared of what the future might bring," he said softly.

And her world fell calmly into place. Tragedy happened sometimes over time and sometimes in an instant. And so did joy.

"I'm not afraid of the future anymore," she told him. "Because it's going to be me and you facing it together."

"No, it's not."

She wasn't wrong about this. "You asked me to marry you, Jon. I'm accepting."

"That was before—"

"You don't want to marry me anymore?" She didn't believe that. Because she knew him.

"No."

"Then I'll hang around until you do," she said.

"I mean it, Lillie." Turning, he looked her right in the eye. "I don't want you tainted by your association to me. You've got a life you love here, the respect of everyone in this town. I can't let you jeopardize that."

"Too late," she said. "I'm already in as deeply as I can be. And it's my choice, Jon, not yours."

Jumping up she massaged her hands up the back of his neck, across his shoulders and down the middle of his spine. He'd let her touch him before. And he did then, too.

Which gave her the answer she needed.

"You're that sure of me?"

She couldn't lie to him. "I'm that sure that I have to see this through," she said, working on his upper arm. "Let's go into the other room."

Jon didn't argue. Taking their glasses, he led her into the living room.

"Lie down on the couch."

"I don't think that's a good idea."

"How else am I going to get your lower back and legs?"

She couldn't have sex with him. They weren't a couple just yet. But she could still find the physical connection she was craving—and knew he needed. It wasn't about pleasure or orgasm. It was about closeness.

Feeling the life in each other.

And maybe, infusing him with some of the same strength he'd given her.

LILLIE'S HANDS WERE driving him crazy. Turning him on beyond anything he'd known before. Even with her.

What if this was his last night of freedom?

Panic rose. Her fists ground into his calves. And he had to have her.

"Stop." The word was as painful as it sounded to his ears. Strangled and desperate.

"Am I hurting you?" The soft warm flesh left his body, leaving him bereft.

"No." Rolling over, Jon didn't even try to hide his hard-on pushing against the fly of his jeans. "Just the opposite. You're making me want you so badly I'm in pain."

Her eyes were smoky. Darker than usual. Her hair fell forward, whispering against the skin on his forearm.

Lillie leaned forward, bringing her lips down to his, opening her mouth to caress his tongue.

"Lil? I'm not strong enough to do the right thing tonight."

"What's the right thing?"

"Leaving you alone to get on with your life. I'm no good for you, not long-term. And certainly not short-term."

"You're perfect for me."

"I can't do this to you."

"It's not like we haven't had sex before," she said, grinning and sounding serious, too. "Not that long ago, as a matter of fact."

It seemed like years. Months. And, as he caught a whiff of her shampoo, merely hours.

Lifting one hand, he slid it up inside her scrub top. Cupping her waist, he ran his hand across her midsection, and then up and around to undo her bra.

"No strings attached," he reminded her. "I'm not going to hold you to any promises you make tonight." If he went down, he wasn't taking her with him.

Or Abe, either.

He wasn't going to run. Not anymore. He was innocent. He had a lawyer who wanted to help him. And he was going to go the course.

Because it was what he'd have Abe do, if his son was ever falsely accused. He couldn't subject the little guy to a life on the run.

Or teach him that when life got tough, the thing to do was run.

Lillie's faith in him, her willingness to stay regardless

of the consequences, meant more than she'd ever know. She was giving him what he should have given himself.

Faith in himself. He was a good man. He knew it. And he had the right to live like it.

Moreover, so did his son.

He had until morning to live as a free man. After that, who knew? "God help me, if you're willing, I need you to help me get through the night."

"I've got news for you, Jon."

He stopped.

"I need you to help me get through the night, too."

Choked up, and turned on all at once, Jon pulled Lillie up on the couch on top of him, pressing his body upward into hers and covering her mouth at the same time.

Lifting her head, Lillie kissed his lips gently. "You've taken a vacant space inside me and filled me with life, Jon. You've changed everything about me for the better. Made my eyes see better. My ears hear better. I notice smells and tastes more acutely. That's why I have to help you through this, no matter what.

"I don't want tonight to be commitment-free. I want it to be our contract, our promise, to spend the rest of forever together."

The unfamiliar lump in Jon's throat made it hard for him to speak.

But he had to.

Because he loved her that much.

"I can't sign on that line tonight." He'd known the pain would be unbearable. "Not with the possibility of my being arrested. I can't do that to you. I won't do it to you. And if that means I sleep alone tonight, that's okay. Tonight and every night. Because I will not have you spend your life as the wife of an Arizona state prison inmate."

It wasn't going to come to that. He hadn't done anything wrong.

But life had a way of surprising him. And she was too precious for him to take a chance with her.

He'd waited too long to find her.

"Okay, Jon, you win," she said, but the finality of her words didn't match her tone. Or the sexy smile on her lips. "For tonight, it's just sex. But tomorrow, I'm going to be right here. And the day after that, too. Until our forevers are here and we're still together."

Sounded to him like she'd just brought them right back to that contract, couched in different words, but Jon couldn't afford to be picky.

Tonight he was a beggar. Not a chooser.

CHAPTER THIRTY

LILLIE WENT TO the door when the knock sounded early the next morning. Dressed in the cotton pajama pants and T-shirt she'd brought over with her and thrown on when Abraham woke up, she looked through the peephole, and wanted to bolt.

To grab Jon's duffel and run out the back door with the two people she loved, who were currently in Abe's room getting Abe's diaper changed.

The knock sounded again.

You took Bray, you can't have Jon, she silently told the fates that seemed to be always knocking at her door.

Reminding herself that she had choices and will, and would fight this thing until they won, she pulled open the door.

"Lillie." Sheriff Richards's face was grim as he glanced at her casual dress and then away. "Is Jon here?"

Of course he's here, Sheriff. Where do you think he'd be? On the run? Well, he's not. He's with me. And Abe. Because he belongs to us. With us...

Her thoughts raced as she stood there, garnering her strength. Her instincts were telling her she was going to need a lot of it.

She would not let Jon down again. She had a heart full of love and she was going to find the courage to give every bit of it away.

"Is he here, Lillie?"

"Lillie? Is someone at the door?"

Dressed only in his cartoon pajama pants, Jon came around the corner with Abraham on his hip. And froze.

His eyes were slightly wild looking as he glanced at her, spurring her to action. Hurrying to his side, she took Abraham, settled him on her hip and slid her free hand up Jon's side, landing directly over his heart.

"I'm going to dress Abraham and take him to the day care," she said lightly. "You take care of the business at hand and I'll call Addy."

His color ashen, he glanced at the sheriff, who'd stayed outside the screen door, listening to the exchange.

"Jon?"

He looked down at her again and, as she'd taught him to do with Abraham, she got right up into his face until he couldn't help but focus on her.

"I'm right here," she said. "I'm not going anywhere. You found me, Jon. You go with the sheriff for now, and you believe."

Sheriff Richards cleared his throat. Jon swallowed.

"Promise me, Jon," she said, a hand on his arm holding him back with her.

"Promise me."

"I promise."

He said the words, but they sounded empty.

Lillie held back her tears until he was gone.

THE SUCTION IMPRINTS had been an exact match with the ones taken from Lillie's glass door. In a court of law the findings were as good as fingerprints.

By eight o'clock that Tuesday morning, Jon had already been charged with six counts of burglary, one count of robbery for the home invasion involving the elderly lady in the home, impending an investigation, and various other trumped-up charges.

Some of the counts would be dropped, but a conviction on only one of them would mean prison time.

Believe, Lillie had said.

He wanted to. He just didn't know how.

The Shelter Valley jail had two cells, the one he sat in and an empty one off to the left of him. He had a cot, a sink and a john.

Believe.

He knew he hadn't committed a crime. And he believed he was going to be convicted, anyway.

Hell, he'd convict himself, given the evidence.

How in the hell had someone used his rubber cups to break into all of those homes? They were in the back of his truck. Always. Until he'd thrown them away. And there hadn't been a break-in involving the cups since. There'd only been one, period. Involving a broken window.

Greg Richards was certain that Jon had used those cups himself. Jon had told him about disposing of them and why he'd done it. But it had been too late. He'd already lost all his credibility with the lawman for lying in the first place.

He had to get rid of Lillie. She couldn't see him like this. He wasn't going to taint her beauty with his dirt.

The sound of a key in the cell door got Jon's attention. A deputy he hadn't seen before called him out and motioned him toward the interrogation room he'd spent so much time in the day before.

Addy was standing by the table as he entered the room. The door closed behind him and they were alone.

"Have a seat," she said.

Wordlessly, Jon complied.

"We have a lot to go over, but the first thing I want to do is talk about each of the nights in question," she said, sitting down next to him this time, rather than across from him, and opening her portfolio. Pen in hand she looked over at him, her gaze open, compassionate. Not the least bit doubtful.

She thought they were going to beat this?

Believe.

He was sitting in jail with a top-notch attorney fighting for him. For free. Because she considered him a friend. While Lillie, beautiful Lillie, who'd spent the night in his bed, watched over his son.

Believe.

"I need to know where you were every minute of the dates and times in question," Addy said. "If you remember what time you went to sleep, what homework you did… maybe you were on the internet and we could establish an alibi with a search of your IP address."

Believe.

His job was to concentrate so he could recall the information Addy needed.

After more than an hour of mental backtracking, all they'd come up with was that Jon had been at home every single night that there'd been a break-in.

If Jon's suction cups had been used, they'd been taken from his truck while it was parked at the duplex.

The bed of his truck was covered.

"Do you keep it locked?"

"Of course."

"What kind of lock?"

"A keyed lock."

"One that could be easily picked?"

His foster brothers could have picked it. But he didn't keep *anything* of any real value to him back there. Just tools that didn't fit in the storage space he had in the apartment. Tools that he could replace if he had to.

Addy called the sheriff. Jon could only hear her side of the conversation, but it sounded as if Shelter Valley's sheriff was taking her seriously.

And as if he knew something pertinent, some new information, that Addy and Jon hadn't known.

Before Addy could tell him what he'd said, her phone rang again. It was Mark calling, she said.

"Do you mind if I fill him in on the details here?" she asked Jon before she picked up. "He wants to help, if he can."

"You can tell him anything you want," Jon responded. "I have nothing to hide."

"Hold on." Addy spoke into the phone, and then said to Jon, "Mark and Lillie are here. They've asked me to come out to the lobby. Sit tight." She stood and, putting her phone in her pocket, left the room.

He was alone again with four windowless walls. Jon leaned back in the chair, remembering Lillie in his bed the night before, laughing as he ran his tongue along her belly.

Believe.

WALKING WITH PURPOSE, Lillie went straight to the door Greg Richards had indicated and pushed her way inside, closing it behind her with a distinct click.

She'd been given permission to be there. And she was fighting for her future.

"Lillie?" Jon stood, wearing the jeans and T-shirt the sheriff had allowed him to pull on before bringing him in that morning. His eyes wide, he looked surprised, but embarrassed, too. He'd been sitting alone in the room for more than an hour.

"I asked you to believe, Jon."

He watched her, unsmiling. She was undaunted.

"I want to know your choice. Right now. This minute. Will you marry me or not?"

"I won't tie you to a convict—"

"Will you marry me or not?"

He wouldn't be able to turn her down. She really believed that. But he had to believe in himself, too. Or they'd never have a fighting chance against what might come their way.

And one thing Lillie knew was that she had to have a man beside her who would stand in the fire with her. Not leave her there to burn alone, if the occasion arose.

"You aren't going to—"

"You aren't going to make my choices," she said gently, still standing at the door. She couldn't get closer to him until she knew she'd won. Until he acknowledged that he was hers.

There was always an out with Jon. Always a reason why he couldn't quite commit. She'd heard it in the stories from his past.

He sacrificed for others. And used sacrifice as a crutch to keep his emotional distance. Keep him safe. She knew. Because she'd been just like him.

He'd even been willing to hand his son over to her. He wanted what was best for his son. But what about for himself?

Her mind raced, as it had been doing most of the day and night before. And all of the morning.

For a man who believed his time with her was limited, he was wasting a lot of it in silence across the room.

"Life is about choices, Jon. I get to make mine. That's the beauty of it all. And I *have* made my choice. I choose you. And I need to know your choice."

She wasn't going to cry. Or plead. She wanted him to

come to her himself. To dare to reach for what he most wanted. To allow himself to shed his past and be whole.

Because if he didn't, if he couldn't, she'd never have all of him.

"Let's wait and see what happens here, Lil. I have to know I can be there for you."

"Your choice is about whether or not you'll be willing to let me be there for you, Jon. Do you have the courage to open your heart and let me in?"

"Lil…"

"I'm not telling you what to choose. But I am telling you that I want to know your choice. Now. Because this is what real love is all about. The bad as much as the good. I have to know that no matter what, we're in this together. Because it's pretty much a guarantee that there are going to be some hard times in the future, regardless of what happens with this case. Are you going to protect me then, too, by removing the emotion from the situation? Because it's never the pain that goes away, Jon. It's only the love that gets lost."

It had taken her a long time to get the lesson, but she'd finally seen the light.

"What's it going to be?"

Answer me, you stubborn man….

"Believe."

"What?" She wasn't sure she'd heard right.

"Believe," Jon said again. "I have to believe, Lil. I'll marry you. Now. Tomorrow. Next week. Next month. Whenever you want."

It was like a dam burst inside Lillie, throwing her across the room and at Jon, knocking him backward. With her arms around his neck, she clung to him, burying her head against his warm, strong chest, and started to cry.

She'd been holding on for so long. And hiding, too.

"Lil?"

"I'm fine," she said, remembering where they were. "I'm just happy," she said, her eyes still blurry with tears as she looked up at him. "Come on, baby, let's go home."

He held back, the light in his eyes dimming. "I can't do that."

"Oh, yes, you can."

"I can?" He didn't move.

She nodded. "Yep."

"I don't understand."

And he still didn't quite believe. She could read the doubt in his eyes. In the slight droop to his shoulders.

So they had some work to do. They had a lifetime ahead of them to do it.

"You're not alone anymore, Jon. And I don't just mean me. You've got friends who care about you, who are fighting for you."

"I'm under arrest, Lillie."

It was time to tell him. "I was sent in here to tell you that the charges were dropped," she said.

"What? Why?"

"I was telling Mark that you wouldn't have an IP address alibi because you don't go on the internet at night because of the baby monitor."

Nodding, he said, "I told Addy the same thing."

"Well, Mark's a bit of a techie, did you know that?"

"Yeah."

"He said that the monitoring software doesn't just monitor in real time, it saves the files somewhere in the program, kind of like a security camera in a store. I took him to your place and he went on your laptop and found the files. They're time and date stamped. And you, bless your heart, visit Abe's room so often that you were captured on video on two different nights there were break-ins."

His mouth gaping, he stared at her. "I'm free."

"Yeah."

Jon's grin was like an ocean. And a sky filled with brilliant sunshine.

BEFORE JON COULD do more than grin stupidly, there was a knock on the door and Greg Richards came in, followed by Addy.

"We got him, Jon." The sheriff spoke immediately upon entering. *Jon.* As though they were friends.

The lawman had told him about Abraham's well-being when he didn't have to. Then again he'd also judged Jon by his criminal past.

"You weren't the only freshman at Montford who came to town with a criminal record," Addy said over the sheriff's shoulder. "The other guy had an alibi for the nights of the break-ins, but the sheriff dug deeper because something didn't feel right."

"He'd be telling you that himself, but technically, because the case is ongoing, he can't," Mark said, coming up behind Addy. The sheriff's head bobbed in a slight nod.

"When I told Greg about the fact that your truck was at home every night of the break-ins, he told me that his other suspect lived in your complex—and would have been able to get the tools out of the back of your truck and return them without you being the wiser. Greg went back to the other guy and while we can't say what transpired, or how or why, he ended up with a confession."

"It helped that my investigation of you turned up some other evidence that fit him," Greg Richards added.

The sheriff didn't say what it was. Jon figured he'd have to wait until the case went to trial to hear all the details.

"When I'm sure I'm right, I'm usually pretty good at

getting a guy to crack," Greg said with a bit of a grin in Jon's direction.

"Yeah, well, a guy shouldn't crack unless he's guilty," Jon shot back.

The sheriff nodded. And Jon figured that maybe they'd just taken their first step toward mutual respect.

"This is yours," the sheriff said, pulling a wad of bills out of his pocket and handing it to Jon. "But I'd suggest you keep it in the bank from now on."

"And unpack that bag," Lillie added. "You've got no reason to run anymore."

It was too much for Jon to take in all at once. That four-walled, windowless room, filled with people he cared about. People who cared about him. But he suspected he had years ahead of him to relive the moment. And he knew he would, too. Over and over again.

Savoring it.

Like he'd once savored dreams of what might be in the future.

JON SUGGESTED LEAVING Abe at the day care until after lunchtime so he and Lillie could have a little time to themselves at home, to discuss their future, before they gave all of their focus to the little guy who had no idea how much better his life had just become.

They talked about a quick marriage, officiated by Becca Parsons. She happily agreed to perform the ceremony but insisted that the Heroines of Shelter Valley, as the town's matriarchs had been affectionately dubbed, would need a couple of weeks to pull the celebration together.

And they'd talked about Clara Abrams, too. Addy was drawing up papers to allow Lillie to legally adopt Abe, in conjunction with Jon, which could be done with only

Jon's permission since his was the only name currently on Abe's birth certificate.

And for the fourth time in an hour, Jon brought up that morning. When he'd been alone in that sterile little room and she'd come to see him.

"Why didn't you just tell me when you first walked in that I was free?" he asked her, running his hands up and down her arms as though he couldn't believe she was real.

That he could touch her whenever he wanted to.

They were standing together in Abe's room, had been discussing a new bed for him when they moved him into one of the bedrooms in Lillie's house. They planned to store the crib in her garage. For the next time they'd need it.

"I didn't tell you because I needed to know that you weren't just committing to me in the good times, Jon. I needed to know you'll let me be there for you through the bad, too. And that you'll stick around through the bad. You aren't going to shut down on me and go your own way like Kirk did."

Because she had her own scars. Her own issues.

But she'd faced them now.

Through Jon's mirror.

And was ready, able and committed to being happy.

He studied her face for a long moment and grinned.

"Makes sense to me," he said.

And in that moment, everything made sense to her, too. All that had been. And all that would be.

Her life had brought her to this moment, to Jon's arms, because that was where she was meant to live and grow and love forever.

* * * * *

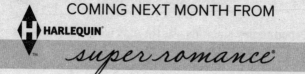

*New York Times bestselling author Brenda Novak
began her impressive writing career with
Harlequin Superromance. Join her now in the town of
Whiskey Creek, California, the setting of her award-winning
contemporary romance series, published by
Harlequin MIRA.*

*In this excerpt, longtime resident Noah Rackham has just
rescued Addie Davies from an abandoned mine—the very
mine in which his brother died fifteen years before…*

HOME TO WHISKEY CREEK

Brenda Novak

"**H**ave we met?"

How could she tell? What she'd seen of him so far had
been dark and indistinct. He was tall and muscular; she'd
gathered that much from his general shape. He was strong,
too, or he couldn't have lifted her out. But that was all she
knew. She couldn't even see the color of his hair.

"Maybe," she said. "Who are you?" Chances were good
she'd recognize the name. Gran owned Just Like Mom's,
one of the more popular restaurants in the area, and she
used to help out there.

She'd anticipated *some* degree of familiarity, but the
name came as a shock.

"Noah Rackham."

She said nothing, *could* say nothing. It felt as if he'd just punched her in the stomach.

"My father used to own the tractor sales and rental place a few miles out of town," he explained, to provide her with a frame of reference.

Fresh adrenaline made it possible to scramble to her feet, despite the pain the movement caused her scraped and bruised body. "Cody's brother?" She had the urge to rip off the sweatshirt he'd given her.

Noah stood, too. "That's right. You knew him?"

He sounded pleased, excited. She might have laughed, except she was afraid that if she ever got started she'd end up in a padded cell. Of all the people who could've come by and offered her aid, it had to be Cody's fraternal twin. There wasn't a greater irony than that.

"You and Cody were friends?" he prompted, trying to interpret her reaction.

She was glad she couldn't see his face. That would be like meeting a ghost, especially here, at the mine. "Not really," she said. "I was behind the t-two of you in sc-school, but…I remember him."

She'd never be able to forget him, but it wasn't because they'd been friends.

Noah is the last person Addie hoped to meet on her return to Whiskey Creek. For both of them, and for several other people in town, what happened in the past hasn't stayed in the past. And complicating everything is the attraction Noah and Addie feel for each other…

HOME TO WHISKEY CREEK *is available from Harlequin MIRA, starting August 2013.*